"Came did I t[...]
most beautiful object I could find.

Ahi'aorina inclined her head. "You desire to give me a gift? That is indeed thoughtful of you, Sir Imp."

Kuzgu's head bobbed up and down in agreement. "Came from far I did to see you," he said again. He reached into his jacket pocket. "Brought this I did for you."

In his palm rested a perfect flower.

Ahi'aorina gasped. She had never seen a flower like it. Its petals were tipped in palest pink, but the color became darker and more vibrant closer to the center, where the petals were deepest crimson. The middle of the flower was yellow as the summer sun, with an orange dot resting in its very center. An emerald-green stem with two perfect heart-shaped leaves supported the resplendent bloom.

She reached out for the flower.

Kuzgu grinned even more widely and stepped forward quickly, pushing the flower toward Ahi'aorina.

"Mum!" shouted one of the handmaids. Ahi'aorina could not tell which one.

All around the clearing, imps appeared out of the undergrowth. Each of them held a spear or a bow.

The whine of an arrow hissed past Ahi'aorina's head . . .

King's Quest is the #1 bestselling computer game series of all time, with over two million copies sold. Now, Boulevard Books presents a new series of fantasy novels based on the characters from the King's Quest games.

DON'T MISS THE FIRST SPELLBINDING *KING'S QUEST* ADVENTURE
The Floating Castle

The King's Quest *Series from Boulevard Books*

KING'S QUEST®

-KINGDOM-
OF SORROW

KENYON MORR

BOULEVARD BOOKS, NEW YORK

KING'S QUEST: KINGDOM OF SORROW

A Boulevard Book / published by arrangement with
Sierra On-Line, Inc.

PRINTING HISTORY
Boulevard edition / January 1996

ISBN: 1-57297-033-2

BOULEVARD
Boulevard Books are published by The Berkley Publishing Group,
200 Madison Avenue, New York, New York 10016.
BOULEVARD and its logo
are trademarks belonging to Berkley Publishing Corporation.

PRINTED IN THE UNITED STATES OF AMERICA

10 9 8 7 6 5 4 3 2 1

-KINGDOM-
OF SORROW

· 1 ·

Ahi'aorina, Queen of the Old Wood, ran her fingers through the long spring grass. Her fingers were slender and milk-white, the nails cloudy as if made of pearl. Bare tracings of green veins lined the back of her hand. She patted the broad leaf of a mayapple and it bowed in deference to her, its green deepening with pleasure.

Ahi'aorina smiled. No matter that it was always spring wherever she was, she never grew bored of the brilliant colors of the buds or the fragrance of the blossoms. How could she? The colors, the fragrances, the shine of the spring moon, all were hers. She *was* spring. As long as there was spring, there was Ahi'aorina. As long as there was Ahi-'aorina, there was spring.

Bright laughter skittered across the glade. Ahi-'aorina glanced over to her handmaids. The faery girls sat in a huddle, heads bowed to catch phrases they whispered behind their hands. White pointed ears with pink-tinged tips projected from under their silky tresses. One of them had a jonquil stuck behind her ear. Their spider-silk dresses were of spring colors—light green, yellow, and palest blue. The pink of the lilies and the lavender of the violet.

"What amuses you so?" asked Ahi'aorina. Her voice floated on the gentle breeze like the bubbling of a brook.

The handmaids glanced up, mischievous gleams brightening their eyes.

"Spring Feste, mum," said the girl with the jonquil.

Ahi'aorina nodded. "And you are wondering who will be chosen for the Tree Trimming?"

"I think it will be Old-Oak-by-the-Stream," said the smallest of the girls in a voice no louder than a mouse's squeak. Her raven-black hair was graced with a garland of violets that matched the color of her dress.

"No," said the girl with the jonquil. "It will be Willow-Who-Stands-Tall-as-a-Mountain. I'm sure of it."

The girls fell into a fit of self-conscious giggling. Every tree of the Old Wood wanted to be chosen for the Spring Feste Tree Trimming, but only Ahi-'aorina could choose the one so favored. Every year, the young girls vied for her attention, hoping to influence her by naming the best and most beautiful of their tree friends.

Ahi'aorina looked back to the grass and ran her hand through it again. The spring grass was so soft, so warm.

Ahi'aorina closed her eyes and breathed in the

scent of the irises that stood tall and proud nearby. All around her, bees buzzed in their search for pollen. Ahi'aorina opened her eyes to watch them.

A dragonfly settled on her shoulder. Its body shone in brilliant hues of blue and green. It hesitated a moment and then took flight.

"Mum?"

Ahi'aorina looked over to her handmaids. "Yes?"

"Someone comes, mum," said the girl with the violets in her hair. A deer ate berries out of her hand.

Ahi'aorina stood. Her willow-thin body towered over the smaller figures of her faery handmaids. The faeries looked delicate and petite, but next to them, Ahi'aorina appeared stretched out and impossibly thin. She was almost as tall as a human.

She was certainly as tall as what walked into the glade. An imp. The deer took fright and bounded away.

The imp, like all of his kind, had skin as rough and brown as the bark of an oak. His yellow eyes blinked in the brightness as though used to less light, though imps were not usually cave dwellers. He was stocky in body, especially around the middle, but his arms and legs were twig-thin. He moved in jerky, twittery steps that were almost comical.

The imp stopped in front of the handmaids,

who had arranged themselves in a double row in front of Ahi'aorina.

"Ahi'aorina?" he asked with a slight bow.

Ahi'aorina hid her annoyance at an imp calling her by her bare name. Not one of her subjects would so dare. But imps were often ill-mannered.

"Mind your tongue," scolded the girl with the jonquil. "You may address our mistress as my lady, or Your Majesty."

The imp made a deeper bow. His eyes blinked more rapidly. "My Lady," he said. "My ignorance of faery customs I beg you to forgive."

The imp's sarcastic tone was at odds with his contrite words and actions. Ahi'aorina had never understood imps. Faeries, though often deceitful, were never really untruthful. A faery might conceal the truth with a clever tongue, while an imp merely ignored it.

"Kuzgu am I called, My Lady," said the imp. "No titles have I, no honors. From far came I through many lands to visit you."

Ahi'aorina brushed a silver strand of hair away from her face with a pale hand. "And so you have visited me," she said. "But why should that be important to you?"

Kuzgu grinned. His pointed teeth gleamed in the bright spring sun. Bits of his last meal were stuck in between his teeth. Ahi'aorina kept a pleasant smile on her face though inwardly she flinched. She had heard what imps considered edible, and did not approve.

"You are the most beautiful woman of all, it is said," said Kuzgu. "So came I had to, to see your beauty."

"So you have seen our mistress," said the girl with the jonquil. "You are dismissed."

Kuzgu was neither impressed nor abashed. He bowed again. "Came did I to give the most beautiful one a gift. The most beautiful object I could find."

Ahi'aorina inclined her head. "You desire to give me a gift? That is indeed thoughtful of you, Sir Imp."

Kuzgu's head bobbed up and down in agreement. "Came from far I did to see you," he said again. He reached into his jacket pocket. "Brought this I did for you."

Kuzgu brought out his hand and held it out to Ahi'aorina. In his palm rested a perfect flower.

Ahi'aorina gasped. She had never seen a flower like it. Its petals were tipped in palest pink, but the color became darker and more vibrant closer to the center, where the petals were deepest crimson. The middle of the flower was yellow as the summer sun, with an orange dot resting in its very center. An emerald-green stem with two perfect heart-shaped leaves supported the resplendent bloom.

The flower shivered in the breeze as if cold. Ahi'aorina felt a great desire to hold the flower close to her heart and comfort it as she would a blossom from her own garden. She reached out for the flower.

Kuzgu grinned even more widely and stepped forward quickly, pushing the flower toward Ahi-'aorina.

"Mum!" shouted one of the handmaids. Ahi-'aorina could not tell which one.

All around the clearing, imps appeared out of the undergrowth. Each of them held a spear or a bow.

The whine of an arrow hissed past Ahi'aorina's head. The missile struck the handmaid with the garland of violets. Bright green blood spilled out of the wound in her chest and she dropped silently to the ground, a frozen "oh" on her face. Her gaze sought Ahi'aorina's, but then the mist overtook it and the soft brown eyes faded to white in death.

Ahi'aorina jerked her hand back and would have stepped away, but Kuzgu jogged forward and slapped the flower against her face. A yellow powder sprang from the flower and enveloped Ahi-'aorina's face.

The powder smelled of the forest floor, of decay and death. Ahi'aorina sneezed and pushed the flower away. She planted her bare feet firmly in the spring grass and drew the power of the spring into her body.

But it would not come. Instead, a terrible lassitude leeched into her bones. Ahi'aorina sank to her knees.

Kuzgu bent down to stare at her eye to eye. "Came from far away I did," he said. "Just for you. Just for you. Spring make you here. Now spring make you there."

Ahi'aorina could not understand what he meant. She blinked her eyes and tried to clear the cobwebs that fogged her mind.

Kuzgu chortled and stepped aside. The last thing Ahi'aorina saw before blackness overtook her was the body of the faery girl with the jonquil. She lay, burdened by frost in the manner of all faeries at their death, on her side, her hand placed under her chin as if she were merely asleep. Her jonquil lay beside her. It had been snapped in two.

Then the darkness claimed Ahi'aorina and she beheld no more.

Graham, King of Daventry, stood at the tallest parapet of the castle. At his side was William, the young son of the castle seneschal. It was William's birthday, and as his present from the king, he had requested to visit the parapet. Normally, Graham and his lady wife Valanice forbade any of the children who lived in the castle to play in its upper reaches, lest the children fall to their deaths. But today Graham made an exception. William was ten years old. Old enough, surely, to know to be careful. And Graham would be there to watch him.

"Can you see the whole kingdom from here?" asked the boy. His sandy shoulder-length hair blew about his face in the breeze. Bright blue eyes took in everything.

Graham smiled down at the boy. For a moment, he started to reach out and ruffle William's hair, but he remembered how much he had hated that gesture when he had been a child. Besides, William was not his son.

A sharp twinge of sadness ran through Graham.

Graham's own son, Alexander, had been kidnapped while no more than an infant. If he had still been at home, he would have been about the same age as this boy. With the years that had passed since Alexander's disappearance, the pain of his loss did not come as often. Days went by now in which Graham thought of Alexander not at all—which only compounded his loss with guilt.

"Your Majesty?" the boy said. "Can you see it all?"

Graham shook himself from his reverie. "Yes, William," he said. "The whole of Daventry."

"Wow." The boy leaned against the stone wall that lined the parapet. "The whole kingdom."

The awe in William's voice was enough to make Graham stifle a laugh. William was still young enough to think Daventry a large place. But Graham had traveled much in his youth and knew the world was far wider than a single kingdom. Daventry was but a small spot among many larger lands. Still, it made Graham feel good that the boy was impressed.

"Ready to go down?" asked Graham. Though it was late spring, there was still a bite to the wind. He shivered and drew his woolen cloak more tightly about him.

The boy didn't seem to notice the cold of the wind. He shook his head. "No, Your Majesty," he said. "I could stay here all day."

The view *was* splendid from here, Graham had to admit. The clean white stone of the castle and the dark gray slates of the roof glittered in the sun as if inlaid with millions of tiny gems. The bright blue uniforms and gray caps of the castle staff complemented the colors of the building itself. Far below, in the courtyard, a horse trader was bringing in his string of steeds. A majestic roan stallion pranced at the head of the string while a nasty-tempered chestnut near the rear aimed a kick at one of its handlers.

"Ooh, isn't he beautiful, Your Majesty?" asked William, pointing down to the courtyard. "The roan, I mean."

"He certainly is," said Graham.

The boy gave Graham a sly look. "Do you think my Dah would buy me a horse? I mean, you could tell him it was a good idea."

Graham folded his arms across his chest. "Now, Master William, don't think you can corrupt me into helping you against your own father." He tried to keep a stern face, but he couldn't hold the expression and broke into a grin. "I'm sure your father will see that you've a horse when you need a horse. Besides, wasn't *this* supposed to be your birthday present?" Graham stretched out his arms, indicating the parapet.

William shrugged and returned the king's grin, but he couldn't take his eyes off the roan.

Graham looked farther out, past the silver ribbon of the Merelee River, past the tiny village that stood in the shadow of the castle, past the newly plowed fields that spread out from the castle in all directions. Out beyond the fields in the east was the Old Wood, where faeries and other fantastical creatures dwelled. Though it was no more than a league away, the Old Wood lay beyond the border of Daventry. Graham had no authority beyond the limits of the fields, and no desire to rule more.

"Hey, you can see my Gran's house from here!" said William. "Hey, Granny!" The boy jumped up and down and waved his hands over his head.

"She's not going to be able to hear you from up here," said Graham, amused. Unlike Graham, who had taken the throne of Daventry little more than a decade before, this boy had family that stretched back into the roots of this land. His father was seneschal, and so had been his father before him. Perhaps William would take that post someday, when Graham's daughter Rosella sat on the throne of Daventry. Or perhaps Alexander . . .

Graham shook his head to clear another bout of sadness. He shivered again, glad he had thought to bring the heavy woolen cloak. Or, rather, he was glad Valanice had reminded him to bring it.

"I think it's time we get down," he said. "Your parents will be wanting to see you, and you know we'll be inviting the village children into the castle tonight for a birthday dinner. You'll need to get ready."

William sighed, but he nodded his head. "Yes, Your Majesty. But I do love it up here."

"Well, maybe you can come back again," said Graham.

The boy seemed content with that. "Yes, Your Majesty, I would like that." He drew back from the edge and stood up straight as a rod.

Graham nodded. He could see the image of William's father in the boy's young features. Though he was only ten, William knew his station and how to behave in a royal house. Graham himself often had a difficult time, mostly because he had not been born to the velvet of a king's station. He had been born a nobody. Were it not for Valanice keeping watch over him, Graham would not have known the first thing about how a king should behave.

Graham ushered the boy down the circular staircase back to the upper floor of Daventry Castle. He paused and carefully locked the door, lest the boy get some idea of making a surreptitious return to the parapet. They walked along the chill hallway past other locked doors leading to dusty rooms. Those rooms were far too cold and drafty to live in during the winter, even with fireplaces and shutters. Soon William's father would direct the staff to air out those floors for summer living.

Finally they reached the main staircase leading down to the heart of the castle. Graham took his time with the circular staircase. He was not old or weak, but it was easy on the steep steps to turn an ankle or a knee. It was vanity, Graham knew, but he didn't want to be seen limping around the castle just because he'd fallen down some stairs.

William bobbed impatiently. Graham was sure the boy knew that he should follow behind his king, but that didn't keep the lad from fidgeting. Graham smiled. It was a relief to see that he wasn't the only one that sometimes had trouble with the rules of his position.

Once in the hallway, Graham stripped off his woolen cloak. The air in the hall was close and warm, even though the windows were open. Now that spring was almost on them, they would doubtless be able to cut back on the wood used in the castle's many fireplaces.

The corridor floor was polished gray marble and the walls had been paneled in oak stained a light blue. A portrait of the late king hung on one side, a boar's head on the other. A small strip of red cloth hung from the boar's mouth. Graham had always wondered at the story behind it, but there was no one around who remembered what that story might be.

Castle staff in their blue uniforms passed him and nodded. Graham did not insist on a lot of formality as some monarchs did. As long as his staff were doing their jobs, Graham saw no reason for them to be distracted by extraneous bowing and scraping. Such actions didn't just keep his staff from their proper tasks, they also embarrassed him.

A few of the staff gave a wink to William as they passed. They knew it was the boy's birthday, and they had all been making a fuss over him. Graham did his best to make sure each of those who worked at Daventry Castle felt that his or her position was more than a task. This was their home as well as his. Even the lowliest kitchen sweeper did a better job and took more pride in his work if he knew the king remembered his name and took time to think of him now and then. Birthday dinners for the children and a few gifts on holidays were a small price to pay for a happy staff.

Graham's wife, Queen Valanice, stood in front of their private quarters, talking to one of the maids. As Graham and William approached, she dismissed the maid and turned to them. A frown marred her beautiful features.

As always, Graham was stunned by her beauty. Her light brown hair fell in ringlets to her waist— or it did when they were alone and she unbound her hair. Right now, her hair was constrained by a golden net. A silken rose-colored dress trimmed in gold thread covered her from shoulders to ankles. The train of the dress was tied up to a small cord that wrapped around one of Valanice's wrists, keeping it from tangling or impeding her movement. The dress was one of Graham's favorites.

Valanice crossed her arms and tapped her foot. The foot was wrapped in a slipper dyed a darker rose to match the dress. "And where have you been?" she asked.

Graham fought a grin and tried to look stern. It was a game they played. Valanice was always teasing him this way—indeed, the mischievous gleam in her eyes belied her angry appearance. Besides, Valanice knew very well exactly where he'd been.

"We went questing, madam," he said with a bow. "For the mysterious Birthday Beast. It had last been spotted in the rose garden eating the first blooms of spring, but by the time we got there, the beast had retreated to colder climes. So the brave lad and I tracked it to the parapet . . ."

Graham paused. He wasn't very good at making up stories on the spot, and Valanice generally let him spin his tale until he got stuck, then teased him about it later when they were alone.

William seemed confused by their jesting. "Birthday . . . Beast?" he said.

Valanice had mercy on the boy. "It was only a jape, William." She patted him on the shoulder. "You had best run on. Your parents will be preparing for your birthday." She bent in low and spoke in a whisper. "I suspect they may have come upon a few presents."

William bowed quickly. "Yes, Your Majesty." He started off down the hallway at a pace just under a run.

Graham chuckled. "We'll see you tonight at your birthday dinner," he called after the boy.

Valanice cast a sideways glance to Graham. "Look at you," she said. "The first of spring, and you're wearing a tunic that should have been thrown out last autumn."

Graham shifted his weight in embarrassment. He had worn his favorite tunic this morning— blue cotton with silver piping and flowers embroidered in gray along the neck and waist. But the tunic was old and some of the flowers were unraveling. Bits of embroidery thread stuck out around Graham's neck.

Fortunately, Valanice was of similar mind concerning formalities around the castle. She was only teasing him again. If Graham wanted to wear a threadbare tunic on a morning stroll around the castle, his wife didn't care.

If he tried to wear the tunic to a council meeting now, *then* there'd be trouble. No doubt about it.

That was one reason he needed her. Loved her. Valanice had a wonderful sense not only of propriety, but also of proportion. She had class without the stuffiness Graham had often seen in others of the nobility. Valanice was organized and intelligent, and could manage the castle and kitchen staffs without half trying. Sometimes Graham thought she ought to be the king, but when he said so to her, Valanice only laughed and shook her head.

"You know," Graham said wistfully, "if Alexander was . . ."

"Yes," said Valanice. "I know." She moved to Graham's side and enfolded him in a tight hug.

It felt good to hold her in his arms and smell her perfumed hair again, even though they'd been separated for only a bare hour. Just being with Valanice could not help but lift his heart. "You know," he said lazily, "I think I forgot to tell you I loved you this morning."

"Only this morning?" said Valanice. "And who is your love now?"

Graham laughed and stepped away. Valanice winked at him. Except during formal council sessions, she couldn't keep from teasing him. It had gotten so Graham could barely imagine a day without listening to her verbal pokes. In fact, he looked forward to them. Valanice might tease, but she was never cruel, and her jibes were a loving antidote to the weights of kingship.

"Are you still planning to have the dinner outside?" asked Graham. "There's a bite to the wind today. It might be too cold."

Valanice took his hand and together they walked down the corridor. Sunlight streamed in through the stained glass windows. "The seneschal already spoke to me about that," said Valanice. "He had noticed the cold, too, and he suggested we move the party into the small council room off the conservatory. It's big enough for the children but not overwhelming like the great hall or the ballroom. And it's close to the kitchen and has a lot of windows."

"Good," said Graham, not surprised that Valanice had things well in hand before he could even ask about them.

"And you, my king," said Valanice, "do you still intend to attend the dinner? The children would enjoy seeing you."

"Yes, I believe I might." Graham suspected that there were few kingdoms where the ruler might play host to a child's birthday dinner. He was glad that Daventry was one place where such things were common.

Valanice stopped by an open window. A confused frown crossed her round face. "Oh my," she said.

"What?" asked Graham.

Valanice pointed out the window. Graham went over and looked out.

A single perfect snowflake fluttered in the window. Others like it fell outside.

"It's awfully late for snow," mumbled Graham. "At least you've already moved the party inside."

"Yes," said Valanice. She seemed distracted.

"What is it?" asked Graham.

Valanice shrugged. "I just don't recall snow this late in the spring before. It's strange."

Graham looked outside again. The snow had stopped. "It's just a few flakes," he said. "A freak cold wind probably."

"You're probably right," said Valanice.

Graham and Valanice continued down the corridor. This wing of the castle housed the royal tutors and most of the castle staff. Portraits of various tutors hung on the walls. A portrait of Master Rokaill, their daughter Rosella's tutor, graced the left wall. The portrait had been commissioned on his sixtieth birthday. The artist had captured the tutor's sharp blue eyes, large beaklike nose, and thin pinched lips perfectly.

Master Rokaill looked the part of a stern headmaster, but he was anything but. Rosella loved him, and the old man returned the affection in full measure.

Graham and Valanice turned the corner and walked together into a small courtyard where Valanice grew her rose garden.

"My word," said Graham.

"Oh, dear," said Valanice.

The courtyard was ankle-deep in snow.

· 3 ·

Graham stood still, hardly daring to believe his eyes as more snow fell. On the other side of the courtyard, Rosella and Master Rokaill stood looking around in confusion.

Rosella, only seven years old, had never been the epitome of poise. She stomped her foot and tossed her blond ringlets. "Oh, poo," she said. "I don't want snow. I want flowers. It's *spring*." Rosella saw her father across the courtyard and ran to him.

"Daddy," she said. Rosella had always refused to call Graham anything more formal than Daddy. "Daddy," she said again, "make the snow stop. The flowers are sad."

Graham hugged his daughter. "I'm sorry, pipkin," he said. "Kings can't control the weather."

"Well, why not?" demanded Rosella. "You're the *king*."

Valanice held out her hand and Rosella took it. "There's a limit to what even kings can do," said Valanice. "You can be sure that if your father could do something about the snow, he would."

"Of course I would," said Graham.

Master Rokaill walked at a stately pace across the courtyard. "Your Majesty," he said. Cold air fogged out of his mouth and nose.

"Let's step back inside before we freeze," said Graham. The others nodded and they all turned back and went into the castle.

A maid just coming by glanced outside and her hands flew to her face. "Oh, Your Majesty," she said to Valanice. "Your beautiful roses. The snow will kill them."

"I don't suppose it will last long," said Valanice, though the snow fell thickly and already their footprints were filling up.

The maid shook her head. "And the shutters have been taken down and put in storage, too. It'll be a cold night in Daventry Castle tonight, Mistress."

Valanice sighed and nodded. "See if you can find the seneschal and tell him to come to me. If the snow lasts through the afternoon, we will have to make some alternate plans. The grounds-keepers may have to put up their rakes and take their shovels and snow brushes out of storage."

The maid bobbed a curtsey and departed.

"Why's it snowing anyway?" asked Rosella. "Aren't we supposed to have . . ." She paused and put a finger to her chin in thought. "Winds from the western sea and warm rain in the Daventry springtime?"

Master Rokaill patted his young pupil on the

shoulder. "I'm glad you remember your lessons so well, Princess," he said in a quavery voice tinged with warmth and strength.

A groundskeeper, pruning shears still in hand, ran into the corridor from the courtyard. "Your Majesty, Your Majesty! An elkrider!"

"What?" gasped Master Rokaill. "An elkrider? *Here?*"

"Why?" asked Valanice. "Why would they come to us?"

"Where is he?" asked Graham.

"Heading for the Great Hall," said the groundskeeper.

Graham took a step toward the Great Hall, but Valanice grabbed him by the elbow and stopped him.

"Not in that tunic, you're not. Elkrider or no elkrider, no King of Daventry is going to hold court in a shabby tunic."

"I can't keep him waiting," Graham protested.

Valanice's gaze was firm. "Far worse for you to insult him by arriving in such a state. What kind of impression do you want to give a member of the faeryfolk?"

"An impression that I'm never late," said Graham.

Valanice crossed her arms and tapped her feet, and this time she was *not* amused.

"All right," said Graham. "I'll change. But go on ahead and make my apologies for me."

"Can I come, Mama?" asked Rosella. "I've never seen a faery."

"No, love, you can't," said Valanice. "This is no casual visitor, to be introduced to children and entertained. If the faeryfolk have seen fit to send a messenger, there's some urgent matter that needs to be discussed. Go continue your lessons with Master Rokaill."

"Mama," complained Rosella. She stamped her small foot again.

Valanice's expression darkened. "Never do that again in my presence, Rosella. It's not ladylike, and certainly it's not anything a princess would do."

Rosella pouted and hung her head.

Graham left them there, knowing Master Rokaill would take good care of Rosella while Valanice and Graham saw to the elkrider.

Graham threw open the doors to the quarters that he and his lady wife shared. The front room was where they received certain special visitors. Their sleeping quarters were farther back.

Graham hurried to the wardrobe in their sleeping quarters and opened it. He unbuckled his belt and let it drop, then pulled his old tunic off over his head and threw it on the bed. He chose a new tunic, purple with gold piping and delicate leaves embroidered in gold thread along the neckline, and put it on. He grabbed a purple velvet belt and wrapped that around his waist and buckled it. The gold buckle held a dark ruby in the center.

On top of the tunic, Graham put on a purple velvet cloak. The cloak fastened at his neck with a gold catch.

Graham went to the table by the window and grabbed a tortoiseshell comb. He ran it briefly through his short blond hair to make sure it all lay flat, then combed out his short beard. Satisfied he looked his best, he turned to leave.

The sight out the window stopped him. The groundskeepers outside struggled in snow that was now knee deep.

Graham let out a worried breath, hoping the elkrider had some news of this strange change of weather. Hoping the elkrider knew how to *stop* this strange change of weather.

Graham left the royal quarters and walked to the Great Hall. The cloak billowed out behind him as he went.

Graham stopped just short of the double doors that opened onto the end of the Great Hall where his throne sat. Not his *official* throne, the stone one inlaid with gold and gems. That was only for coronations and sat in the drafty, smaller Throne Room. The throne in the Great Hall was wooden and padded and comfortable to the backside—a blessing when Graham had to sit in it for hours at a time during Council sessions.

A royal aide in purple silk cleared his throat and threw back his head. "The King of Daventry approaches the throne!" he shouted into the Great Hall.

Graham had long ago learned not to be embarrassed by this display and had become resigned to the apparent silliness of it. As Valanice often reminded him, the people needed ritual. It reassured them and enhanced their pride in their kingdom.

Graham stepped confidently into the Great Hall and strode to his throne. Valanice already sat on her own throne, which was just to the left of his. She inclined her head to him as he approached, no hint of teasing in her features.

Graham bowed to her slightly, arranged his cloak, and sat down.

Another royal aide approached from the far doors that separated the Great Hall from the large courtyard outside. The aide walked down the entire length of the room and knelt at Graham's feet.

"Your Majesty, an elkrider has appeared in the castle and wishes an audience with your royal person," announced the aide. He was shivering. No doubt the silk of his summer uniform was very uncomfortable today.

"Bid the elkrider approach the throne," said Graham. "And extend my greetings to this representative of the faeryfolk."

The aide nodded, got up, turned around, and walked back down the entire length of the room. When he was newly crowned, Graham had once suggested in Council that the aides only have to walk from the side door to the throne, but the opposition to changing the tradition had been so strong, he had never suggested it again.

Still, his impatience grew as the aide walked. He wanted to know why the elkrider was here. He would have preferred just to go outside and greet the faery, and *ask*. But the formalities had to be observed. Valanice had been right to make him change. Faeries took appearances very seriously.

The aide went through the doors. A moment later, a large stag's head poked its way in. Then the rest of the animal followed.

The elk stag was magnificent. His head was raised proudly, and his rack of antlers was huge. Although it was not season for deer to bear ant-lers, Graham knew the variety the faeries rode never dropped theirs.

The shaggy dark brown fur of the elk's neck was thick and frosted with snow. For all the stag's size—the massive rack, the heavy neck and shoul-ders, the stocky body—its legs were thin and del-icate in appearance. They ended in four very small cloven hooves.

On the elk's back sat a diminutive man. He was dressed in green trousers and boots. His tunic was stainless white as the snow, as was his hair. His eyes—

Graham could not look away from the faery's eyes. The eyes were dark and deep, without whites, the stare as distant as a cat's. Whatever lurked behind those eyes was alien to Graham.

The faery rode the elk down the length of the

room. Graham supposed he should have been insulted, but he had no doubt the elk walked faster than the little man that rode it, and anything that hurried up news of the storm, Graham welcomed.

The elk stopped a few feet away from the throne and the faery hopped off. He was no taller than Graham's waist.

The tiny figure bowed. "King of Humans," said the faery in a high, piping voice. The voice sounded of birdsong and the chirp of the cricket.

"Sir Elkrider," said Graham. "You honor my court with your presence."

The faery cocked his head but said nothing.

"Please, sir," said Graham, "tell me the purpose of your visit. Do you have any information on the strange weather that has come upon us this day?"

The faery's face looked grave, though his eyes remained as dead things. "Aye, that I do, Human King. But even though I know the cause of the trouble, I have been charged not to speak it. I have not been asked to be the messenger of bad news."

"Then why have you come?" asked Graham. "If not to give us knowledge of the unseasonable snow?"

"I bear you an invitation," said the faery. His pink-tipped ears stood out from his snow-white hair. "From my king, Quilli'ehennan. King of the Old Wood. He has invited you and your lady queen to his court. He himself wishes to share the grave news of the snow with you."

"Grave news?" asked Graham. "If we must travel to the Old Wood to hear it, then the news must be bad indeed."

"Aye," said the faery, bowing his head. "The Wood grieves today as it has not for ten thousand years or more."

Graham ran his hand through his beard, considering. Faeries were not evil creatures, but they were also not necessarily truthful, nor did they hold much goodwill toward humankind. Faeries were more likely to mislead a human from the path in the woods rather than show him a straight road to their woodland palace. It was safest never to cross their path, and to only speak softly to them, for faeries were said to be easily insulted. And an insulted faery was a dangerous enemy for a human to have. Best to steer clear of them entirely.

Still, an invitation from the King of the Old Wood could not just simply be dismissed. Not only did Quilli'ehennan know the secret of the snow, but he was a king whose borders touched Graham's own. To turn down his invitation or even to suggest sending another in Graham's place would be unforgivably rude.

Graham glanced over to Valanice. She wore a pleasant look and a small smile. She usually wore such an expression while on public display in the Great Hall, keeping her true thoughts and feelings to herself, where the people could not see.

Graham depended on her to remain calm and pleasant at all times so that he could occasionally rant and rave and then pretend to be dissuaded by Valanice from some rash act. It was a routine they used only when necessary, but it often got results when formalities ground negotiations or other processes to a halt.

Despite her skills in diplomacy, Graham did not want to put Valanice in harm's way. It would be all right for him to accept Quilli'ehennan's invitation, but could he risk taking Valanice to the forest?

Valanice saw his glance and inclined her head. "I am honored by the King Quilli'ehennan's invitation," she said, tripping slightly over the trill in the middle of the name. Valanice nodded once to Graham. So. Valanice thought the knowledge that might be gained was worth the risk.

Graham looked back to the elkrider. "My queen has the right of it," he said. "At what time does King Quilli'ehennan expect us?"

The elkrider hopped onto the back of his strange steed. The elk blinked in a bored fashion and shook its head. Graham was glad he was not within reach of its sharp antlers.

"As soon as possible," said the elkrider. "King Quilli'ehennan says the matter is urgent and you should make haste."

Although the faery made no obvious gesture or command, the elk turned and trotted down the length of the room. It eased its way out the door and was gone.

A visit to the King of the Wood. Graham's stomach turned and bunched into knots. And bad news on top of it.

Graham tried not to dwell on these inauspicious tidings, but he couldn't help it. Everyone knew faeries were not to be trusted.

He had no choice but to go. With the snow continuing to fall and showing no sign of abating, he had no choice indeed.

· 4 ·

Graham stood up, as did Valanice, indicating to his aides that the audience was over. She came to him and took his hand. Together, they walked out the side door.

"The king has left the Great Hall," shouted the aide. Graham rolled his eyes and Valanice giggled.

"You know you love it," she whispered to him.

Graham shook his head, in no mood for levity. He and his queen walked back toward their quarters. They would have to change their clothes if they were to survive what had become a howling blizzard outside.

"I don't want you to go," he said.

Valanice frowned. "I know the danger. I've heard the stories that are told about the faeries. But I don't think the faeries are the danger this time. If King Quilli'ehennan has the answer, we must go to see him."

"I know," sighed Graham. "I just wish you weren't in danger."

Valanice threw back her head. "Humph," she

said. "I can face danger as well as anyone."

Graham squeezed her hand. "I know you can. I'm worried about the children. If something happened to just one of us, it would be bad enough for Rosella. But for both of us to be out in this storm—with faeries, no less—"

"I know," said Valanice firmly. "But it can't be helped. Neither of us can afford to turn down Quilli'ehennan's invitation. Not only is he our neighbor, but he's the king of the Old Wood. You don't want to know what would happen if the king of the Old Wood were angry with us."

"What?" asked Graham. "What would happen?"

Valanice poked him in the side with an elbow. "I just told you, Husband, that you don't want to know."

A shivering servant in blue opened the door to their quarters for them. Matilda, Valanice's lady-in-waiting, stood in the front room. Her ample figure filled up her blue castle uniform. A gray scarf was tied around her white hair.

"I came as soon as I heard about the snow, milady," she said after a curtsey. "I expect you'll be needing a warmer change of clothes. I've had the maids up to the storage areas to bring the winter dresses back down."

"Yes, Matilda," said Valanice. "But first I'll need riding clothes. The warmest ones we have."

"Riding?" asked Matilda, her plump face drawn up in a frown. "In this weather? Surely milady does not mean to go out of the castle today."

"I can assure you this lady does," said Valanice. "The king and I must go to the Old Wood at once."

Matilda crossed her arms. "Forgive me, milady, but that is the daftest idea I've heard in years. Go to the Old Wood? It's a dangerous place at any time. Certainly it will be a dangerous enough journey with the snow, let alone the faeries and fays and whatever other beasties live in the woods proper!"

"Do you always speak so to my lady wife?" asked Graham.

Matilda turned a dozen shades of red and fell to her knees. "Oh, no, Your Majesty. I didn't mean to say that milady *was* daft. It's just that . . . I mean, the Old Wood. Sir, you can't seriously be thinking of allowing your wife to go there."

Graham stepped forward and took Matilda by the elbow. "Get up, Matilda," he said, "before you hurt your knee again. And yes, I know it's daft to go the Old Wood, especially in this weather. But we have to. The king of the Old Wood himself has issued an invitation to Valanice and myself. He wishes to see us both and to tell us the true nature of this strange storm we're having."

Matilda stood with some difficulty. She had come with Valanice when that woman had first journeyed to Daventry. Years of climbing castle steps from lowest dungeon to highest parapet chasing after Valanice—first as a child, then as woman and queen—had worn her body down. But Matilda was not one to complain. She loved Valanice like a daughter. Graham knew that, and he knew it was that love that prompted Matilda to speak so directly to his queen.

"The king of the Old Wood?" asked Matilda. "Quilli'ehennan himself?"

"Yes," said Graham.

"But, but, *sir*," protested Matilda. "He's an evil creature, it's said. A stealer of children, they say."

"Well, no worries about that," said Graham. "Rosella will be safe here with you and Master Rokaill."

"Yes," said Valanice. "Rosella will be fine. Won't she, Matilda?"

Matilda wiped her face with the back of a hand, flustered. "Why, yes, of course. Of course, milady. I just . . . the king of the Wood!" Matilda shook her head. "I pray I see you again soon, milady Valanice," she said. Using Valanice's name only showed how deeply Matilda was upset. "They say once one goes into the Old Wood, there's no telling how long it will be before you come out. It might seem an hour to you but be a year here. Or more."

"Well, we can't help that," said Valanice matter-of-factly. "The riding clothes, Matilda—can we have them now, please?"

Matilda managed a shaky nod and went to fetch the clothes. Valanice's wardrobe was so large, it was not kept in their quarters. In fact, Valanice's summer wardrobe alone took up a set of apartments down the hall that had housed royal nieces and nephews and cousins of all sorts in long-ago times when the royal family had been larger.

Graham went back to the wardrobe and accompanying trunk where most of his woolen things were stored. He opened the trunk and rooted around in the neatly folded clothes. At the bottom of the trunk he found his favorite pair of woolen pants.

Graham pulled out the pants and several cotton shirts. He took another look at the raging storm outside and got out a second pair of pants. It wouldn't be possible to be too warm today.

Graham put on several pairs of socks, both pair of pants, and all three cotton shirts. He slid his feet into his well-worn leather boots. Then he opened the wardrobe and pulled out a wool jerkin that was coarse, undyed, and most importantly, thick. Warmth would be more important than fashion once they were outside. He pulled that on over his head and cinched it around his waist with a leather belt.

The sound of the outer door opening and closing meant Matilda had returned with Valanice's clothes. Graham heard Valanice and Matilda talking, but he couldn't tell what they were discussing. He fished around in a small trunk he kept by the bed for scarf, mittens, and a fur hat. Matilda and Valanice would go to the queen's dressing chamber and leave him alone here until Valanice was properly clothed.

Graham sat down on the bed and pulled on the mittens. The black wool mittens were warm—at least inside. In fact, Graham was beginning to feel very warm indeed. He took a deep breath and got up, barely restraining himself from pacing. It wouldn't do to start sweating under all these clothes, just to have the sweat chill on him later. At least wool would keep him warm even if wet.

Graham hoped sheep realized how lucky they were to have such a wonderful substance provided for them by nature. He was certainly grateful to have sheep for their wool. Graham liked mutton, too, but he could live without that. But life without wool? Not in this region.

Graham got a belt knife, checked it for sharpness, and then tied the sheath onto his belt and put the knife into it. He also rooted around in his small chest and pulled out a tinderbox. In cold weather, it was always good to have a bit of dry cloth and flint with you. Graham looked around the room, but didn't see anything else he'd need except for a wool outer cloak.

The cloak had an inner pocket. Graham put the tinderbox in the pocket and threw the cloak about his shoulders. The cloak had been dyed black with the royal sigil of Daventry—a gyrfalcon—embroidered in white and gold on the back.

Graham walked to the outer chamber. In the

next room, Matilda scolded Valanice on some point or other.

"I'm going to the stable," Graham called out.

"I'll meet you there," said Valanice.

"Daft," muttered Matilda. "My poor lady, out in the snow. Tsk, tsk. What will I do with you, lady?"

Graham smiled and left the room. He walked as quickly as he could to the stables, regretting putting on the cloak before getting outside. He was really starting to overheat now.

Graham stepped outside into the expanse of the large courtyard that separated the castle proper from the stables and other outbuildings. The cold sting of the wind in his face felt good at first. It took away the heat he had built up under the wool.

The castle staff, though clad only in thin silk, had been busy shoveling snow. The drifts on the outer edges of the courtyard were waist deep, but in the courtyard itself, the snow was only ankle deep.

A single groundskeeper remained, sweeping snow away from the castle front steps. He shook so badly, he could barely hold his broom.

"M-m-majesty," stuttered the man. Mini icicles dripped from the man's short black beard.

"Get inside, man," said Graham, searching his memory in vain for the man's name. "Before you freeze. Clean steps aren't worth your life."

"Th-th-thank you, M-m-majesty," sputtered the man. He fled inside.

Graham walked across the deserted courtyard to the stables. Inside, it was warmer. The animals put off a lot of heat. Not only their breath, but their very bodies steamed in the frigid air.

Long, curious equine noses popped out over stall doors as Graham walked by. Large tulip-shaped ears were cupped toward him and bright pairs of eyes watched his every move. Graham moved down the long line of stable doors until he came to his own steed.

The buckskin gelding greeted him with a whicker shaped by a velvet-soft nose. Graham patted the nose and the horse nosed Graham's chest.

"No snacks today," he said. "Another time. Today we have work to do."

As if the horse understood him, he snorted and stomped a foot. He was probably just cold.

"Your Majesty," said the deep voice of the chief stabler.

"Stabler," said Graham. "I need him saddled as soon as possible."

The stabler, a large bald man with great meaty paws for hands, rubbed his hands together to warm them. "A steward came by and said you'd be here, Your Majesty," said the stabler. "I was just coming to get him."

"My lady wife's horse must be saddled as well," said Graham. "I'm sure she'll be wearing a split skirt, so you won't have to put on the sidesaddle."

"A sidesaddle would be a foul thing indeed in this weather," said the stabler. Graham nodded in agreement. He had always detested the things, even though he had never, of course, had to ride with one. But the sidesaddle forced all a woman's weight into its left stirrup, unbalancing both horse and rider. In the snow, that could be very dangerous.

Graham had searched for months to find a stabler who was of his mind on the subject of sidesaddles. Every other stabler wanted to put the court's ladies in sidesaddles only—no ifs, ands, or buts. This man, however, had a sense of proportion. Put a lady in a sidesaddle when she rode through the streets of the village in her finest dress for the Midsummer Fair. That was fine.

But when a lady actually needed to *ride* a horse somewhere, this stabler banished the sidesaddles to the spare tack room where they belonged. Graham had hired him on the spot.

Now Graham stood aside while the stabler went about his work. The buckskin was saddled quickly.

"How about supplies?" asked the stabler. "You don't want to get caught out."

"We are not going far," said Graham. "Only to the Old Wood. It's, what, four miles?"

"Far enough in this weather," said the stabler. "I'll put some saddlebags on here and have the lad fill them with food and wine."

"Fine," said Graham. "That is an excellent suggestion."

The stabler nodded and left to send his assistant to the kitchen for supplies. When he returned, he led Valanice's mount by a line.

Valanice's mare was dapple gray with a strange black smudge on her nose, as if she'd brushed up against charcoal. The mare was even-tempered and had smooth paces, essential in any animal forced to wear a sidesaddle for even the occasional formal affair.

The stabler saddled Valanice's horse with the requested saddle and put on the bridle. Soon his assistant came back, balancing overloaded saddlebags in each hand. The stabler took the bags and fastened a pair to Graham's saddle horn, and the other pair to Valanice's.

"There," said the stabler. "That should do you."

"Thank you," said Graham. "As always."

The stabler smiled and nodded. "Your Majesty." He waved the boy away.

Graham took the reins of his buckskin and swung into the saddle. The stabler came over and helped Graham spread his cloak out over the horse's rump. The stabler was careful not to get too close to the horse's rear hooves. The buckskin had a habit of kicking when he was annoyed, and to judge by the set of his black-tipped ears, he was certainly annoyed right now. Graham supposed he would be, too, if someone had roused him from a warm box stall and expected him to cart someone about on his back in this frightful cold.

It couldn't be helped, but the horse didn't care.

The stabler led Valanice's gray forward. Just then, Valanice strode into the stable.

Valanice wore an outfit that matched Graham's. Woolen cloak with royal sigil, heavy jerkin—and pants. She also wore leather boots, a fur hat, and an overcloak. Hers was pale green. It complemented her light brown hair.

Graham couldn't help but stare. He'd never seen Valanice in pants before.

Valanice swung into her saddle and took the reins from the stabler. "Thank you," she said to him.

The stabler bowed and stepped back. Valanice looked over to Graham, a defiant tilt to her chin.

"Well?" she asked. "Are we going or not?"

"I, uh, well, of course we are," said Graham. "Um, whose pants are those?"

"Yours, of course," said Valanice. She kicked her horse in the ribs and the gray mare trotted gamely out into the blowing snow.

"Of course," echoed Graham. He kicked his buckskin and the gelding followed the mare out into the Daventry spring.

· 5 ·

The first blast of cold air to hit Graham's face as his horse took him out of the stable stung like a slap. Graham blinked quickly in surprise and shivered. It was much colder than before. Suddenly, four miles seemed like four hundred. They'd never make it in this weather.

Valanice pulled her cloak's hood over her head and bowed her head over her horse's neck. The gray mare shook her head and stopped at the edge of the courtyard, where the snow was deeper, but started again when Valanice urged her forward.

Graham's horse followed the gray, his ears plastered back to his neck. The horse was decidedly not happy about this.

Well, neither was Graham. He urged his horse to keep up with Valanice's. The buckskin responded with a trot that took him only a few yards before he slowed to a walk again.

Outside the courtyard, the snow was so deep, Valanice's gray had trouble negotiating it with her shorter legs.

"Here," shouted Graham into the cold wind, "let me go ahead. My horse is taller than yours."

Valanice pulled up the gray and let the buckskin pass. The buckskin snorted, apparently preferring to follow a trail already broken through the snow than to have to make it himself.

Graham urged his horse forward again and the buckskin plunged into the snowdrifts that filled the road leading into the courtyard. The horse took Graham through the village of Daventry, which sat outside the castle gates.

The snow wasn't quite as deep in the village— the closely crowded houses and narrow streets seemed to keep the snow from drifting as badly as it had in the large open courtyard. The buckskin and gray made good time through the narrow streets.

Wary eyes peered at them from every window. The citizens of Daventry cowered in their homes and watched the royal couple ride through the streets of the village. Graham couldn't blame them. The chill in his teeth was giving him a headache and his toes already felt numb—and he'd only been riding a few minutes. He, too, would prefer to be indoors.

In the center of the village were the large circular grounds used for the market as well as for the Midsummer Fest Dance. A lone figure stood in a shabby cloak in the center of the dance grounds. The wind whipped the cloak around him like a kite in a storm as the figure swayed from side to side.

Graham tugged on the reins and the buckskin changed his course to intersect the cloaked figure. When he got close, Graham shouted, "Hail, citizen. Why are you about in such weather?"

The cloaked figure turned to him and Graham recognized the local seer. The old man's few wisps of white hair stuck out of his cloak's hood and blew in the wind. A scrunched-up toothless face peered up at Graham. The old man was so ancient, no one even remembered what his name was. He was just the Seer. Unlike many of those who came and went over the years claiming to be able to see the future, the Seer was no fortune hunter, no con artist ready to take folks for their last gold coin.

No, the Seer of Daventry was the real thing. Exactly where he lived and slept, no one knew. During the day, he wandered the village. No children or dogs ever bothered him, and people considered it good luck to spare the old man a meal.

Graham had always suspected the old man lived that way because his gift of seeing left him too unbalanced to do anything more. The Seer lived a hand-to-mouth life, and didn't seem to notice. He often acted as though no one else were around him. Even his prophecies were often spoken to empty air, as if he were forced to speak of his visions when they happened and where they happened with no regard as to if there was anyone around to hear.

"Spring," said the old man. He looked right through Graham as if the king weren't there.

"Yes, I know," said Graham. "It's supposed to be spring. It was spring this morning, anyway."

"Faery magic," said the Seer. "There's faery magic here. An elkrider."

"That's the past, Seer," said Graham. "Have you seen the future?"

"I have yellow legs and a tail," said the Seer. "I am a creeper and a crawler. I hide in small places. I am the savior of the spring."

"What's that he's saying?" asked Valanice. "Savior of spring? That would be you, right?"

Graham looked at her, annoyed at her teasing now, but the gentle look in her eyes stopped him from saying anything.

"I am the Sticky-Toed Wonder," said the old man, "who crunches his dinner. I am the opener of the cage."

Valanice leaned forward. "Can you tell us anything of the snow?" she asked.

The Seer pulled his tattered cloak around his emaciated frame. "I see the faeries in their mourning clothes. Ashes of willow wood and rough cloth of flax, grief and despair do they know. I see a golden cage with an ivory key clutched around the heart of sorrow."

The old man wandered away. "Run, run," he

said, shaking his head. "Run up the wall. Run up the wall."

The wind blew up a sheet of snow, and when it cleared the old man was lost in the gray shadows of the storm. "Should we go after him, do you think?" asked Valanice.

"No," said Graham. "He has minded his own way longer than any other in the kingdom. I'm sure he knows where he's going. Besides, we'd better get on the road before the snow gets even worse."

Valanice nodded. Graham tapped his buckskin's sides and set the horse on the road to the Old Wood.

Fortunately, the wind was at his back and the sting of the falling snow was no longer in his face. Graham sighed, thankful for small favors at least.

The road out of the village wound around the farmlands of Daventry. They should have seen the green shoots of spring barley, and the first tiny sprouts of rye clearing the dark earth. But no trace of the fields remained—a white blanket of snow was all that could be seen. Only the road markers and Graham's own familiarity with the road kept them on track.

Graham and Valanice had traveled barely a mile, however, before they lost all track of their location. In the blowing snow, Graham could not tell one direction from another. First the snow blew in from the right, then the left. The wind was at his back one moment, then came around to hit him in the face the next. Ahead, the Old Wood was too far away to see, and Daventry too far behind to make out in the blizzard. Graham pulled up the buckskin. Valanice brought her horse up to stand next to Graham's.

"Now what?" asked Valanice. "The Old Wood has to be ahead somewhere."

"I know," shouted Graham back to her. The wind whipped his words away. He hoped Valanice heard him. "But I can't tell where we're going!"

"We'll have to stop," said Valanice. "We can't go any farther."

Graham glanced ahead. Blankets of white flakes falling and swirling in the air were all he could see.

"Just a little farther," he said. "Surely we'll be able to see something soon."

Graham looked at Valanice. She wore a worried frown. "All right," she said. "A little farther. But I'm not sure we can even get back to the castle in this!"

Graham nodded and pulled his fur hat down over his ears even more. He kicked the buckskin, who shook his head and snorted as if he couldn't believe what was being asked of him. But he stepped forward as requested.

They had only traveled a few more yards before Graham knew they were hopelessly lost. Without any landmarks to judge by, Graham could not tell anything about where they were. He hit his fist against his thigh.

"Curse this weather," he said. "We'll have to stop."

"We have to go back," shouted Valanice.

"Go back? Go back which way?" asked Graham. He gestured behind them. The horse's tracks were already filled with new snow.

Valanice's expression was set in grim determination. She urged her horse to walk around in slow circles.

Graham wanted to ask her what she was doing, but knew she wouldn't hear him over the wind, even though she was barely ten yards from him.

The gray mare walked obediently in circles for several minutes. Valanice looked up and gestured for Graham to come over.

The buckskin twitched his skin and stomped his foot in apparent delight as soon as he entered the small area tamped down by his stablemate. He lowered his head and searched through the snow for some grass.

Valanice hopped off her mare and took down the saddlebags. "Come on," she said. "Put the horses on the outside of the clearing, and we'll stay in between them."

It seemed a good idea. At least, Graham had nothing better to suggest. He swung his leg over the buckskin's saddle and took down his own saddlebags. He rifled through one until he found a small flask of port. He drank some and handed the rest to Valanice. The sweet wine warmed his stomach at least.

"Can you make a fire?" asked Valanice. She threw the empty flask on the ground.

"Not in this wind," answered Graham. "If it stops blowing, then we can."

Valanice sighed. "I almost wish we had a fire amulet with us."

Graham nodded. He knew what Valanice meant. A fire amulet could make a fire that looked cheery and smelled wonderfully of burning pine. But the magical fire it created gave off very little heat. It was illusion rather than true flame. Still, even the *sight* of a fire right now, illusion or not, might make Graham feel better.

Valanice tugged her cloak about her as the wind tried to whip it away. Graham did the same and leaned against the buckskin's flank. The horse was warm. Though very little of the horse's body heat got through to Graham, he was grateful for every bit he could get.

Graham had no idea how long he stood there. A strange lassitude crept into his bones, and the numbness he felt from the cold seemed to leech out of his bones all desire to move.

He felt contented, relaxed. He could sleep . . .

"No, Graham!" shouted Valanice.

Graham woke up with a start and looked over at his wife. "What?"

"Don't go to sleep, Graham," urged Valanice. "It's dangerous. You'll never wake up."

Graham stood straight in fear. He'd heard tales of travelers who lost their way and fell asleep in the snow, never to awaken. He could understand now how it happened. The weariness in him seemed so wide, so deep. He wanted to give in to it so badly.

Graham clenched his hands into fists. He didn't want to die. He was King of Daventry! He had a kingdom to rule, a spring to save.

A daughter who waited at home for him.

Graham nodded to Valanice. He would not sleep. He would *not*!

Valanice nodded in return and looked up. She gasped. "What's that?"

Graham glanced up. A small green sphere of light hovered over their heads.

"Come, silly humans," said a high-pitched whistle voice. "King Quilli'ehennan awaits."

"We do not know the way from here," said Graham. "We are blinded by the snow."

The green sphere whistled a mocking tone. "It is just this way, humans," it said. "Where the *lo-'ahimasa'evannan* awaits. Waits for you!"

The green sphere expanded rapidly until it enveloped Graham, Valanice, and the horses. Inside the sphere, the wind did not blow and the snow did not come. Graham could see through the sphere, but it was like looking underwater. Everything outside the sphere looked strangely distorted.

At the top of the sphere hovered a hummingbird. The hummingbird flitted down to look Graham in the face.

At close range, Graham could see it was not a bird at all, but a miniature person with dragonfly wings that beat so quickly they were just a blur. The little winged person was covered by a green dress. Her blue hair was bound up in braids on top of her head.

"What are you?" asked Graham.

The little person crossed her arms. "Humans don't know anything," she said. "I'm a sprite. I visit blooming flowers and transfer their pollen to other flowers. When there are no blooms, I sit on the lily pads and make music with the frogs. You see—a *sprite*."

"Ah, yes," said Graham. "Of course. Well, Mistress Sprite, can you show us the way to King Quilli'ehennan?"

"My name is Jiilii'a," said the sprite. "Not Mistress Sprite."

"Jiilii'a," said Graham, having some trouble reproducing the piping sounds. Were all faery names this hard to say? He'd thought Quilli'ehennan difficult enough.

"Close enough," said the sprite. "Thick human tongues can't say faery names right."

The sprite left Graham to hover in front of Valanice. "Pretty one," said Jiilii'a. "I'd like you to stay in the Wood with us. You'd be young and beautiful for a long time then, not like out here in the human's world. You'll get old so quickly here."

Valanice bowed, gracious as always. "I thank

you, Jiilii'a," she said. "Your invitation is most kind. But I have my duties to my own people, just as I know you have your own. I cannot turn my back on my duty."

The faery hovered a moment. "Duty, yes," she said. "All faeries know what *duty* is. Didn't know humans did, too."

"Well, we do," said Graham. "And our duty now is to get to King Quilli'ehennan. Can you help us?"

"Of course," said Jiilii'a. "You travel with me. I'll keep the snow off of you. And the wind, too."

"You are indeed powerful," said Graham. "For such a small thing."

Jiilii'a buzzed right up to his face. "Size doesn't matter," she said in a stern tone. "Even the smallest faeries are more powerful than any human."

Graham nodded. "I meant no disrespect," he said. "I know that all faeries are powerful."

Jiilii'a was apparently content with that. She zipped back up to the top of the green sphere. "Then come on," she said. "This way."

Graham and Valanice replaced the saddlebags on their saddles and mounted their horses. In a few moments, with Jiilii'a in the lead, they were on their way.

· 6 ·

While it was true that Jiilii'a's magic kept the
snow and wind off of them, it did nothing for the
bone-numbing cold. Graham shivered under his
many layers of cotton and wool and longed for a
fire. Or a deep down mattress covered by down-
filled blankets, and a warm brick at his feet. He
sighed.

Suddenly, it grew brighter. "What happened?"
asked Graham.

"We are in the Old Wood now," piped Jiilii'a.
"Faery magic is always stronger here. *I'm* stronger
here."

The sprite whistled a merry tune that cheered
Graham. The music made him feel light and care-
free. He sat up straight and drummed his fingers
against his thighs, happier than he'd been in days.

He had no reason to worry. What was the snow
to him? Graham grinned and bobbed his head in
time with the sprite's whistle. In fact, why didn't
Graham just get off his horse and walk into the
Wood? Get off the path.

Yes, that was what he wanted to do. He wanted

to let the horse free to wander on its own as it was meant to do. He wanted to run through the Old Wood and laugh with the faeries and swim with the beasts of the water.

He wanted to dance, and dance, and dance. For joy, for . . .

"Stop!" commanded Valanice. "Stop that whistling!"

Graham frowned. He didn't want the whistling to stop. It was beautiful. It was comforting. It made him forget his troubles.

It was faery magic.

The music stopped and a strange grogginess assaulted Graham's senses. "What's going on?" he asked.

"She bespelled you," said Valanice. Graham heard anger in her voice.

"Humans succumb so easily to faery tunes," whistled Jiilii'a. "Makes them happy and they forget their humanness for a while. What could be better?"

"Forget being a human?" asked Graham. "What's good about that? May such a terrible thing never happen to me!"

Jiilii'a whistled a sorrowful note. "What could be good about being human?" she asked. "Living so quickly, being born and dying in a flicker of time. In the wink of an eye, you're here and you're gone. What good is that? Better to be a faery and live forever."

"I'd get bored," said Graham. "There's not

enough of the world to spend forever in. Besides, faeries always live in the same place. You can't leave your Wood. At least not for long. Spend forever in the same patch of forest? That sounds bad to me.''

"I suspect," said Valanice, "that if you are content with being human, and Jiilii'a is content with being a faery, then you are both luckier and wiser than most."

Jiilii'a flitted down just in front of Valanice's face. "That is a wise-hearted thing to say, lady human," she said. "I had no idea humans could know such wisdom. What is your name?"

Valanice hesitated. Graham couldn't blame her. To give a faery one's name was supposed to give the faery power over you. At least that's what the old wives' tales said.

"I am Valanice, Queen of Daventry," said Valanice at last.

Jiilii'a fluttered around Valanice's head for a few moments. "Valanice," she said softly. "Valanice. It is a good name. It sounds like a faery word—*vaal'inisia*. Do you know what that means?"

"No," said Valanice. "I don't know any faery words."

"It is the wisdom of the grass," said Jiilii'a. "The wisdom that tells the grass to bend before the wind and not to stand tall in the face of it. The wisdom to endure the storm rather than fight it. The oak has the strength to stand proud and tall, but falls before the wind. The grass humbles itself by bending its head to the ground before the wind, but it never falls."

"That is a good word," said Valanice. "How did you say it again?"

"*Vaal'inisia*," said Jiilii'a. "You may use it if you like. It is an ordinary enough word. There is no magic in it."

"*Vaal'inisia*," repeated the queen. "Thank you, Jiilii'a."

Jiilii'a flitted ahead of them again. "It is nothing," she said. "If you have the wisdom, you should know the word for it. It is a simple enough thing."

"How close are we to King Quilli'ehennan?" asked Graham.

"The time it would take me to fly there is the time it takes for the elk to run from the Stream of Yilia'mureia to the Dale of Solitude," said Jiilii'a.

"Yes, but how far is that?" asked Graham.

Jiilii'a whistled a harsh note. "How am I supposed to know human distances?" she asked. "We are not there yet, that is obvious. We will be there shortly."

Graham didn't say anything, but he felt that the faery's idea of what "shortly" was might differ significantly from his own. Still, what else could he do but follow until Jiilii'a brought them to Quilli'ehennan? They were at the sprite's mercy.

Jiilii'a continued to lead the way in silence. Graham tried to peer out of the green sphere to see what the Old Wood might be like, but he could not tell if the twisted and tortured shape of the trees was their natural state, or merely an illusion cast by Jiilii'a's magic.

Graham glanced back to Valanice. She winked at him and nodded. So. She was all right. Graham knew she would be—she was the strongest person he knew when it came to enduring bitter trials or terrible danger—but that didn't keep him from worrying about her.

At last, Jiilii'a stopped. "We are almost there," she said in a hushed whisper. "The *lo'ahimasa'ev-ennan* waits just ahead for you. Good-bye!"

With a single bright flicker of wings, Jiilii'a zipped away and was gone, as was their protective bubble. Graham and Valanice found themselves in a small clearing where the snow lay in only a slight dusting on the ground and ice crystals danced in the air.

The sky was blue but Graham saw dark clouds gathering around. It seemed the snow had not yet attacked the Old Wood in force, but it would only be a matter of time.

The dancing ice crystals glittered like tiny glass prisms, throwing off wonderful small rainbows all over the clearing. The ice crystals flew to Graham and Valanice and their horses and surrounded them.

Graham could have sworn he heard the ice crystals laughing. He tried to single one out and stare at it, but all of them moved much too quickly for him to track a single one. Perhaps these were tiny versions of sprites.

A faery maid stepped into the clearing. Her raven-dark tresses fell in a forest of braids from her head to her ankles. Her eyes were dark and empty like the elkrider's. Her curved, pointed ears stuck out of her hair and almost touched the top of her head. Her skin was palest white, with bare tracings of green veins showing at her neck. She was about as tall as the elkrider, waist high or so, and clad in shimmering white.

"Welcome to the Old Wood," said the faery maid. Her voice was low and deep for one so small and seemed to emanate from the very ground itself. "I am Eleni'iulena. I will lead you to the King of the Wood. You may leave your horses here. No one will harm them in this glade."

Graham and Valanice dismounted. The gray mare looked around the clearing once, then dropped her head and began to munch on the sweet spring grass.

Graham bowed to Eleni'iulena. "Madam, may I present my lady wife, Valanice." Valanice bowed to the faery.

Eleni'iulena's ears flattened against her head. Graham was surprised. He had not known faeries could move their ears as the horses did. "I know who you are," said the maid in her low, sweet voice. "King Quilli'ehennan's invitation is known to all the folk of the forest."

Eleni'iulena turned and walked away. Graham hesitated. Normally, he would have let Valanice go before him, but he hated to have her in danger. Should she follow Eleni'iulena first or should he?

But then, better to have her in front of him where he could see her and any who might threaten her. He bowed to Valanice and she went before him. Graham followed.

The Old Wood seemed to clutch at Graham. The branches and twigs of the trees almost seemed to reach out. He constantly had to pull his cloak away from briars and branches.

"The forest is not happy we're here," he said.

"Of course not," said Eleni'iulena. "How could it be? The Wood is indeed Old—it remembers a time before humans. Before faeries, even. But over the aeons it has grown used to my kind. Your kind are still ill-favored in this place. Though not all your kind are as unwelcome as others."

Graham could see what Eleni'iulena meant. The briars and branches did not target Valanice. Like Jiilii'a, the forest must think of her as something beautiful to admire, something to keep safe forever.

Graham shivered, and this time it had nothing to do with the cold. This place was just too strange, too alien. The Wood seemed to have eyes that watched him and judged him. Accused him, even, and he didn't know for what except that he was a man. A *human* man.

And that was enough.

Graham had never felt anything like it. His bones ached as if he, too, were tall and unbent before the onslaught of time. As if he, too, had weathered aeons upon aeons in silence. A silence pervaded only by faery songs and the laughter of the waters of the streams.

Eleni'iulena stopped and turned to Valanice. "You, I know, will be able to pass," she said. "For the forest covets your beauty. But you," she said, looking up at Graham, "may not be able to pass. If you cannot, you will be alone here on the trail in the Old Wood. If so, you must not move. If you so much as step off the trail, you will be lost here forever."

"You could not find me and bring me back?" asked Graham.

"When mortal flesh becomes lost in the Old Wood, no power on earth can find it and retrieve it safely," said Eleni'iulena. "Do not step off the path. If you cannot pass, then eventually I will return to you and guide you back to your horse."

"And King Quilli'ehennan, does his invitation mean nothing then?" asked Graham.

"Passing the barrier has naught to do with invitations of the *lo'ahimasa'evannan,* mighty though he is," said Eleni'iulena. Her eyes betrayed not a spark of life or emotion. "It is a test of the Old Wood. If you do not pass, you will not see Quilli'ehennan, you will not speak to Quilli'ehennan. You will have to stay here until I can return and guide you to your horse."

"All right," said Graham. "Let's go."

Eleni'iulena stepped behind a tree. Valanice followed. Graham walked forward and tried to do the same.

He froze. Every muscle in his body tensed in fear. Cold sweat broke out all over him. Graham glanced around, panicked, without moving his head. He couldn't go forward.

That was silly. Valanice had taken this step easily enough. Graham forced his foot another inch forward.

His fear doubled. Heart racing, Graham panted for air. Run! Run! His instincts threatened to override his reason, ready to force his legs to carry him pell-mell through the forest, away from this awful fear.

Graham gritted his teeth and suppressed the desire to scream. This was a test. It was only a test.

Graham squelched his fear as best he could and slammed his foot down. Instantly, he found himself in a long, narrow clearing. Tall oaks lined the sides, their branches intertwining overhead to make a sort of roof.

At the far end of this living hall sat a veiled figure in a chair made from antlers. Before the chair stood Eleni'iulena and Valanice. Graham walked forward with as much dignity as he could find and bowed to the figure on the chair.

"King Quilli'ehennan?" he asked. "I am Graham, King of Daventry, your neighbor. I have honored your request and stand before you ready to discuss a danger which seems to affect us both.''

The figure lifted the thin, white gauze veil and threw it back over his head. A young boy sat on the chair. He looked to be no more than a teenager—maybe thirteen, maybe fourteen. Darkly green hair had been cropped close to his head. Eyelashes and eyebrows of the same color surrounded eyes as dark and empty as every other faery's eyes Graham had seen.

Graham suppressed his surprise. He had expected Quilli'ehennan to appear older, wizened with years. Instead, a youth sat before him.

''I am Quilli'ehennan, Heart of the Wood,'' said the youth. ''King of the Wood. I welcome you to my court, King of Daventry.''

Eleni'iulena turned her face away from her king but Graham could not help but stare. Quilli'ehennan was more beautiful than anything Graham had ever seen. Even Valanice paled before such timeless, ageless beauty.

''I . . . ,'' began Graham. He got no farther. A sudden dizziness came upon him and he dropped to the ground.

· 7 ·

"Graham? King Graham?"

Someone was calling him. Graham thought he recognized the voice, but he wasn't sure. He opened his eyes reluctantly.

A faery maid stood over him. It took a moment for Graham to place her name. Eleni'iulena. That was it.

"Yes?" he said, his voice barely above a whisper.

"It is not healthy to stare at the *lo'ahimasa'evennan,* especially for a human," said Eleni'iulena. "His beauty is beyond that which can be tolerated in this world."

Valanice knelt beside him and took his hand. She appeared contrite.

"What's wrong?" Graham asked.

Valanice wouldn't look at him. "I knew not to look," she said. "But I failed to warn you. I'm sorry."

Graham smiled. "You grew up in an area where there were fairies. I didn't. You can't be blamed for that."

Graham pushed himself into a sitting position.

Warily, he glanced toward the throne, but Quilli'ehennan was thoroughly veiled, and a gray cloak covered his shoulders. The hood of the cloak fell down to cover part of his face.

"It is I who am sorry," said Quilli'ehennan. "It is considered rude among us to speak with a veiled face, but it had been so long since I spoke with a mortal, such as yourself, that I had forgotten the effect I would have upon you."

"No rudeness, surely," said Graham. "To wear a veil if it is necessary."

Quilli'ehennan gestured toward another antler chair like his own. "Please, King Graham, sit with me and hear my tale of woe."

Graham stood, a bit shaky. He went to the antler chair and sat, expecting to get poked. But the chair was as comfortable as his chair in his own Great Hall.

"Queen Valanice," said Quilli'ehennan, "please, join us." A second chair was brought out to sit by Graham's.

"Thank you," said Valanice. She sat gracefully.

"Now, what tale would you tell me?" asked Graham. "I hope it has something to do with the snow."

"It has everything to do with the snow," said Quilli'ehennan. "For my wife, the *oelevanor'li'ahimaseia*, the Spring of the Wood in your tongue, has been captured and taken."

"What?" asked Valanice. "No wonder spring has left our land."

"What do you mean?" Graham looked from Quilli'ehennan to his wife.

"I've heard of the queen of the Wood," said Valanice. She clasped her hands together in her lap. "She is the spring, the flowers, the gentle rain."

"She is all those things and more," said Quilli'ehennan in agreement. "Without her, there can be no spring."

"What happened?" asked Graham.

Quilli'ehennan gestured to Eleni'iulena. She bowed and departed. "Hear from the lips of one who was there," he said. If anything, his voice, though still beautiful, was even more flat and emotionless.

Within moments, Eleni'iulena returned with another faery maid. This one had hair of gold and a dress of purest rose red. She stepped nimbly on the grass to stand before Quilli'ehennan.

"My king?" asked the maid.

"Tell what happened to my Queen Ahi'aorina. Tell the humans what has been done," commanded Quilli'ehennan.

The maid turned to Graham and Valanice but did not raise her eyes. "It was early yesterday," she said. "The queen, myself, and some dozen others of her handmaids were in the woods when we were approached by an imp. No sooner had he come, than several others of his kind jumped out of the forest and took the queen. We fought to save her, I and the others. All the others died in the attempt. Only I live to tell of my shame, that I could not protect my queen."

"Shame indeed," said Quilli'ehennan, "for your queen to be taken and you to live. For that, our law condemns you to death. You know this."

The faery maid bowed her head farther.

"But," said Quilli'ehennan, "if you had not lived, we would not know what has become of my queen. You shall be punished, yes, but you shall not be killed."

"As you command, my king," whispered the faery.

"Then it is so," said Quilli'ehennan. He raised his hand, a simple gesture, but no sooner had he done so than the faery maid writhed and fell to the ground. In a moment, what had been a faery was a creeping vine. Eleni'iulena bent over to pick it up gently.

"If my queen returns, you shall live in her garden and be tended by her forevermore," said Quilli'ehennan. "And perhaps, one day, she will pity you and return you to your own form. If my queen does not return, you shall climb in the trees without hope of release, and fend for yourself as best you may like any other growing thing."

Eleni'iulena carried the vine away. Graham swallowed hard at the swiftness and mercilessness of the other king's justice.

"Do you marvel at the harshness of my sentence?" asked Quilli'ehennan. "When you know the terrible nature of what has been done, you will not think me so cruel."

"Then tell me," said Graham.

"My queen is gone, and she is the springtime," said Quilli'ehennan. "Until she returns, no spring will ever come again to the Old Wood or to the surrounding lands."

"You mean, it will snow forever?" asked Graham.

"Perhaps not forever," said Quilli'ehennan. "Perhaps for only an aeon or two, until nature balances out on its own. But that will be too long for even a faery to wait. We will perish. Humans will perish first, of course, but so, too, will the faeries. Even the Old Wood might be in danger— it's hard to say how much the Wood has become dependent on my queen since faeries first came here. In any case, certainly no human and no faery will be able to live here for ages to come if my queen does not return."

Graham was silent. He had never considered a time when spring itself would be endangered, every human in Daventry doomed. And all because a faery had been stolen from the Old Wood.

"What can we do?" he asked Quilli'ehennan at last. "What can any of us do?"

"You can go to my queen," said Quilli'ehennan. "Rescue her from this imp and return her to the Wood."

"Forgive me, but why can't you go?" asked Graham. "If she is your lady and faeries are in danger . . ."

Quilli'ehennan raised his fist. "Don't you think I want to?" he shouted. "Don't you think I want my lady and my queen back? But I can't leave the Wood. Just as Ahi'aorina is Spring of the Wood, so I am Heart of the Wood. To leave it, even if only for an hour, means my death."

"And your people?" asked Graham.

"They can leave," said Quilli'ehennan, "but their magic fades the farther they get from this place. By the time one of them reached my queen, he or she would be too weak to help her."

"And so you need me," said Graham.

"Yes."

Graham thought. If he said yes, it certainly wouldn't be the first time he had gone questing. He could take care of himself, he knew. But it was no longer just himself he had to worry about.

He looked over to Valanice. Her eyes had filled with tears but she did not shed them.

Graham remembered his words of this morning—he had promised Rosella that if he could do something about the snow, he would. He had meant it.

Graham nodded. "I will rescue Queen Ahi'aorina," he said, never taking his eyes off of Valanice.

She hesitated, but nodded. She knew that if rescuing the faery queen would stop the snow and save Daventry, Graham would have to go.

Graham turned back to Quilli'ehennan. "Is there anything else you can tell me—the direction the imps took, for example."

"East," said Quilli'ehennan. "The trees watched. Past the border of the Old Wood, the imps continued on toward the Glass Mountains."

Graham nodded. "Then I'd better get started." He turned to Valanice and took her hand. "Explain to Rosella that I'll be home as soon as I possibly can. And please tell William I'm sorry I can't attend his birthday dinner."

Valanice nodded and pressed her lips together. A single tear escaped her control and dripped down her cheek.

"A birthday dinner?" asked Quilli'ehennan. "Forgive me, but what is that?"

Graham faced the king, but kept hold of his wife's hand. "Every year on the anniversary of our births, we celebrate and keep count of the years."

Quilli'ehennan shook his head. His veil swung side to side. "Every year?" he asked, incredulous. "How can you keep track of so small a thing as a year?"

"It's not so small a thing to us," said Graham. "We have so few to count."

Quilli'ehennan bowed his head. "I'm sorry. I mocked you and your kind just after you agreed to aid me in this time of sorrow and trouble. My apologies. It is simply that faeries keep track of aeons. Years slip by us without our noticing."

"I'm sure they do," said Graham. He couldn't imagine the kind of time Quilli'ehennan could count back. How long was an aeon? How many of them had Quilli'ehennan seen?

Graham stood and bowed. "Then I shall be on my way, Your Majesty. I shall rescue your queen and return spring to the Wood. And to Daventry."

The figure on the antlered chair bowed where he sat. "As I knew you would," Quilli'ehennan said. "I knew you to be a brave and wise man. Brave enough and wise enough to retrieve our *oelevanor'li'ahimaseia,* my queen."

Valanice rose and bowed as well. "I shall return to my own land," she said. "And take care of it as well as I can until my husband's return."

"You shall return no later than you left," said Quilli'ehennan. "This is within my power to grant. For time moves strangely around my kind, and often years slip away unnoticed even from mortals when they visit us. But you shall find not a minute gone when you depart this place."

"Thank you," said Valanice. Relief spread across her face, and Graham knew she had been thinking on Matilda's words, that those who visited faeries would not return for years.

Eleni'iulena returned.

"My daughter will show you to your horses," said Quilli'ehennan.

"Your daughter?" asked Graham.

Eleni'iulena bowed slightly. "Quilli'ehennan and Ahi'aorina are my parents," she said. "I thank you for agreeing to go after my mother."

Though her words were kind, Eleni'iulena's eyes remained flat and vacant. Graham shivered.

Though the faeries had been courteous, they were still far too alien for him to grow comfortable in their midst. He had no wish to stay a moment longer than necessary among them.

Eleni'iulena led Graham and Valanice back out of the hall to the path. The snow fell through the tree branches now.

"Even the Old Wood is touched by the winter now," said Eleni'iulena. "So will it be until the *oelevanor'li'ahimaseia* is returned to us."

"Which will be soon, I hope," said Graham. "For the sake of my people, who will die under this snow."

Eleni'iulena nodded. "For my people, too," she said softly.

The faery led them back to their horses. The buckskin raised his head and looked askance at Graham as if to warn him the horse did not want to go back out into the snow.

"You will have to walk from here," said Eleni'iulena, "so your lady must lead your horse back to the castle."

"I'm not sure I can get there in all this snow," admitted Valanice.

"Jiilii'a will guide you home," said Eleni'iulena. "We will not strand you here now."

Graham hugged Valanice and helped her into her saddle. He handed her the buckskin's reins. "Take care, my love," he said.

"And you," Valanice said simply.

Jiilii'a flitted into the clearing. "I will lead you

home now," she said. "Pretty one. It makes me sad you will not stay with us. But I understand *duty*."

Valanice nodded and turned the gray mare away. Graham watched them go until his wife and the horses were lost in the darkness of the Old Wood.

He sighed and turned back to Eleni'iulena.

"All right," he said. "Show me the path I'm to take."

Eleni'iulena nodded and turned, leading Graham deeper into the grasping, clinging branches.

Ahi'aorina looked about her dully. Since the imps had taken her from her Wood, she had felt weak and sick. Clumps of hair had fallen out of her head, and her white skin had turned the yellow of old bones.

Ahi'aorina sighed and brushed her silver hair out of her face with a trembling hand. More hair came away in her hand and floated to the bottom of her cage.

"Stop that!" shouted Kuzgu. "Faery no good, pull all her hair out. Soon no more the most beautiful she will be!"

Ahi'aorina turned away from the imp. In the past three days, he had mocked and taunted her endlessly. At first, his attentions had angered her, but she had learned to ignore them.

"Sing, faery queen," called another of the imps, a smelly creature Kuzgu called Zuzak. Zuzak was a bit shorter than Kuzgu, and rounder about the middle. Among all the imps, this one seemed most interested in food and song. "Faery songs so wonderful, they are. Want to hear one, I do."

Kuzgu put his beaklike nose up to the wooden bars of Ahi'aorina's cage. "Hmm, maybe a good idea this is," said Kuzgu. "Bring spring to us, you could."

Ahi'aorina turned her head and contemplated the thin hands in her lap. Though they were her hands, she barely recognized them, they had changed so much after leaving the Wood.

Kuzgu grabbed the wooden bars of the cage and shook them. Ahi'aorina cowered on the floor of the cage, terrified Kuzgu might touch her, might cause her more sickness and pain than he had already.

"Sing," demanded Kuzgu. "Sing a faery song."

Ahi'aorina did not lift her head, but she sang a low note, the first note in the faery song to the autumn full moon. She sang the song very slow and in a minor key, quite unlike the way she would have sung it, high-spirited and brightly chorded, if she had been home in the Wood.

Even though the song was sung sadly and in a dreary key, the imps smiled in pleasure and closed their eyes. Zuzak linked his fingers across his ample stomach and sighed loudly.

Ahi'aorina finished the song and the imps smiled at each other.

"Sing another," said Kuzgu. "Sing a happy song."

"How can I sing such a thing?" asked Ahi'aorina in a voice hoarse with weariness. "For there is no joy in me and will never be again until I return to my Wood and my love."

"Rest she should," said a taller imp. "Not look good does she."

"Shut up you should, Lugmut," said Kuzgu. He sauntered around the cage. "Looks good enough, does." The imp grabbed the bars of Ahi'aorina's cage and glared in at her. "Sing another song," he said in a voice that brooked no argument.

Ahi'aorina glanced around her wooden prison. She would sing a song to the wood. Even this wood, dead and dried from years in the sun and wind, might respond to her.

Ahi'aorina sang the song of the growing stem, the song of the branching twig. She poured her heart into the song, hoping desperately there was some memory of nature left in the dead bars of her prison.

It seemed there was not. Ahi'aorina held out the last note of the song and touched a wooden bar, but it did not bend to her will. She sighed.

"Good, good," said Kuzgu. "Look, spring you have made."

Ahi'aorina glanced out of the bars. Daffodils had sprouted around her cage, and a songbird fluttered in a newly budded tree nearby. A gentle, misty rainfall touched the cage and the imps for a moment and then was gone in a burst of a rainbow.

One of the imps made a grab for the songbird and it flew away. The daffodils bowed their heads, spent already. Ahi'aorina's eyes filled with tears for the flowers. She had called them forth into a cold world, and already life had left them. A flower's life was short, indeed, but at least a bloom had a few days to enjoy the sun. These had had life for only the length of her song.

It had been a cruel thing to do to the flowers. Even the tree shed its buds now, returning to its interrupted winter sleep.

Ahi'aorina wept.

The imps laughed. "Beautiful," they said. "Sing again! Sing again!"

"No!" shouted Kuzgu. "Go on we must. Songs there will be at a later time—when we return to Sorrowing Court. Songs we will have then, as many as we wish."

The imps bobbed their heads in agreement. "At Sorrowing Court," said Zuzak. "Spring then we will have. Spring forever."

Four imps approached Ahi'aorina's cage and picked it up. The cage had been constructed so that a pole could be mounted on both ends. Four imp bearers carried her ever closer to the Glass Mountains. Ahi'aorina had caught quick glimpses of the mountains through the bars. She shuddered. The Glass Mountains were said to be even older than the Old Wood, and even less amenable to living creatures. Nothing grew there. Nothing ever had.

Ahi'aorina had never been able to imagine the loneliness the mountains must feel, never to hear a faery sing or feel the gentle brush of a deer's muzzle. But she thought now she might be able to grasp it. Being taken from her Wood, and her family, was more than she could bear.

Unbidden, the face of Quilli'ehennan floated in her mind's eye, gentle and beautiful. For countless thousands of years they had lived in the Wood, Heart of the Wood wed to Spring of the Wood. And there was her daughter, Eleni'iulena, whose dark hair reminded Ahi'aorina of the velvet blanket of night over the forest.

Her garden was another one of her loves. Each leaf of grass, each bud and root, was hers. She knew them and cherished them always.

"Kuzgu!" shouted an imp with a tattered ear.

"What is it, Buzgut?"

Ahi'aorina roused herself enough to peer out at the imps. Most of the nearer imp's form was obscured by a wooden bar, but she could see Kuzgu clearly.

Buzgut held out a small crystal. The crystal glowed with a cheery rose color. Ahi'aorina's eyes drank in the sight. She hadn't realized how much she missed seeing *colors*. The imps wore brown and gray, with only the yellow of their eyes relieving the sameness of it all. And everywhere Ahi'aorina had been taken since the Wood looked dull and dead to her. But the crystal was not. It glowed. It *lived*.

"Something happens in the path we left," said Buzgut. "Red the crystal glows. Faeries of the Wood some action have taken."

Kuzgu laughed. "What can they do? If they leave their Wood, they will weaken, and be easy to see and catch."

"Could be tasty, too," said another imp. Ahi-'aorina did not know his name. "Never tried faery."

"Ha," another one said. "So old they are, stringy they must be. Marinate and slow-cook one would have to do."

"A chance to find out maybe we will have," said Buzgut. "If following us the faeries are, catching them we will do, and eating them, too!"

The imps laughed loudly at that. Ahi'aorina sat back in her cage and thought furiously.

It could not be Quilli'ehennan who followed, for to leave the Wood meant laying down his life. Surely Quilli'ehennan would not have sent one of their people to follow. The imps were right on that—a faery outside its own Wood was weak.

So who followed?

Or did the imps even know how to use the crystal?

"May I see that?" asked Ahi'aorina.

"What?" asked Kuzgu. "The stone you should not see. Magic it is."

"I would just like to look at it," said Ahi'aorina. "It is so beautiful."

"Beautiful as you it is not," said Kuzgu. "Buzgut keeps. Perhaps later show it to you he will."

Ahi'aorina nodded. Sitting back, she reached for the dreamless slumber of the faeries, where only darkness surrounded and touched her.

It was a darkness she knew and cherished, especially over the touch of the imps. Ahi'aorina sighed and let herself slide over, over beyond the pale of hope and the sting of despair.

· 9 ·

Graham followed Eleni'iulena to the edge of the Old Wood. They arrived much more quickly than he had supposed they would—it was barely evening.

"The Wood seems small," he said.

"It is big enough," said Eleni'iulena. "Besides, mortals have difficulty traveling the forest. It might be that you would walk in a straight line for days and not see the other side, or walk in circles for a few hours and find yourself at home."

"A perilous place. I am grateful, lady, for your guidance," said Graham.

"Such is my duty, to lead a mortal king out of our land," said the faery. "Most who blunder into our Wood wander lost under leaves. They remain alone and sorrowing until they die."

Graham shivered at that. He stepped out beyond the edge of the Wood, glad to have it behind him. Ahead of him were wide open plains dotted with small clumps of trees and brush.

Graham turned to thank his guide again, but she had disappeared without a sound. Graham was happy enough to have her gone. Although Eleni'iulena and her people meant him no harm, they were cold, comfortless companions. Even Quilli'ehennan, who had wanted to appear pleasant and courteous, had seemed alien to Graham.

He supposed it was just that faeries lived forever, and could not be bothered to display much courtesy or concern over human ways. Graham was glad the faeries of the Old Wood were not his enemies, but they were at best uncomfortable friends.

On this side of the Wood, the snow was not yet deeper than Graham's knees. Only a few flakes fell, but gathering clouds threatened more storms. And soon.

Graham struggled forward, glad he'd thought to wear several pairs of socks. Even so, his toes were numb with cold.

He walked until the sun set and the full moon rose above the horizon. By its pale light he headed toward a nearby clump of trees, hoping to find shelter for the coming night. He was getting a late start and hadn't come more than eight or ten miles from the Old Wood, but he was tired and needed a rest.

Graham stooped under a willow and gathered a few twigs for his fire. He pulled out his tinderbox and struck a spark with the flint. The spark fell onto the dry twigs, but failed to catch.

Hands shaking with the cold, Graham tried again. And again. Finally, a spark landed on his twigs and took hold. A small flicker of flame appeared.

Carefully, Graham fed the new fire with grass and small twigs until it was large enough to eat more substantial things. He built a fire of larger branches around and over the blazing twigs. His fire consumed them eagerly.

Graham removed his mittens and held his hands out to the fire, glad to have a chance to warm them. He set up a small, flat rock near the fire and laid his mittens on it. They steamed as the fire leeched them of their accumulated moisture.

Graham leaned back against the tree, and, despite his worries, he was asleep in moments.

A sharp staccato crack awakened him. Graham sat bolt upright and looked around. The area was empty of all but him. He stretched and retrieved his mittens. His fire had gone out and the mittens were cold now, but at least they were dry.

Graham put his mittens back on and rubbed his hands together until they warmed up. He stood and stretched again, then kicked some snow over the dark coals of his fire. He didn't suppose there was any danger of the fire spreading, but he would rather be sure.

The crack sounded again. This time, Graham realized it came from above. He looked up. A woodpecker, white with black head and tail, stared down at him for a moment, then pecked again at a dead tree trunk.

The bird gave up and flew away. The flutter of its wings was the only sound Graham heard.

Graham set his feet toward the rising sun and began walking. The sky was cloudless and blue as only a winter sky could be. Graham breathed in the cold, refreshing air, grateful there was no snow.

"Hail, traveler!" said a cheery voice.

Graham turned to a clump of trees. A lanky man sat by a meager fire. The man's red hair caught the morning sun. He was dressed in summer-weight clothing: a light tunic, pants, and low boots. The man didn't even have a hat on, yet he did not seem to be shivering.

"Hail," said Graham. "Um, pardon me, but aren't you cold?"

The man laughed. "Cold doesn't touch me," he said. "At least, not often. Still, it does take something out of you. The cold, I mean. After a while."

"You get sleepy," said Graham. "It happened to me yesterday."

The man nodded. "Snow sleep is a dangerous thing. Come, share my fire, stranger."

"Thank you," said Graham, "but I must be going."

"What's the hurry?" asked the man. "It's awfully early to be so late."

"I'm following some people," said Graham. "And I have to catch up with them—I hope to do so on this side of the Glass Mountains."

The lanky man nodded. "Then you have either much room to catch them or far to go. The Glass Mountains are at least a week's walk from here."

"So you see why I must keep moving," said Graham. "Though your invitation is kind."

The man stood and bowed. "I am Shallan, a traveling minstrel," he said. "Perhaps you would allow me to share the road with you a while."

Graham hesitated. "I don't know," he said. "I'm in a hurry."

"Where there's a hurry, there's a story," said Shallan. "And stories are food and drink to a minstrel like me."

The minstrel stared at Graham in a pleasant, disarming fashion.

"Uh, I'm Graham," said Graham. "King of Daventry."

Shallan's eyes grew wide. "A king, yet. Your Majesty." Shallan bowed even more deeply.

"Please, don't do that," said Graham. "I'm in no mood for formalities—I can hardly stand them at court, let alone here. I'm sorry, but I have to go."

Shallan kicked snow into his fire. "I'm ready," he said.

"What?"

"I said, I'm ready," repeated Shallan. "A king out of his court, in a hurry to meet the dawn, means a *big* story. No minstrel worth his lute-strings would pass up such an opportunity."

"Um," said Graham.

"So let's go," said Shallan. "After you, Your Majesty."

"Graham," said Graham. "Really, I'm only king in Daventry, and this area is far beyond my borders. I'm no king here. Besides, if you're set on coming with me, it will get tedious to have to listen to you saying Your Majesty all day."

Shallan smiled. The smile started with his mouth and spread across his whole face. Finally, he laughed. "I like that," he said. "A king who doesn't want titles. But," Shallan held out a cautionary hand to Graham, "I warn you ahead of time, heroes of ballads always take their titles with them."

"I'm no hero of any ballad," said Graham. "And I have to go now. If you're coming, come on."

Graham started back east. Shallan jogged over to walk beside him.

Seated, Shallan had looked merely lanky. Standing, he was *tall*—at least a foot taller than Graham, though he probably weighed no more than the king. The minstrel had less trouble in the snow than Graham, as Shallan had both longer legs and bigger feet.

"Now, why are we going to the Glass Mountains?" asked the minstrel. "They are a perilous place indeed. The mountains have no love for any creature, even the smallest and most humble."

"I'm after some imps. They have taken the faery queen away from her Wood, and so we have snow instead of spring," said Graham. "It will never be spring again in my land until she is returned."

Shallan whistled. "A mighty task, indeed, Graham. But good for ballads. A king on foot, chasing imps guarding a stolen faery queen. Eternal snow and the Glass Mountains. I tell you, this will be the ballad that will make my career."

"You'll have to come to Daventry and sing it at court sometime," said Graham. "Providing I'm successful. If I'm not, there won't be any Daventry anymore."

Shallan nodded. "Should I live to tell the tale, I'll come to your court. Who knows, maybe you'll offer me a job."

"Who knows," said Graham. "But then, I haven't heard you sing yet—so how do I know what kind of minstrel you really are?"

Shallan laughed. "Very good," he said. "Well, judge for yourself."

Shallan launched into a merry song about a fat king who couldn't get up from his throne. One after one, his courtiers tried to pull or pry him out, to no avail. Eventually, the chief cook came up with the solution—grease the king down with butter. The courtiers did and out popped the king.

By the second time the verse came around, Graham was singing along with the minstrel, adding his own baritone voice to the minstrel's clear tenor.

The last note of the last verse died away. Graham sighed. "A song like that helps the heart," he said. "Thank you."

Shallan bowed slightly as he walked. "I'm glad you're pleased. But now, I must rest my voice awhile."

Graham slogged ahead and the two of them traveled in silence for the better part of the morning. At noon, Graham called a halt at the top of a hill.

Below them in a deep valley was the silver ribbon of a river. Between them and the river were fields full of deep holes and great boulders.

"Now I see why I had to come on foot," said Graham. "I didn't know why the faeries wanted to separate me from my horse. But if the terrain ahead is any indication, I'd have had to let the horse go, or at least lead it, for the rest of the trip."

"Better to walk, anyway," said Shallan. "Loosens a man's feet and fires the appetite."

"Speaking of which . . . ," said Graham.

"Ah, not to worry," said Shallan. "I passed a lovely little farmhouse a couple of days ago, and for a song or two, the farmer and his wife parted with a sack full of food. Mostly day-old bread and salted meat. But you'd be surprised how good those things can be after a day on the trail."

"I can repay you when we return to Daventry," said Graham.

"Bah," said Shallan. "Who needs payment for

something which comes from the earth for free?"

"Hardly free," said Graham. "Since it takes a great deal of toil to tease the crop out of the earth and make it bountiful."

Shallan shrugged. "There's more than one story behind everything," he said. "It seems free to me, so eat what you will."

Graham and Shallan made their way over to a low boulder and sat on it. Here, there was almost no snow, and the rock was dry. But still very cold.

Shallan brought out meat and bread and even a few pieces of bruised fruit. Graham ate with relish. Before he knew it, all the food was gone.

"Don't worry about the food," said Shallan. "Somehow, the world always provides for minstrels. Perhaps it's a magic talent we have."

Graham nodded, glad his stomach was full after half a day of walking without a stop. He rested on the boulder for a few minutes.

He stared down at the river. "Will we have to cross it to get to the Glass Mountains?" he asked.

Shallan nodded. "It's possible to reach the Glass Mountains without crossing it, but we'd have to follow it back a hundred or more miles. And from your tale, I suspect we haven't got that kind of time."

"No, we haven't," said Graham. "So let's go."

"Let's," agreed Shallan.

The two men made their way carefully down the slope. Loose rocks were everywhere, as were pits that were deeper than Graham was tall—

maybe deeper than Shallan was tall, even.

Halfway down the slope, Graham's foot slipped out from under him. A shower of small, round stones fell down the slope. Graham fell to his knees and threw out his arms.

Shallan grabbed Graham's wrist and held on as the king, off balance and teetering over the brink of a deep pit, fought for control. Graham's heart raced and he was afraid he would either fall into the pit or slide the rest of the way down the slope.

But Shallan held on, and Graham managed to step away from the pit and regain his balance.

Graham sat down. "Thank you," he said, panting for breath. "I owe you my life."

"Well, perhaps you do," said Shallan, "but maybe you don't. If you'd gone in the pit, I could have pulled you out. But if you'd gone down the slope . . ."

"Yes," said Graham. "That would have been very bad indeed."

"So be grateful it didn't happen that way and let's move on," said Shallan. "We should cross this river before nightfall, don't you think?"

"Yes, we should," said Graham. He stood up and pressed on.

Graham and Shallan made it the rest of the way down the slope without further incident. To Graham's disgust, Shallan seemed to have the balance and dexterity of a mountain goat—he never stumbled or dislodged stones. The king, on the other hand, couldn't seem to move without incident.

By midafternoon, Graham and Shallan stood on the banks of the river. The river wasn't very wide—perhaps twenty or thirty feet. But it flowed swiftly by. Driftwood and plants that were trapped in the current moved past Graham and were gone almost before he could identify them.

"Now what?" asked Graham. "Have you crossed this river before?"

"Once upon a time," said Shallan.

Graham looked at the minstrel and frowned. Shallan shrugged.

"Trade joke," he said. "But, yes, I have crossed the river. A few miles upstream there's a ferry. I don't know what's downstream."

"Then upstream it is," said Graham. With aching feet, he turned and trudged up the stream bank.

Shallan was right. Only two or three miles from where they started by the river, they found the ferry.

So had some others. A party of imps.

·10·

"These wouldn't happen to be the ones you're looking for, would they?" asked Shallan. "There *are* an awful lot of them."

Graham counted ten imps at the ferry. One of them seemed to be arguing with the ferryman. The ferryman was a singularly short and stocky individual. He wore a black cloak. Large blue-skinned hands gestured toward the imps.

"I don't think so," said Graham thoughtfully. "They don't seem to have anyone with them."

"True enough," said Shallan.

The men trudged forward toward the ferry. Soon, they were close enough to hear what was going on.

"Twelve we paid you for," insisted the imp. "But only ten of us came across. Go back you must for the others."

"What others?" asked the ferryman. "Do you see anyone over on the far shore?"

The imps muttered among themselves. Some cast worried glances to the far shore. Whatever they saw there, it did not make them happy.

"Be there they must," said the imp. "Two companions we have who still must get across."

"Then show me where they are," said the ferryman. "Point to them."

The imps looked at the far bank and then looked at each other. "There they are not," one of them said. "Maybe back home they went."

"Home?" asked the imp who had argued with the ferryman; he seemed to be in charge. "Not home is Sorrowing Court. Time to leave that place it was. Heading home now are we. Back to the land of Zakizga. Home *that* is."

The others milled about, but said nothing. Some still glanced back across the river.

"But the others . . . ," said one.

The imp in charge turned back to the ferryman. "All right, so come with us our two companions did not. For two fares do you owe us, then."

"No refunds," said the ferryman. A long blue muzzle rose up out of the cloak. Many long white teeth glistened in the jaws of the muzzle. "Anyone who wants a refund has to take it by force."

The imp facing the ferryman raised a fist. The ferryman opened his mouth and hissed.

The imp hesitated, then thought better of it. He lowered his fist and stepped back. "Thief," he said.

"You got across the river, didn't you?" asked the ferryman. "Be grateful for that. Now get out of here."

The imps hesitated a moment more, then fled. Graham and Shallan approached the ferry.

"How much for passage?" asked Graham.

"What do you have?" asked the blue-skinned creature. Graham could see his hands and snout. The rest of him, even his eyes, was covered by his black cloak.

"I have this." Graham pulled a ring off his finger. It was a gold band inlaid with pearls, a gift from Valanice. He felt a pang as he handed it over to the ferryman. But Valanice would understand. And it was only a ring. He could sacrifice a piece of jewelry if it meant getting closer to the imps who'd taken Ahi'aorina, the imps who had doomed Daventry to a slow, cold death.

The blue hand closed over the ring. "A beautiful item," said the ferryman. "A treasure fit for a king."

"Can it buy passage across the river for my friend and me?" asked Graham. "And the answer to one question?"

"Passage, yes," said the ferryman. "The answer—well, I'll have to hear the question first."

"I saw those imps coming from the far bank of the river, but have you ferried others to the east, as well?" asked Graham. "These imps would have had a faery woman with them."

The blue muzzle contracted back into the hood of the cloak. "Yes," said the ferryman.

"Good," said Graham with relief. He was still on the right track. "How long ago was that? How many of them were there?''

"Those are questions two and three, and not covered under our bargain," said the ferryman. "Please, step onto the ferry. I will get you across the river."

"But . . . ," began Graham.

"Thank you," interrupted Shallan. He turned to Graham. "Shall we go?"

Shallan looked worried. Perhaps Graham would not be wise to press the ferryman—at least not until they were across the river.

Graham nodded and stepped onto the ferry. Shallan followed him.

The ferryman said nothing, but pulled on the rope that bound the ferry to each shore. Though it must have been very difficult—Graham doubted he could pull the ferry across by himself—the blue-skinned creature did not seem burdened by the task.

In only a few minutes, they were across. Graham and Shallan stepped down. Many imp tracks marred the mud on this side of the river. Though there had been enough comings and goings to obscure the true number, Graham suspected that far more than a dozen imps had passed this way in recent days.

"Do you know what happened to the imps who were left behind?" asked Shallan.

The ferryman chortled. "I'll give you that one for free. Yes, I do. See that you don't meet the same fate, travelers."

"Thank you for the warning," said Graham, though the ferryman's explanation was far from helpful. "And thank you for easing our trail."

The ferryman bowed slightly. "You have only to pay and I will take you across as many times as you like."

"Once was enough for me," said Shallan. "Well, maybe twice, if I come back this same way."

Graham and Shallan continued their journey. The land on this side of the river was rolling hills covered with forest. The trees were stunted and bare.

"An entire forest of dead trees," said Shallan. "This is simply a charming place. I must make an effort to get here more often."

"Dead thorn trees," muttered Graham as a thorny branch nabbed his fur hat. He pulled the hat away. It came back to him, thorns still sticking out of it.

"A sticky place," said Shallan. "Or, a place that sticks to one. Let's hope we don't stick to *it*."

The sun set behind them at dusk, leaving a faint touch of silver on the eastern horizon before descending for the night.

"The Glass Mountains," said Shallan. "They glimmer in the sunlight. They're still days away from us, though."

"We have to catch up to those imps," said Graham. "I hope we can do it before we reach the Glass Mountains. I don't suppose there is anything like a ferry there to carry us across the peaks?''

"No, there is not," said Shallan. "None that I've heard of anyway. You'd need a flying ferry in any case. But we don't have to worry about that for days. Perhaps not ever, if we catch up with those imps soon.''

Graham gathered wood for a fire. Thorns continued to prick his fingers until they bled.

"I'll be glad to feed a few of these bloodthirsty twigs to a good fire," he said.

"Yes, the trees here do seem particularly unfriendly," said Shallan. "Still, most living things love a song, don't you think? I'll sing to them.''

Graham started the fire while Shallan sang a sad tune about a princess trapped in a burning forest. The trees and animals tried to help her, but to no avail. The princess finally climbed the highest tree and threw herself down from that height just before the fire reached her.

At the song's end, Graham realized he was crying. Quickly, he wiped tears from his face. "Tragic song," he said. He struggled to regain his composure.

"Yes," said the minstrel. "But sad songs often touch the heart more readily than a happy one. A happy song can banish thought while a sad one binds people together in their thoughts and their feelings.''

Graham threw another branch on the fire. This one did not scratch him first.

"Maybe your idea worked," he said. "I wasn't harmed that time. Try again."

Shallan shrugged. "All right," he said. "Let's see."

After a moment, Shallan began another sad tune, this one about a young boy who ran away from home after being beaten by his father. One day the boy found an injured faery. In return for his aid, the faery granted him one wish. The boy wished to be without trouble. The faery turned him into a swan and he flew away, without memory of his human life, but without the pain and sorrow he had had, either.

"Enough," said Graham. "You'll think me mad, a king that always cries at sad songs."

"These are touching songs," said Shallan. "Those who love are always affected. You could say they're a kind of test, really. If you didn't cry, I would know you for a hard-hearted man. But you have proved yourself a kindhearted, gentle man."

"Hm," said Graham. It seemed a strange test.

"Sssing another," whispered a dry, hissing voice.

"Yesss," agreed a second voice, this one higher pitched. "Sssing for usss."

"Who's there?" asked Graham. He looked around in alarm, but the thorny trees were all he saw.

"Sssing," asked the first voice.

"Only onccce more," said the higher pitched

voice. "We know your voiccce must be tired."

"All right," said Shallan. "But then you must show yourselves. Agreed?"

"Yesss," hissed the voices.

"I'll sing something a bit cheerier," said Shallan. "Is that all right?"

"Yess," said the first voice. "There isss no joy here. Sssing to usss of joy."

"Very well." Shallan started another song. This one was about a ball where a young prince and princess met and fell in love. The song was long and beautiful. It was not sad, but it tugged at Graham's heart just the same. He couldn't help but remember Valanice.

"Ahhh," sighed the voices when Shallan had finished. "Ahhh, that was good."

"Now show yourselves," said Graham.

Rustling in the undergrowth. Suddenly, two pony-sized forms slipped from between the twisted dead trunks of the trees. Spiders. Yellow fangs hung down from their mouths and their bodies were covered in coarse black fur. A multitude of eyes sat on each of their heads. The eyes reflected the light of the fire.

"That wasss good," said the larger of the two—the one with the higher pitched voice.

"Very good," echoed the other.

"I think we just found out what happened to those two imps," said Shallan.

"Oh my word," said Graham. "Oh my."

"Yess," said the smaller spider. "We took the

imps. They were juicy." The spider clicked its fangs against its lower jaw. "Very good impsss."

"What about us?" squeaked Graham. "Are we good to eat, too?"

"Yesss, humansss very good eating," said the larger spider with cruel humor. "But we are full now."

"Could kill you and ssstock you for later," said the smaller spider. "Alwaysss good to have ss-something in the larder. But you sssang for usss."

"We will not eat you," said the larger spider. "Becaussse we are not hungry now and you have pleasssed usss."

"I'll remember that," said Graham. "If I ever pass through these woods again, I'll make sure you're well fed first.'"

"A good idea," said the smaller spider.

The spiders melted back into the undergrowth. Graham looked over at Shallan, who shrugged.

"Always good to have an appreciative audience," said the minstrel.

Graham nodded, but didn't laugh. He felt as though he were being watched. Watched by dozens of flat black spider eyes. He shivered. The spiders were even more alien than the faeries, and they had been strange enough.

Shallan curled up by the fire and slept. His red hair fell in his face and was blown up and down by his breath.

Graham didn't sleep. He waited by the fire, and tended it, until dawn touched the horizon and the stars faded into the sky.

· 11 ·

Graham added some more wood to the fire as the sun came up. The fire ate the sticks greedily, sending forth warmth and smoke in equal measure.

Shallan yawned and stretched. He sat up and rubbed his eyes.

"You slept well," Graham observed.

Shallan shrugged. "When you're a traveling minstrel, you sleep well wherever you're at, or not at all."

"Well, at least nothing happened during the night," said Graham.

"I didn't suppose anything would," said Shallan. "I believe our arachnid friends would have seen to any trouble."

"I don't think it's wise to depend on spiders for our safety," said Graham. He was hungry and cold, and inclined to be irritable this early in the morning. "What if they decide they're hungry?"

Shallan smiled. "In my travels, I've found that anyone who appreciates a song is loath to let anything happen to the singer. We were safe enough."

"Well, at least you were," said Graham. "I didn't sing any songs."

"That all depends on how well spiders can tell individual humans apart," said Shallan. "We probably look the same to them."

"Yes, I'm sure we do," said Graham. "Tasty."

Shallan wagged a finger at the king. "You seem to be particularly grumpy this morning. Could it be because we've no breakfast?"

Graham sighed. Yesterday's midday meal seemed a lifetime ago.

"Never fear. Such details of life work out for traveling minstrels like—"

"Like you, yes," said Graham. "But what about traveling kings?"

"I guess we'll just have to find out," said Shallan. "Shall we go?"

"Why not."

"Wait," said a high-pitched voice from behind the thorny trees.

"Show yourself," demanded Graham. The tangled underbrush was so thick, the spider could have been mere feet from him and he'd have never known.

"Sssomething for you, in return for your sssong," hissed the spider. Two great black hairy legs stuck out of the underbrush. The legs pushed several bunches of grapes into the small clearing.

"Grapes?" asked Graham. "In this season?"

"I know humansss eat sssuch things," said the spider.

"Thank you," said Shallan. He took a grape and popped it in his mouth. "Delicious."

The spider legs retracted back into the undergrowth. "Perhapsss you will return to sssing to usss again," said the spider.

"One never knows these things in advance," said Shallan. "If so, I shall have a new song for you to hear."

There was no answer.

"I guess that's that," said Shallan. He ate another grape. "Slightly bitter, but no worse than that."

Graham took a grape and stared at it as if its dark purple surface could reveal some secret.

"If you won't eat, that just leaves more for me," said Shallan. He ate a handful of grapes and picked up the rest.

Graham ate the grape. It was, as Shallan had said, slightly bitter, but still plump and full of juice. Shallan handed him a bunch.

"We can eat while we walk," said Shallan.

Graham nodded and the two of them set off. The forest of thorny trees was left behind quickly.

Graham was stiff and sore and in no mood for Shallan's perpetual levity. He remained silent for the better part of the day despite the minstrel's nonstop chatter.

By midafternoon, Graham and Shallan had come across plowed fields dusted with snow.

Ahead of them to the east, the sky was dark.

"Snow ahead," said Shallan. "As we get closer to the mountains, it will probably get worse."

Graham nodded. "We may have to find a place to stop soon," he said. "If it begins to snow, I'd rather be inside. Perhaps a farmer will put us up for the night, or at least allow us use of a barn. And perhaps someone has seen something—I don't even know if I'm going quite the right way."

"Well, we've seen no tracks, but that means nothing," said Shallan. "The imps have a couple days' head start on us, didn't you say?"

"At least two days," said Graham.

"Well, then, we'll just have to stop somewhere and ask," said Shallan. "You know, you can find out a lot that way."

"And maybe we'll find something more to eat than grapes," said Graham.

"Now, now, don't turn up your nose at our breakfast just because the giver was large, hairy, and eight-legged," said Shallan. "It's never wise to spite a gift given freely."

"You're probably right," said Graham.

"Of course. When you've been on the road as much as I have, you learn a few things about gift-giving and gift-givers."

"And how long is that?" asked Graham.

"A while," said Shallan. He laughed and ran a hand through his red hair. "A long while."

Graham and Shallan walked across plowed field

after plowed field as the sky grew darker. Finally, it began to snow.

"Bah," said Shallan in disgust. "Now I'll be wet. Cold's not so bad as long as you're dry."

Graham brushed snow off of his cloak. "You could borrow my cloak," he said. "I've got several layers on under it. You've barely anything on."

Shallan nodded. "All right. I accept."

Graham unclasped the cloak and handed it to the minstrel. Shallan wrapped the cloak around his shoulders and sighed. "Ahhh, that does feel good," he said.

"You should have said something sooner," said Graham, abashed. "I wasn't thinking of you and what you were wearing."

"You needn't be concerned about me," said Shallan. "I've lived by my wits for years, and I'm still around."

"Doesn't the cold hurt your voice at all?" asked Graham as he wiped snow away from his shoulders. "Wouldn't you rather spend your life inside with a fire?"

"I'd rather spend it inside with a woman," said Shallan. He laughed. "No, really, I've tried the settled life and I prefer to roam. Even if I sing for you at your court, I'm sure I won't be able to stay long before I get the urge to walk again."

"As they say, it takes all kinds of people," said Graham.

"They say right," said Shallan. "By the way, now would be a good time for you to thank whomever you thank for good luck."

"Why?"

"Because I do believe I spy a farmhouse up ahead," said the minstrel.

Graham peered into the blowing snow. Less than a mile ahead he saw a light. "Could be," he said. "I hope so."

"Let's hope what's on the fire is good," said Shallan.

Graham and Shallan trudged to the light. As the minstrel had predicted, it turned out to be a lantern hung outside a large farmhouse.

Graham knocked on the door. Inside, a dog barked.

The door opened. A rotund woman, her hair hidden under a yellow scarf, stood on the other side.

"Please, ma'am," said Graham. "We're travelers caught in the snow. Do you have a place where we could spend the night?"

"That's all you want?" the woman asked pleasantly. "How about some supper?"

Graham's stomach growled. "Whatever's on the fire is fine with us," he said.

The woman stepped aside. "Don't get too many visitors way out here," she said. "But come in, come in."

Graham ducked his head under the low doorway and stomped snow off of his boots. A big yellow dog sniffed his hand and wagged its tail.

"Hi there," Graham said to the dog.

Shallan came in behind Graham and the dog went to him. The woman closed the door.

"It's an evil night," she said. "All this snow after the spring thaw. Shouldn't be. Something's wrong."

"Something is indeed wrong," said Graham. "But I hope something can be done about it."

The woman gestured toward two chairs by a roaring fireplace. "Sit yourselves down," she said.

Graham sat down and put his feet nearer the fire and removed his hat, scarves, and heavy mittens. The snowflakes that clung stubbornly to his boots melted quickly.

Graham looked around. The farmhouse was spacious. Herbs hung from the ceiling. Whatever was in the pot on the fire smelled delicious. The woman grabbed some leaves from one of the herbs dangling from the ceiling. She crushed the leaves in her hand and threw them into the bubbling pot.

"You have to know just when to add the spices, you know," she said. "Otherwise your stew won't turn out."

"Cooking is a mysterious art," said Shallan. He smiled at the woman. "One I have never mastered, much to my dismay. But if the smell coming from your pot is any indication, you are a master cook indeed."

"Yes," said Graham. "It smells delicious."

The woman grinned, obviously pleased. She

bowed her head and blushed. "I do my best, sir," she said.

"My name is Shallan," said Shallan. He bowed where he sat. "My companion is Graham, or, rather, I am his companion. We are on his quest. I am a minstrel."

The woman clapped her hands together. "Oh, I do hope you will sing us a tune, then, sir."

"My pleasure," said Shallan. "Something to whet the appetite."

He promptly launched into a song about a king whose court seer prophesied that he must have a feast, a feast so large the king and his court couldn't eat it all. Until this happened, the king would never be wed. Nor could he ever be wed until all the food was gone. The king called in his cooks and told them about the prophecy.

The cooks prepared the feast. The king and his court ate and ate, but couldn't eat all the food. The king called in his people, and they couldn't eat it all. The king brought in the horses and the dogs from the stable, and they couldn't eat it all, either. One portion remained. Finally, a young girl from a neighboring kingdom came looking for work in the kitchen. The cook sent her out to the feast. She finished the feast and married the king.

The song was hilarious—especially the way in which Shallan sang in different voices for the different people. His falsetto for the maid-turned-queen had Graham laughing until his sides hurt.

While the minstrel spun out his song, others had come into the room to join them. Four burly men now sat by the woman's table, nodding their appreciation for the song.

"Beautiful voice you have there, minstrel," said one in a deep bass. A scar cut his left eyebrow in two, but the eye beneath it was as bright and blue as the other.

"Aye," agreed the other three.

"Stew's ready," said the woman before Shallan could respond. She brought bowls to the fire and carefully ladled stew into each one. She served Shallan first, then Graham, then the other four. At last, she took her own bowl.

"Bad weather to be out in," said the man with the scar.

"Yes," agreed Graham. "I'm certainly glad we found this house."

"Don't recall seeing you around here before," said another of the men. He had dark hair cut close to his head. "You just passing through?"

"Yes," said Graham. "I'm on the track of some imps that passed by here a couple of days ago. Did you see them?"

"I don't think so," said the man with the scar. "You see anything, Hogshead?"

"Nope," said Hogshead. He was a beefy blond man with dark eyes and a farmer's tan. "How about you, Ramsquarter?"

"Nope," said Ramsquarter. He was the dark-haired man. "How about you, Lambsfoot?"

"Nope," said the fourth and last. The thin wavery voice didn't match the large body. "Haven't seen imps around here for many a year."

"And you, ma'am?" asked Graham.

The woman shook her head. "I'd remember if any imps came by. You must be going the wrong way."

"This is the right way," said Shallan. "For the imps are taking something to the Glass Mountains, and this is the way to the Glass Mountains, is it not?"

"Depends on where you're from," said Hogshead.

"From Daventry," said Graham.

"Never heard of it," said Hogshead. "You heard of it, Ramsquarter?"

"Nope. How about you, Lambsfoot?"

"Nope. How about you, Brindlenose?"

"Nope," said the scarred man. "Sorry, we don't know where Daventry might be."

"But the Glass Mountains *are* east of here?" asked Graham.

"They certainly are," said Brindlenose. "But the trip's a hard one. Rocky hills and thick forest between here and there. But, yes, the mountains are certainly east of here. Aren't they, Ramsquarter?"

"Oh, yes," said Ramsquarter. "Don't you agree, Lambs—"

"Thank you," said Graham. Although he was grateful to his hosts, their incessant quizzing of one another was beginning to get on his nerves.

Both Graham and Shallan had a second helping of the stew.

"This is marvelous," said Graham. "I wish my cook had such skill."

The woman blushed again.

Shallan handed his bowl back to the woman and yawned. "I agree. The stew is magnificent. However, it's been a long day on the trail," he said. "Long and cold, with only the comfort of companionship to warm our way. Is there a place where we can sleep?"

"Certainly," said the woman. "Come this way."

Graham put down his empty bowl, full and content. He followed Shallan and the woman into a back room. The back room was cold and drafty, but at least no snow blew in. A large bed took up most of the room. The only other piece of furniture was a tall wardrobe.

"I know it's cold," said the woman. "The fire only warms the front room. But there's a down blanket on the bed that will keep you toasty enough."

"Thank you, ma'am," said Shallan. He removed the cloak that Graham had loaned him and spread it over the bed to form an extra layer of insulation, then slipped in between the covers.

Graham climbed wearily into the large bed and was asleep before the woman left the room.

·12·

Graham was awakened by someone hauling him out of the bed by the collar of his wool jerkin.

"Tie him good," said someone. It sounded like Brindlenose.

Graham tried to focus on what was happening, but the room was spinning around him. The motion made his stomach do a queasy roll.

Graham's hands were forced behind his back and tied. So were his ankles.

"Got this one trussed up nice," said another man. That one sounded like Ramsquarter.

"This one, too," said Lambsfoot. "How about you, Hogshead?"

"Nice and tight," said Hogshead. "They're not going anywhere."

"The Laburnum will be grateful to us for such a prize," said the woman. "See the sigil on the cloak of that one? That's the crest of the royal house of Daventry. They're bluebloods."

"All the same to the Laburnum, I would suppose," said Brindlenose. "Blue or red blood, makes no difference."

"Fool," snapped the woman. "The Laburnum were not pleased by that stringy guardsman and that half-dead troll you threw down last month, now, were they? Isn't royal blood better than any of that?"

"Royal blood or no, they've plenty of meat on them if eating them's what's on the Laburnum's minds," said Hogshead.

"Who knows what the Laburnum do with what we give them?" asked the woman. "And who cares? Just so long as they leave us and our fields alone."

"Do you think they'll make the winter go away if they're pleased with these two?" asked Lambsfoot.

"Who knows," said the woman impatiently. "Maybe."

Graham wanted to say that the winter wasn't being caused by the Laburnum—whatever they were—but his tongue was thick and he couldn't speak clearly. All he managed was an "uhh" sound.

"This one's awake," said Hogshead. "What'll we do now, Tilly?"

"Same as always," said the woman. "Leave them here until dawn. We'll send them down into the pit then."

Graham was thrown down onto the bed. Without the down comforter, he was soon shivering with cold. But whatever was clouding his mind had a sharper grip on him than the cold, and he fell into black dreamless sleep.

His sleep was interrupted by someone hauling him out of the bed.

"Sun's up," said Brindlenose from behind him. "Rise and shine."

This time, Graham could see the room clearly. Whatever had fogged his mind was gone. Across the room, Hogshead and Lambsfoot held Shallan like a limp sack between them. Ramsquarter held Graham's feet.

The woman, Tilly, came into the room. A red scarf covered her hair today. She nodded. "Good. Let's take them, then."

"Where are we going?" asked Graham as Brindlenose and Lambsfoot carried him out into the front room.

"To the Pit of the Laburnum," said Tilly.

"What are the Laburnum?" asked Graham. "I've never heard of them."

"They've been here longer than anyone knows," said Tilly. She held the outer door while Brindlenose and Lambsfoot brought out Graham. Graham assumed the others followed with Shallan.

"Longer than anyone knows," agreed Brindlenose. "Right, Lambsfoot?"

"Right," agreed the other. "Isn't that so, Hogshead?"

Hogshead grunted. Apparently, Shallan was more a burden than he seemed. Graham was glad at least that carrying the minstrel broke off the men's round of question and answer.

"Yes," said Graham, "but what *are* they?"

The men carrying him grunted with the effort and said nothing.

"I don't know," said Tilly from somewhere behind Graham. "All I know is they want offerings. As long as we give them what they want, they leave us alone."

"Yeah," said Hogshead. "One time we didn't throw down a traveler for over three months—heck, hardly anyone comes this way. Was too long for them, we guess. In a single night, they destroyed all our crops, killed all our animals, poisoned our well—we almost had to leave."

"Why didn't you?" asked Shallan. Graham was relieved to hear the minstrel's voice.

"Why didn't we what, leave?" asked Tilly. "Because this land is free for the asking. Grows any kind of crop you want. Climate's never too dry, never too wet. Farming's almost no work at all out here."

"You just have to pay the price," said Graham. "Killing travelers that come to your door is a high price to pay."

"Well, I'll miss the minstrel," said Tilly. "But life doesn't get better than it is right here, me and my brothers all know. Right, boys?"

"Right, Tilly," chorused the four men. At least they said it all at once.

The men carried Graham and Shallan down into a small valley. At the very bottom of the valley was a well. The yellow dog danced around them as they went, bouncing through the snowdrifts and running back and forth in front of the party.

Brindlenose lay Graham down on the cold ground at the edge of the well.

Tilly leaned over the mouth of the well. "Laburnum, Laburnum, come and behold," she chanted. "Laburnum, Laburnum, come out of the cold. Laburnum, Laburnum, listen to me. Laburnum, Laburnum, come hither and see!"

Brindlenose put a foot against Graham's throat. "Don't think about trying anything," he said. "Or I'll press down until you pass out. I'm sure you'd rather meet whatever's down there awake, now, wouldn't you?"

"Rather not meet it at all," squeaked Graham.

"Too bad," said Lambsfoot. "All right," he called, "this one's ready to go in."

"This one, too," said Hogshead.

From deep out of the well came a scuttling sound like the sound of dry leaves blowing in the castle courtyard back home in Daventry.

"They're coming," said Tilly.

"Aye, that they are," said Hogshead.

"So they are," said Ramsquarter.

"Here they come," said Lambsfoot.

"They're quick this time," said Brindlenose.

The dry leaf sound faded away.

"Laburnum?" called Tilly down the well. The sound did not return.

"Maybe they're not ready for more," said Hogshead. "Do you suppose we should just let these two go?"

It sounded like a good idea to Graham. But Tilly shook her head. "No. They might not want them right now, but they will soon. We'll put them down and the Laburnum can do as they please. *We'll* fulfill our part."

"Whatever you say," said Brindlenose. He nodded to Ramsquarter. "Go ahead. Drop the minstrel."

Ramsquarter and Hogshead rolled Shallan to the edge of the well and shoved him over. Graham didn't hear him hit bottom.

"Now it's your turn," said Tilly.

Brindlenose and Lambsfoot pushed Graham to the edge. The yellow dog hopped over and gave him a sloppy lick across his face. Then the two men pushed and Graham was falling into darkness. He didn't fall very far—maybe fifteen feet—and landed in something soft.

Graham rolled away quickly, afraid he'd fallen on top of Shallan.

"Shallan?" he asked.

"Over here," said the minstrel from a few feet away. "Trust me not to get crushed."

"Now you'll find out what the Laburnum are," shouted Tilly down the well. "Oh, and, uh, thanks for the cloak."

"Yeah, thanks. We can use it," said Hogshead. "Isn't that right, Ramsquarter?"

"Oh, sure it is. And thanks for the hat. Right,

Lambsfoot?" asked Ramsquarter. Ramsquarter's voice was fainter. Tilly and her brothers must have been going back to the house.

"Yes, and thanks for the knife. Right, Brindlenose?"

"You are so right," said the last of the four. "And for the . . ." The brothers' voices faded into the distance.

"Well," said Shallan's voice from the darkness. "The Pit of Laburnum. And here I thought the thorny forest was a bit depressing."

"Now what?" asked Graham. "I don't feel like lying here waiting around to be eaten—or whatever it is the Laburnum do with their guests." He tugged at the ropes around his wrists.

"As it happens, my bonds seem to be a might loose," said Shallan.

"The luck of the minstrel, no doubt."

"No doubt."

In a few minutes, Shallan had worked free of his own ropes and turned his attention to Graham. Soon they were both loose from their bonds—if no closer to being free of their predicament.

"I think I see a light," said Shallan. "Shall we go that way?"

Graham stood up and peered into the darkness. Now that his eyes had had a few moments to adjust, he, too, saw a light.

"That will probably lead us right to the Laburnum," said Graham, refusing to be cheered.

"Possibly," said Shallan. "But our only other option is wandering around in the dark. Your tinderbox is in your cloak, and our late hosts have that."

Graham sighed. "You are right." Despite himself, he grinned. "Now I sound like one of Tilly's brothers."

Shallan laughed. "They'll make fine grist for a ballad—assuming we get out of here."

"Assuming we get out of here," echoed Graham. "Well, let's head toward the light."

"Age before beauty," said Shallan, and he stepped forward toward the light. And the Laburnum.

·13·

Graham couldn't see around the minstrel's narrow shoulders—the passage wasn't much wider than Shallan and light was at a premium.

"Are we getting closer?" asked Graham.

"Seems so," said Shallan. "Ah, yes, yes, I do believe we are approaching something."

"Something?"

A chittering noise sounded out in the darkness. Graham stopped, but Shallan didn't.

"Wait," said Graham.

"What for?" asked the minstrel.

"Well . . ." Graham had no good answer.

"Look," said Shallan. "We can stand around in the dark or we can go on. Strange sounds are just strange sounds. If we want to find out what they are and how to deal with them, we'd better get to the light."

"Fine," said Graham. He didn't like the idea of just walking up to the Laburnum, especially considering that Tilly and her brothers had never seen anyone *leave* the Laburnum's domain. But Shallan was right—they could wait in the darkness, or they could go to the light. "Lead on."

Graham and Shallan walked on for several minutes. Twice Graham heard scuttling sounds coming from *behind* him. He gritted his teeth and tried not to imagine what might be stalking him from the rear.

Mostly he kept thinking about the spiders they had met in the thorny forest. What if the Laburnum were more of the same? Graham had no wish to be impaled on spider's fangs.

"Are we any closer yet?" he asked, trying to keep the sharp edge of panic out of his voice.

"A bit," said Shallan. "Lucky for us the floor is even. I'd hate to have to worry about climbing over rocks in this darkness."

"You know, just because the floor is even doesn't mean there won't be any pits," said Graham thoughtfully.

"Thanks for reminding me," said Shallan. "I guess if you hear me scream and fall, you'll know not to step forward."

Graham and Shallan trudged on in silence. Graham considered humming to himself just to keep from hearing the unsettling scuttling and chittering sounds, but on the other hand, if something *were* to jump him in the darkness, he'd like to have a little warning.

What use the warning would be, he didn't know. But he kept silent just the same.

"You know, I think that light is a lot closer

now," said Shallan. "Maybe only a hundred yards or so."

"A hundred yards?" asked Graham. "It seemed only that far away to begin with." He panted with effort. It also seemed to him the passageway was going *up*. Between that and his fear, he was breathing heavily.

"It's difficult to judge distances underground," said Shallan. "Unless you have a lot of practice at it—and I'm sorry to say now that I don't—you just can't tell."

"Great," said Graham.

"But we are definitely getting closer," said Shallan. "Really."

Graham and Shallan continued for several more minutes. Now even Graham could see the first faint shimmers of light around Shallan's silhouetted figure.

"Do you think it's a way out?" Graham asked his companion.

"I doubt it," said Shallan. "Why would the Laburnum want travelers thrown down to them just to let them walk away? Besides, this light doesn't look like sunlight. It's more like . . . Well, it's more *green*."

Graham sighed and kept his aching legs marching after Shallan.

"Ah, I think we're almost there," said Shallan. "Yes, I do believe . . ."

The minstrel stopped speaking suddenly and

stopped walking, too. Graham bumped into Shallan's back.

"What?" demanded Graham. "What is it?"

"I'm guessing it's a Laburnum," said Shallan softly.

"Yes, but what is it?" Graham whispered back. Visions of huge spiders or centipedes or some other many-legged horror danced in Graham's mind's eye. He wanted to grab Shallan by the shoulders and shake a description out of the man.

"Well, it's small," said Shallan.

"Yes? And?" Small spiders could be just as terrible as large ones.

"And furry," said Shallan. "Sort of a golden-brown, really. It's actually kind of cute."

"Cute?" Graham shouted. "These horrible Laburnum are *cute*?"

"Well, we haven't actually established their horribleness," said Shallan. "Although I agree they probably do not mean us well."

"Probably?" shouted Graham.

"Could you not do that?" asked Shallan. "They don't seem to like the noise."

Graham clamped his lips together. Shallan took a few steps forward. Graham clenched his fists in frustration and fear and followed.

After twenty or thirty yards, the passageway opened up. Shallan stepped aside. Graham looked forward, half-eager and half-terrified, to see what a Laburnum was.

Three of them stood in front of Graham and

Shallan. They were bipedal but barely came to Graham's knees. Skinny twig legs supported an oblong body and head. The creatures appeared to have no necks; instead their heads and shoulders seemed to be all of one piece, with their arms starting almost level with the top of their heads and ending far above their waists. Large, soft brown eyes regarded Graham evenly.

One of the Laburnum stepped forward toward Graham. He jumped back.

Chittering sounds came from behind him. Graham put his back to the wall and looked around.

More of the small golden-brown creatures came down the corridor. They cheeped and chittered to the ones in front. Seven of them passed Shallan and Graham without a glance, gesturing with their twig-thin arms and small, delicate, furry hands. The ones in front clicked and whistled back.

The Laburnum that had followed walked on into the light. One of them carried the ropes in which Graham and Shallan had been tied. It held up the lengths of rough cord, which brought on another round of chittering from the others that faced Graham and Shallan.

One stepped toward Graham, and another toward Shallan. They held out their hands as if offering to lead the humans somewhere.

"I guess we're invited to tea," said Shallan. He sighed. "And I just hate cucumber sandwiches."

Shallan reached forward and took the upstretched hand of the Laburnum. Graham hesitated. "Might as well," Shallan said. "We haven't much choice after all."

The Laburnum facing Graham chittered and took another step forward. Very slowly and cautiously, it took Graham's hand and gave a gentle tug.

The Laburnum's hand felt very small and fragile in Graham's. The fur was softer even than a rabbit's. Graham took a step forward.

The Laburnum chittered again, its tone somewhere between exasperation and wheedling.

"All right," said Graham. "I'm coming." He allowed the Laburnum to lead him into the light.

Even though he had been walking toward it for some time, the light momentarily blinded Graham. He blinked and stopped. His guide tugged at him, but Graham refused to move forward until his eyes adjusted.

Slowly, the cavern came into focus. The light seemed to be coming from luminous rocks in baskets set around the room. Graham gasped. Hundreds—no, thousands—of the Laburnum scurried about on unknown errands. Some, like his companion, were golden-brown, while others were more cinnamon-colored. Still others were the color of orange mud. Graham could not tell if the colors represented animals at different stages of life or different genders. Besides color, the Laburnum all appeared to be the same.

Their guides led Graham and Shallan slowly toward the center of the cavern. Here, a motley collection of tents stood.

A small group of cinnamon-colored Laburnum noticed the humans' approach and whistled at the guides, who chittered back. Graham and Shallan were led to the cinnamon Laburnum.

One of the cinnamon-colored Laburnum walked right up to Graham. It peered up into his eyes a moment, chittered, then pressed its fingers against his shin. Whatever it felt must have pleased it. It turned back to its companions and clicked and chittered in an excited way.

The Laburnum made the same test of Shallan, and seemed equally as pleased. It gestured to the guides.

The guides kept hold of Graham and Shallan's hands and led them after the cinnamon-colored group. The cinnamon-colored Laburnum walked between some tents and into a small open area.

Graham stopped as soon as he saw what was in the area. It looked like—it *was*—a stockpile of furniture. Furniture made from bones.

The furniture reminded him of Quilli'ehennan's antler chair. But these tables and chairs—Laburnum-sized—weren't antler. Graham hadn't seen many skeletons, but he could tell from size that the tables were constructed of arm and leg bones. The bowls on the tables seemed to be the tops of heads, and the plates looked like shoulder blades.

"Oh, my," said Shallan. "A chop shop. How do

you fancy yourself as a table, Graham? Or perhaps you'd prefer to be a chifforobe."

"I'd prefer to be myself, and alive," said Graham.

Other Laburnum approached them now. One of them reached up to pinch Graham's thigh. Another prodded his calf.

"I think we might be dinner, too," said Graham.

"Very, hmmm, efficient of them," said Shallan. "I suppose they use every part of the animal from the tail to the snout and skin to the bones."

"You mean every part of *us*," said Graham.

"Quite," agreed the minstrel.

"How about getting out of here while they still seem to be considering what to do?" said Graham.

In fact, an argument seemed to have erupted between the Laburnum who had inspected Graham's bones and the ones who had pinched his flesh.

"It would appear they're debating current market value," said Shallan. "I wonder if our guides get a commission for helping make the sale. Well, I don't feel a burning need to have that question answered. I should think this is a good time to make our exit."

"Which way?" asked Graham.

"Who cares?" asked Shallan. The minstrel pulled away from his guide and kicked a cinnamon-colored Laburnum into a table.

Graham yanked his hand free. His guide latched onto his leg. Graham reached down and ripped the creature free.

"Run, Graham!" shouted Shallan.

"I'm trying!" Graham tossed his guide into an approaching group of Laburnum and ran after the minstrel, who was pulling down tents and kicking aside Laburnum left and right.

Graham dashed into the confusion and bowled over a few Laburnum himself. But the angry chittering and scuttling from behind him told him he was being pursued.

Shallan grabbed a basket of glowing rocks and ran into a tunnel. Graham was only a few steps behind him.

Graham ran after the minstrel, his legs aching, his breath coming in ragged gasps. He wanted desperately to stop, but the sounds coming from behind him convinced him to struggle on.

Eventually, the sounds died away. Shallan halted. The minstrel was breathing hard, too.

"Their legs are so short, it'll take them a few minutes to catch up," said the minstrel. "Let's walk a bit."

Graham didn't bother to answer; he just nodded and followed.

All through the day, Shallan and Graham alternated running from Laburnum and taking short breaks. Shallan led them through the maze of tunnels without hesitation.

"I have an excellent sense of direction, even

underground," he said. "You need to go east, so east we go."

Graham was so mixed up, he had no idea what direction they were going. They might very well have been heading back to the main Laburnum cavern. But Graham didn't know the way out— following Shallan was better than nothing.

Graham had no idea how long this went on. Hours. Days. He lost complete track of time. He could barely remember his mission. His legs had long ago gone numb in exhaustion. He simply put his head down and kept himself upright more out of sheer determination than anything else.

"A light ahead," said Shallan at last. The minstrel hardly sounded weary at all.

Graham groaned. "Not back to the cavern," he said. His throat was dry, and talking hurt.

"I don't think so," said Shallan. "Looks more yellow than green." The minstrel hurried forward.

Graham followed as best he could, but he fell behind. Suddenly, a crowd of Laburnum rushed in front of him from a side tunnel. Unlike the creatures they had encountered before, these carried a collection of bone clubs and cudgels. Suddenly, their cuteness was significantly diminished. They looked brutal, and stood between him and Shallan.

"Shallan!" called Graham.

The minstrel turned back. "These creatures are certainly precocious," he said. Shallan waded into the crowd, kicking and shoving the small furry bodies. Clubs thumped against the meat of his thighs and rang against his shins.

"Go on out, Graham," said Shallan. "I'll keep them occupied a few minutes."

"I can't leave you here," said Graham.

Shallan laughed. The sound startled Graham.

"I'll lead them a merry chase, round and around," said Shallan. "Have no fear, King of Daventry. We will meet again. Now, go!"

"No," said Graham. "We'll go together."

He began fighting his way through the horde of creatures toward the minstrel. A bone club whacked into his side with surprising force, but Graham pushed on.

Suddenly one of the Laburnum produced what looked to be a polished length of leg bone. The creature raised the bone to its lipless mouth, and a small white stone blurred through the air to smack against Graham's skull.

The impact left his head ringing. Another club caught him on the leg. Then another missile struck him on the shoulder.

Graham cried out in pain and staggered back. More of the Laburnum produced the white tubes and fired their missiles. One of the little projectiles struck the wall at Graham's side and fell to the floor. It appeared to be a small bone from a finger or toe. A flurry of the little missiles came all at once, whistling through the air. Graham raised his hands, but the bones struck him on the chest, on the shoulder, the arms. Club-wielding Laburnum closed in.

"Run!" shouted Shallan.

"You're sure you'll be all right?" asked Graham.

"Of course," said Shallan. "Everything works out for minstrels. Now, go on. I'll catch up soon."

With the pain from the Laburnum's weapons, Graham needed little persuading. He jumped over the heads of the nearest creatures, kicked another one out of his way, and ran as fast as he could toward the light. Flying bones thudded to the ground behind him.

The light grew closer and closer and the tunnel shorter. Finally, Graham was crawling. But he only had to crawl a few yards and then—

Outside!

Graham crawled a few feet from the Laburnum's hole and collapsed onto the cold ground as the sun rose over the Glass Mountains. In the sunlight, hopefully, he would be safe.

Graham waited until the sun was high in the sky, but Shallan did not come out. Finally, Graham walked down the slope to the valley at the foot of the mountains. He found shelter in between some haystack boulders and fell asleep.

·14·

Graham didn't wake up until the sun touched the tops of the mountains the next day. He shivered and sat up. He hoped to see Shallan sleeping nearby, but the minstrel was not in sight. Graham's stomach growled.

"There is no breakfast," he told it. "You might as well be quiet." Carefully, he stretched his legs. Every muscle in his body screamed at him. Where the laburnum clubs and bone missiles had smacked against him, he could feel the bruises without needing to see them. Graham felt as if he could barely move.

Slowly, he pulled himself to his feet and walked out into the open.

The Glass Mountains loomed high and black to the east. Barely a mile from Graham, the mountains rose straight out of the ground. At their very base was a small stream.

Water! Graham hurried forward as fast as he could. When he reached the stream, he dropped to his knees and gratefully drank his fill of the water, which was clear and sweet.

It didn't help his hunger much, but Graham felt much better after a drink. He finished, sat up, and took a look around.

Behind him stretched a ridge of rocky hills, their tops capped with tall pine trees. The Laburnum hole that he had escaped through was about halfway down the grassy eastern slope of the hills. Large boulders populated the bottom of the small valley that lay between the mountains and the hills.

Graham scanned the area but saw no sign of Shallan. Grief gripped him. Shallan had braved the dangers of the Laburnum better than Graham had himself, and had sacrificed himself at the end for Graham and his quest.

Still, it was hard to believe that such a merry individual as Shallan would want to be grieved over. Probably Shallan would laugh if he knew Graham missed him and regretted his death.

But then, without a body, how did he know the minstrel was dead? Shallan had led them both through the Laburnum's tunnels for a day without getting them lost or farther from the Glass Mountains than when they started. Perhaps the minstrel *was* merely leading the Laburnum on a merry chase.

Graham fervently hoped it was true. He turned and looked up the valley, his determination renewed. He could do nothing to help Shallan now. He had to find the imps, and the faery queen.

From here, Graham saw no indication that any

imps—indeed, that anyone at all—had ever been by. He glanced up to the forbidding slopes of the mountains, wondering if the imps had already made it across.

Slope was the wrong word for the sides of the Glass Mountains. They rose, jagged, sharp, and vertical, straight from the valley floor. And they were lifeless. On this side of the stream small sprigs of grass grew between the stones. A couple of small, stunted bushes dotted the slopes of the hills behind Graham.

On the other side of the stream, not a blade of grass, not a hint of green. The Glass Mountains looked dead.

Not knowing what else to do, Graham turned to his left and walked north along the stream. If he walked several miles and saw no trace of the imps, he would backtrack and try the other way.

If there were no trace of imps in either direction, he didn't know what he would do.

After several miles, Graham was tired and even colder than before. Dark clouds gathered at the summit of the mountains.

Perhaps that was a good sign. Daventry had gotten cold when the faery queen was taken, and winter had followed her and the imps east. Tilly and her brothers wanted the Laburnum to end the winter for them, so it followed logically that this weather was not typical for them, either. Whatever it was causing the snow was ahead of him, then.

Graham slogged on, occasionally stumbling

over the smooth stones that lined the stream. He clutched his jerkin close to him and regretted the loss of his cloak.

By midafternoon, the black clouds were directly over him and it had begun to snow. Graham hurried as best he was able, determined to catch up with the imps. He had a chance—they had had a two-day head start two days ago, but the imps had had to cross difficult terrain and negotiate deep forest, while Graham had run half the way on even, if subterranean, ground.

It was just possible he'd catch them on this side of the mountains. Just possible. Graham kept scanning the valley ahead of him, eager for his first glimpse of the imps.

What he was going to do once he caught up with them, he didn't know. But he'd do something—anything to save Daventry.

The sun had touched the tips of the pines on the ridge to the west when Graham saw tracks. Lots of them. The tracks came out of the forest and down the hill to the stream. The tracks then milled about on both sides of the stream before continuing north on the west side of the water.

The tracks were fresh. Cautious now, Graham hesitated. He didn't want just to blunder into a group of imps. The faery maid had seen at least twenty. Twenty against one were uncomfortable odds.

Graham climbed the hill to the forest edge and scanned the valley. Only a mile or so north of him, a group of travelers sat around a roaring campfire.

Graham took cover in the dusk and the relatively lighter growth at the very edge of the forest and made his way north. By full nightfall, he was directly above the encampment.

Graham eased down the slope, taking each step carefully. He didn't want to fall into a broken heap in the imps' laps.

A small group of haystack boulders huddled a mere fifty yards from the imps. Graham peered around the boulders.

Graham could see ten imps on guard from his vantage point. He wasn't too worried that there might be more—the imps had no reason to believe they were being followed, and anyway, imps weren't terribly great at guarding anything.

Slightly away from the fire, and surrounded by four of the eight imps, was a cage. A white blanket covered most of it, but Graham saw the bottom few inches of bars sticking out from underneath the sheet.

This had to be Ahi'aorina. Graham considered his next move.

"Hey, faery queen," said one of the imps. "A song you will make for us!"

Silence.

A second imp walked up to the cage and pounded on the top. "A song you will make. Now. A song we wish to hear, so a song you will sing."

At first, Graham heard nothing. Then, slowly,

the plaintive melody of Ahi'aorina's song carried to him. The beauty of it was heartbreaking. Graham wanted to run forward, wanted to beg for more, but he clutched the boulder and held his ground.

It was a song of loneliness, a song of sorrow. Graham wept at its power.

The imps merely smiled and nodded.

"Good song," said one when it was over. "Good faery queen."

The others rumbled something that was apparently agreement.

"Now I make a song!" shouted an imp. "Sings now Kuzgu of his great deeds!"

The other imps cheered. The imp Kuzgu danced around the fire, a whirling dervish of energy. Graham caught only a few of the words, for the imp's back was often to him. The dance and the song were crude and loud, nothing like the faery's song at all.

Graham shook his head in disgust. These creatures felt they had accomplished something good by capturing the Queen of the Old Wood? They were cruel, nothing more than a degenerate rabble.

Kuzgu finished his dance and sat down. Another imp ran up to him.

"Kuzgu!" shouted the second imp. "The crystal—brighter it glows! Very near our pursuers must be!"

The second imp held out a small something—

Graham supposed it to be this crystal the imp had mentioned. The crystal glowed a brilliant red.

"Bah," said Kuzgu. "No one pursues. How could they? Where we are, no one knows, not even Sorrowing Court."

"I know where you are, Kuzgu the Imp!" shouted Graham. "I and my army know your position. Give up now and surrender the faery queen!" Graham's voice echoed in the valley. The echo off the Glass Mountains was particularly loud and shrill.

The imps screamed and ran around in confusion. Some of them grabbed spears. They formed a circle around the faery queen's cage.

"Show yourself, pursuer mine," shouted Kuzgu. "Show your army!"

"Surrender now or taste the consequences," said Graham. It was all a blunder. He had no idea what to do next. He couldn't rush so many imps with no weapons, after all.

But then, imps weren't particularly clever. He might be able to play with them, much the same way the Laburnum had played with him. Let the imps wonder what was in the darkness past their fire's friendly light.

"Who's out there? Who?" demanded Kuzgu. "Faery queen our prisoner be! Have her no one else will!"

"We'll see about that," said Graham. "We'll see. Beware, imps!" Graham pitched his voice low. The effect off the mountains made his voice sound like thunder. Graham was pleased with it.

If the imps came looking for him, he'd be in trouble. But Graham doubted they'd leave their fire, and they couldn't fight very well encumbered with torches.

The imps spread out to the limit of their fire's light and stopped.

"Show yourself!" demanded Kuzgu again.

Suddenly, another song rose in the darkness— a sweet, sad voice that filled the valley with longing. Ahi'aorina was singing. The imps smiled in pleasure and swayed on their feet.

Graham watched, baffled. The faery queen seemed to have some kind of plan. What was it?

That became evident in only a few minutes. One by one, the imps dropped to the ground, asleep.

The song continued and the imps slumbered. In fact, it sounded as if the song were repeating. And weakening. Graham needed to act fast before Ahi'aorina's strength was gone. Even now, her voice wavered in what sounded to Graham like exhaustion.

"Well, it's now or never," said Graham. He stepped forward cautiously. Ten steps. Twenty. Not an imp twitched.

Graham jogged the rest of the way to the imps. He picked up a spear from the closest one.

Suddenly, one of the imps leaped to his feet. "Our faery queen you will not steal!" he shouted. Despite Ahi'aorina's song, this imp seemed active and alert. He stabbed at Graham with a spear.

Graham parried the thrust with his own stolen spear. The imp stepped closer to him and swung his spear at Graham. Graham ducked and the spear whizzed by over his head.

Graham ran his own spear right through the imp.

Then he staggered back, expecting the imp to fall. The imp did not. It grabbed the spear in both hands and quickly pulled it out from the back. Graham winced at the sound of the spear sliding through the imp's flesh.

"You can't beat Kuzgu that easily," said the imp.

Graham made a grab for the spear, but the imp jerked the weapon out of his hands. Despite its small size, this imp seemed to have tremendous strength.

The imp struck back at Graham. He dodged to the side just in time to miss the point of the spear. The weapon plowed into the stony ground, throwing up sparks and dirt. Graham jumped forward again, but the imp—Kuzgu—spun the shaft of the spear around and smashed it into Graham's ribs. He fell away, gasping from the pain.

The imp laughed. "This is too simple. Can you really be the one they have sent?"

A black fear seized Graham. His heart began to race, and the hairs along his neck and arms stood up stiffly. He turned and ran back up the slope, and the faery song faded into silence behind him.

When Graham reached the forest, he dove in between the trees. Panting in weariness and hunger, he glanced back down the slope.

Kuzgu the Imp walked around the faery's cage, poking at it with the spear. The rest of the imps slumbered on.

Graham turned his back on the valley and wandered into the forest. In a few minutes, he had found a place to sleep.

Graham put his back to the tree, but he didn't sleep. All night long, he kept replaying the incident in his mind.

He didn't know exactly what had happened, but he knew one thing. The imp Kuzgu frightened him.

No, that wasn't the right word. Graham, King of Daventry, was terrified. Terrified of a creature that was half his size. All night long, Kuzgu's yellow eyes haunted Graham.

Graham didn't make a sound or a move until the sun turned the black of the forest into gray.

·15·

Ahi'aorina wept. When she had heard the human's voice, claiming an army in support of him, she had not stopped to think he might be lying. She had only thought of the hope of escape.

The wooden bars of her cage remained dead to her, unbending. But a human with an axe could open them quickly enough, if only the human could get close enough.

And so Ahi'aorina had sung, sung to the imps, sung a spell of slumber. It would not work on the humans—that would be a different song entirely.

But it had not worked. The imps, for whatever reason, had not slept. One of them had fought with the human and run him off. Despair settled around Ahi'aorina all over again.

"Ha—faery queen!" shouted the wretched Kuzgu. "Songs you sang for us, songs to sleep. Very bad. Faery queen make Kuzgu angry."

The imp poked its spear through the bars of its cage, pricking the sharp point against her skin. Ahi'aorina shuddered, but she did not pull away.

Seeing her cringe in fear was one satisfaction she would deny him.

Finally the imp tired of his torment and went away. The night passed and the dawn came.

The imps removed the sheet from Ahi'aorina's cage. She had convinced them that she should not be kept out of the sun too long, or she would die. She didn't think Kuzgu believed her, but he had not stopped her from having a little bit of sun and air.

The Glass Mountains loomed before them. Ahi-'aorina crouched in her cage in fear. These mountains hated living things. Nothing lived in them. Nothing at all. They were supposed to be uncrossable.

The imps must have some alternate route in mind. Four of them loaded her cage upon their shoulders and they crossed the stream that bordered the territory of the Glass Mountains.

The air on the other side of the stream seemed flat and odorless to Ahi'aorina. There was no smell of green, growing things. Her heart pined for the scent of even one small blade of grass.

The imps made for a small cut in the mountains.

"Still here," said one. "Kuzgu as good as his word."

"Said it would be here, Kuzgu did," said Kuzgu. "A pass for us to use."

As the imps moved up onto the side of the Glass Mountain, they stepped into the black stone as if it were no more substantial than smoke. Ahi'aorina felt a new chill come over her as she passed inside the mountain. It was like moving through cold smoke, or through water that was somehow not wet.

The imps carried Ahi'aorina throughout the day without asking her once for a song. She was glad of that at least. Some hours passed before they came though the passage of mist and emerged onto the far side of the mountain. More of the jagged peaks loomed ahead.

The stark blackness of the mountains frightened her. The mountains were indeed glass—brittle and sharp. Jagged edges poked the imps, drove through their boots. But except for stopping occasionally to pull glass shards out of their clothes or shoes, they did not seem to notice.

The imps walked all day and most of the night. They passed a second row of peaks, and a third. Finally, the scenery began to change. On the eastern side of the Glass Mountains were different mountains, just as tall, and just as forbidding at first glance.

But these mountains harbored life. Ahi'aorina could smell it.

"Close we are to Sorrowing Court," said one of the imps. "A warm fire I look to!"

Ahi'aorina roused herself enough to ask, "What is this Sorrowing Court you speak of? Who rules there?"

Kuzgu hesitated for a moment, then gave her a

yellow-toothed smile. "Dunstan rules there," said the imp. "A giant is he. And soon enough you will know Sorrowing Court. Winter is there. Winter of the soul. Spring there you will make."

Ahi'aorina sank back down in her cage as she was carried into the land of the new nameless mountains, where small spring blooms poked their heads out of the gaps between the rocks.

The sight cheered her. Just a little. The human had failed once, but if Quilli'ehennan had sent him, he must be special. He would try again.

He *had* to.

Ahi'aorina reached through the bars of her cage and brushed the tips of her finger against a forlorn shrub as she was carried past. She hummed a brief tune to the bush and watched as it produced a few leaves of bright green.

If the human really was following, she would leave him a trail to follow.

·16·

By morning, it was dreadfully cold and Graham's feet and hands were numb. It seemed so long ago that he had been warm at home, by the fire in Daventry.

Graham got up, muscles still aching from his days of travel. He made his way back to the edge of the forest and looked for the imps.

They were gone. Graham hurried down the hill to see which way their tracks went.

From what he could see, the imps had gone north about half a mile and then turned to the Glass Mountains. They had crossed the stream at a wide shallow spot. Graham hopped across on some stones that rose out of the water. The stones weren't slippery as he had thought they would be. On close inspection he found that there was not a trace of moss on the stones. Perhaps the Glass Mountains didn't allow anything to grow in the stream.

Once on the other side of the stream, the tracks headed directly for the Glass Mountains. Graham walked right up to a sheer black glass surface. The

tracks ended right there—the imps had gone neither to the left nor to the right.

Graham felt the glass. A sharp edge sliced open
his palm and blood dripped down onto the black
stone.

He cried out in pain and stepped back. The
mountain certainly felt solid. And unfriendly. He
held his wounded hand close against his chest.

Graham looked at the tracks again. It looked to
him like the tracks went through the mountain—
in one instance he could clearly see only *half* a
footprint. The other half must have been under
the mountain.

Unless Graham knew how to lift the mountains
and walk under, he had no hope of following the
imps.

Defeated and hungry, Graham recrossed the
stream. He would look in the forest for something
to eat. Perhaps then he could think of something.
Or perhaps he could see a pass from a higher
vantage point.

Graham climbed the rocky slope of the hill and
entered the forest. He walked around for most of
the morning but couldn't find even a single berry.
Most of the forest was pine, but even the occasional stand of oaks and elms did not harbor the
usual edible plants under the shelter of their
limbs.

The sun was high overhead as Graham contemplated digging into the soil for worms or grubs.
Not very appealing, but it had been three days

since he'd eaten anything and he doubted very much that a spider was going to appear magically and present him with more grapes.

Graham caught a whiff of something. Smoke. And something cooking. He sniffed again, but couldn't tell the direction the smell was coming from.

"Hello?" he called out. "Is anyone here?"

A crow peered down from the branches of an oak. It croaked once and flew away.

"Helloo!" called a deep voice. "Hmm. Hmm. Do I hear a traveler in my wood?"

"My name is Graham," said Graham. "I've been traveling for days and have had nothing to eat."

A gnome stepped out of the underbrush. Graham recognized it as such, for gnomes occasionally came to Daventry to sell their wares. Those who did turned a good profit, for gnome-wrought work was well crafted and highly prized. This gnome was almost as tall as Graham's waist, and its head seemed too large for its portly body. A thick white beard grew from the deeply lined face and a brown leather cap sat on the gnome's head. The gnome also wore worn leather pants, boots, and a jerkin.

"Sir Gnome," said Graham. "Could you spare even a small bit of food for me?" He wrapped his arms together across his chest and shivered. His breath came out in a fog.

The gnome's breath, too, fogged in the chill

air. The gnome stared at Graham for a few moments.

"Hmm. Hmm. I suppose I could," the gnome said at last. "I smell a hint of mystery about you, stranger. Hmm."

"Mystery?" asked Graham. "I don't understand."

"Could be where you've been or where you're going," said the gnome. "It's a gnomish talent for finding customers. You in the market for something? Hmm? Hmm?"

"Besides a meal?" asked Graham. "I'm too cold to even think of something. Perhaps more clothes."

The gnome shook his head. "I'm not a tailor," he said. "Though my wife makes a fair seamstress. I'm a cobbler. Hmm."

"I've got boots already," said Graham.

"I still sense a mystery," said the gnome. "My name's Wigglebright. My wife's Glitterthunk. Come join us for breakfast and I'll figure it out. One thing I can't stand—losing a customer because I can't figure out what they need. Hmm. Hmm. Come along."

The gnome turned and pushed his way through the underbrush. Graham followed. Only a few yards away was a tiny house.

"You'll have to step down and bend over to get inside," said Wigglebright. "But the house is cozy enough. "It'll warm you right up."

Wigglebright opened the door and went inside.

"Company for breakfast, my love," he said.

"Then get in here and shut the door," said another deep voice. "Don't let any more of that unnatural cold in than you can help. It'll spoil my thread."

"Yes, dear," said Wigglebright. He turned to Graham. "Come on in. Breakfast is on the table, hmm."

Graham bent low to get in the door and closed it carefully behind him. Inside, several steps led down to a room dug out of the ground. Tree roots covered with a board served as a table. Small wooden stools sat by the table, which was at knee level for Graham. He squatted on one of the tiny stools.

On the other side of the room, next to a roaring fire, sat another gnome. She wore a green wool dress. Her tawny hair was braided and coiled around her head. She nodded and smiled at Graham.

"Eat up," she said. "And tell us your mystery, hmmm."

"Told you," said Wigglebright. "You smell like a customer. You must be a customer. Our talent wouldn't have placed me in your path—or you in mine—if we weren't destined to do business."

It was as strange a speech as Graham had ever heard. He merely nodded.

On the table was a bright copper kettle and a wood bowl. Graham ladled out a portion of whatever was in the kettle into his bowl.

Whatever it was smelled delicious. Graham looked around but saw no silverware. He looked up. The gnome couple stared at him, pleasant smiles on their faces.

"Is the soup not to your liking?" asked Glitter-thunk.

"Ah, I'm used to eating with a spoon," said Graham.

Wigglebright slapped his forehead with a meaty hand. "Of course," he said. "I had forgotten that part about human manners." He looked at Graham and shook his head. "I'm sorry, but we don't have any spoons," he said. "Gnomes drink from the bowl. Hmm."

Graham didn't want to offend his diminutive hosts, and if gnomish manners meant drinking from the bowl, he would drink from the bowl. He was hungry enough to *eat* the bowl. Graham lifted the soup to his lips and drank a long swallow. It was warm and spicy and full of small chunks of vegetables.

Graham ate a second bowl of the soup. And a third. Finally, he was full. He looked at his hosts, somewhat embarrassed for his greed.

Wigglebright and Glitterthunk merely nodded.

"Now, hmm," said Wigglebright. "Where are you going?"

"I'm following some imps," said Graham. "They seem to have gone under the mountains."

"Under the mountains?" asked Wigglebright. "Under the mountains? Hmm. Hmm."

"The Glass Mountains?" asked Glitterthunk.

"Yes," said Graham.

"And you have to follow them to the other side," said Wigglebright. "Hmm. Hmm." A slow smile spread across his face. "Then I know what you need."

"What?" asked Graham.

"Boots," said Wigglebright.

Graham shook his head. "I have boots already."

"But not like this," said Wigglebright. "You have to cross the Glass Mountains. To do so, you need to stick to the mountains like a spider on a web, hmm. I can make boots to do this. If you do not have them, the mountains will slice you to pieces."

Graham turned up his hand and regarded his split palm. The wound was clean and had bled little, but still gapped apart some.

"I already found that out," said Graham.

"Oh," said Glitterthunk. "Come here and let me stitch that for you."

Graham half-walked, half-crawled across the warm room to sit by the gnomes' fire. He held out his hand to Glitterthunk.

"Tsk," she said. "The mountains have tasted your blood. Hmm."

Quickly and neatly, the gnome woman stitched up Graham's hand. She was finished in a matter of minutes. Graham examined her work. Glitterthunk's stitches were small and tidy.

"Pull them out in a week or so, hmm?" said Glitterthunk. "It won't be hard. Gnome thread holds when it needs to and loosens when it's supposed to."

"Thank you," said Graham.

Wigglebright came over and sat on the floor next to Graham. "About your boots," he said. "I can make you a pair like you need—and Glitterthunk can stitch you gloves so that you can climb the mountains easily."

"That sounds good," said Graham. "But I have no coin with me to pay you."

"Hmm. Hmm. Gold doesn't spend very well in the forest, anyway," said Wigglebright. He peered at Graham.

"That's a very nice jerkin you have," he said. "May I touch it?"

"All right," said Graham. "But I don't think I can trade you any of my clothes, or I'll freeze to death before I cross the mountains."

Wigglebright fingered Graham's jerkin. "Good weaving, this," said the gnome. "Glitterthunk could take it and make a shirt for each of us out of it, I'm sure. Hmm."

"I'm sure I could," said Glitterthunk in her deep voice. She beamed.

"Hmm. Hmm. For your boots and gloves, I would want the boots you have now, one of those pair of pants you're wearing, and the jerkin," said the gnome. "Hmm. I can sell the boots to someone, and the pants will give us some wool to make scarves and mittens out of. Interested?''

"I don't want to freeze to death," said Graham. "How about a shirt instead of the jerkin." He pulled up the jerkin to expose the shirts he had on underneath.

Wigglebright fingered the shirts. "Two shirts," he said. "Instead of the jerkin."

"One shirt," said Graham.

"Two shirts and I'll throw in a tinderbox," said Wigglebright.

A tinderbox! Graham needed something to make a fire with. "Deal," he said.

"I'll begin on your boots then. Hmm. Got to find the leather. Got to find my tools. Hmm. Hmm." Wigglebright began to wander around the room, picking up objects, putting them down.

"How long will it take?" asked Graham.

"One, maybe two days for the boots," said Wigglebright.

"Only a day for the gloves," said Glitterthunk. "I've a pair already started I think will fit you."

Graham started to protest, but didn't in the face of the gnomes' pleasantness. If it would take two days before he could go on, then it would take two days. He would still find a way to catch up with the imps.

And this time, they wouldn't catch him by surprise.

· 17 ·

Graham ended up staying four days with the gnome couple. It only took two days for Wigglebright to finish the boots, but the raging snowstorm outside the snug gnome house was too dangerous to venture out in. Graham sat in the main room of the gnome house, apologizing hourly for being in the way. But Wigglebright and Glitterthunk waved away his apologies.

Finally, on the morning of the fifth day, the snowstorm abruptly stopped. Graham ate a hearty breakfast and prepared to leave.

"Stop by again, hmmm," said Wigglebright. "And I'll make you whatever sort of boots you need. Remember the name, hmmm? Wigglebright makes the best shoes anywhere."

"I'll remember," said Graham. Although the gnome couple had been pleasant company, they were somewhat boring, and their constant "hmm hmm" was beginning to drive Graham mad. Besides, there was an important task to perform. He was eager to be back on the trail of the imps. "If you're ever in Daventry, come to the court. I'm sure you could sell some shoes there."

Wigglebright looked offended. "I'm sure I could sell shoes in many places. Hmm. But I am a gnome—my talent puts the right customers on my path at the right time. And I like the woods."

"Of course," said Graham hastily. "I didn't mean to offend you. I only meant I would be glad to see you again sometime when the weather was more pleasant."

"An odd way you have of saying it," said Wigglebright. He shrugged. "Human manners, I suppose. Hmm. Well, safe traveling. Have no worries about your shoes. They'll stick to the Glass Mountains like glue and work like regular boots elsewhere."

"Thank you again," said Graham. He crawled out of the gnome's front door. "And thanks again for all the food."

No answer. Graham supposed that was gnome manners. He closed the door.

The snow was waist deep. Graham quickly regretted the loss of one pair of his pants even more than he regretted losing his cloak. But he supposed it couldn't be helped.

Graham made the western edge of the Glass Mountains before noon, despite the snow. The small stream was frozen over. Graham trudged across it to the mountains' edge.

Cautiously, he put out a hand. The palm of his glove stuck to the rock face. Graham put both hands on the rock and a foot. He eased himself up.

He *did* cling to the mountains. Graham laughed. He could follow the imps now.

Graham climbed up the mountain to the very summit. Perhaps he'd be able to see where the imps had gone.

Beyond the first mountain was a second range. It took Graham the better part of the day to get down the slope of the first mountain to the slopes of the second. The sun had long ago snuck behind the mountain to the west of him, leaving Graham cold and in the dark. He huddled next to the rock face and shivered the night away, as there was nothing to burn for warmth.

At least he had nothing to fear from wild animals or thieves. Or giant spiders or Labernum, either. The mountains were more silent and dead than anything Graham had ever experienced before. Only the wind ventured through these mountains. The wind—and the cold.

In the morning, he pressed on. He didn't climb the tallest peak this time, aiming instead for the lower passes between the peaks. But no matter now many he climbed and descended, it seemed there was always another black glass mountain in front of him.

By the fourth day, Graham was desperately hungry. Enough snow had fallen so that he had water. But he had no fire. No comfort. With no trees on the glass slopes, there was no firewood. Notions of just sitting down and giving up crossed his mind with increasing frequency.

One more mountain. Just one more, Graham promised himself. He chose a tall peak and climbed to the top.

Graham let loose a shout of joy. He was at the end of the Glass Mountains at last. Past the foot of the mountain he sat upon was another stream, and beyond that—plants! Trees! They were leafless and covered in snow, but still!

Graham laughed and hugged himself. He'd made it! He hurried down the last slope just as the sun disappeared behind the mountains to the west.

Graham leaned down and drank of the clear stream water. He wandered to a large bush, crawled under it, and slept better than he had since leaving the gnomes.

In the morning, Graham looked for any evidence of the imps, but he saw nothing. They had a week's head start on him now. He'd fallen too far behind.

Graham abandoned his quest for the imps for the moment and looked for food. By noon he was exhausted and even hungrier than before.

Then he saw it. A single pink flower stuck its head out of the snow. And beyond it, a small blade of grass.

Graham's spirits soared. Perhaps he could still track the imps. Maybe the Queen of the Wood— now that she knew someone was trying to rescue her—had figured out a way to leave a trace of her passing. He hoped so. It was all he had to go on.

Graham followed the trail of flowers and seedlings all day. By evening he came across an entire bush bursting with berries. Graham ate the berries greedily.

As night fell, dark clouds obscured the stars and the snow started again. Graham huddled in the lee side of a boulder and made a small fire. All night he stayed by it and fed it twigs from the dead and sleeping trees and bushes around him.

By morning, Graham was tired and stiff. But at least he wasn't as cold as he had been in the Glass Mountains. Without wood, a fire was impossible there. At least here he could find fuel.

Graham stretched and started out. The berry bush was dead and drooping this morning. The faery queen's magic must not last very long.

Graham walked all morning, following what small smidgens of green he could find. But his trail of green became less important—he could see now where the imps were heading.

Ahead of him was another range of mountains. These were not nearly so tall as the glass peaks he had ascended, nor so lifeless. They were blunt, rough affairs of black stone and twisted trees. Great boulders lay in heaps about their base, and on several of the slopes Graham saw the dark openings of caves.

The imps' trail went right for this cluster of dark mounts. Graham doubled his pace. He ought to be able to reach the strange broken peaks by nightfall.

During the afternoon, it began to snow. Graham hugged his arms to his chest, bowed his head to the wind, and slogged on. At dark he pushed through the boulder fields around the base of the first black hill. The path of the imps was still clear, and even in the failing gray light he was able to follow their course around the slope and into the pass between one mountain and the next.

Past the dark peaks he caught his first glimpse of a small hidden valley. Somewhere down there had to be the goal, the place where the imps' long march had finally come to an end.

But Graham was at the limits of his strength. The snow blew harder and harder until he could barely see his hand in front of his face. He needed to stop, to build a fire, get his bearings, and rest his aching legs. He had no idea where to turn or if there might be shelter anywhere nearby.

Graham wandered around aimlessly, searching for a tree, a rock—anything to put between him and the icy bite of the wind. But there was nothing. He finally crouched where he was and let the snow blow over him.

·18·

The sharp crack of a burning pine knot startled Graham from his dreams. He raised his head and looked around his campsite.

When the storm finally lifted, Graham had managed to press on until he found a few broken limbs from which to build a fire, and a meager place of shelter behind a pile of rubble. There he had huddled through the night while the wind carried the clouds away and bought on a chill moonless night.

Except for the small crimson stain that the firelight cast across the snow, all was darkness, silence, and cold. High overhead, the stars hung in the sackcloth sky. Their tiny flames seemed as cold as the snow.

Graham was about to lie down and return to his slumber when he noticed how small the fire had become. The spare supply of wood he had been able to gather had not lasted as long as he had expected. In no more than another hour, the last of the kindling would fall to ash and the fire would go out. Then there would be nothing but the frigid wind. If it hadn't been for the timely warning of the noisy bit of pine, Graham wondered if he ever would have awakened at all. He might have fallen back into the deadly embrace of the snow sleep.

With a groan, he sat up and beat his cold hands together until some feeling returned to his frozen fingers. He picked up Glitterthunk's gloves from a stone near the flagging fire and pulled them over his stiff hands. He missed his heavy, warm mittens. He missed his cloak. He missed the shirts that Wigglebright had taken in payment. While he was at it, he missed his horse, his family, and his nice warm castle filled with nice hot meals.

Graham took the last bit of tinder and fed it to the fire. The flames licked it away like a child attacking rock candy. Graham's legs tingled as if they were being burned by a thousand tiny fires of their own, but with a few minutes of painful effort, he got to his feet and moved slowly around in the circle of firelight, looking for more wood.

There was nothing. He extended his search into the darkness around the light, but still he found no wood. His feet felt heavy and cold as the stone of the mountains. Behind him the firelight dimmed, slipping from bright red to a dull, smoldering crimson as the last of the fuel reached exhaustion. The warmth and good feeling he had enjoyed at starting the fire now seemed like a distant dream.

Graham shuffled his feet through the snow and

managed to locate a small branch jutting through the drifts. With hands that were little better than clubs, he was able to grip the branch and tear it free. Though it was scarcely bigger around than his smallest finger, and green with sap from the interrupted spring, it was the only wood he had. He returned to the smoky remains of the fire, snapped the branch into three small lengths, and dropped them among the glowing coals. With a few careful breaths, he coaxed the tip of one piece into flame. In a few moments, sputtering yellow fire jetted from the wood.

He pulled off his gloves, held his icy hands over the tiny fire, and rubbed them briskly. For a moment, Graham's thoughts turned again to Daventry. To Valanice and Rosella. To the wonderful fireplace in the grand hall of the castle.

Graham only hoped that someone had thought to restock the wood bins. Otherwise, that fireplace would not do them much good. He had thought of having it restocked some weeks ago, but spring had begun and they had not expected to need it. And then there were the windows on the upper floors. The shutters that covered the windows in winter had already been removed. With them down, Castle Daventry would be drafty and cold. Someone would need to see that they were returned and kept up until this second winter was ended.

"I should be there to take care of them," Graham muttered. His words emerged in puffs of frozen crystals. "Of course, if I was there, and not here, then this winter might never end. But if they're in danger . . ." His thoughts grew muddy. He was too exhausted to think clearly. He only knew that he was frozen, tired, and lonely. The idea of being home with his family seemed like a vision of paradise.

By the time dawn tinged the tips of the Glass Mountains with shades of orange and purple, the fire was gone. Graham stood and surveyed the valley he had only vaguely glimpsed in the failing light of the previous evening.

It was not a cheery place.

Undulating dunes of snow spread out from the base of the broken mountains to a distant stand of scraggly, twisted trees. Beyond the narrow strip of forest rose more ugly hills of dark stone. Graham knew that every place looked less inviting in the winter, but he did not believe that this valley would look much better even in the midst of spring.

If the imps had taken Queen Ahi'aorina to some place in this valley, that destination was far from clear. That was, if he could assume the imps really had reached the end of their trek. Perhaps they were still moving. Perhaps they would carry the faery queen on and on with Graham always trailing behind. There was nothing he could do but go down and hope to pick up the traces of the imps' trail. Graham got his frozen feet in motion and trudged off through the snow.

Though the seasons were definitely askew, the return of winter didn't seem quite so harsh on this side of the Glass Mountains as it had been in Daventry. Where the snow on the other side of the mountains had often been knee deep, here it only rarely reached the tops of Graham's boots and sometimes was no more than a dusting over exposed knobs of black rock. It might only have been that the mountains provided shelter from the storms, but Graham chose to take it as a good sign. Like the blooming flowers and trees he had passed from time to time, the lessening snow could mean that Queen Ahi'aorina was being held somewhere near. Graham's search might finally be nearing its end.

He had exactly that happy thought in mind when the sole of his boot slipped across a patch of exposed ice.

Graham had just enough time to utter a brief startled cry before his head slammed down on the stone and the king of Daventry was left sprawled unconscious in the snow.

When Graham opened his eyes, he was moving again. Though he was not sure how.

He was quite certain that his own feet were not doing the work. From what he could tell, his feet were not even on the ground. His head was, though. The tender spot at the back of his skull was sliding over the cold stone and snow with considerable speed. At each bump, thump, and lump on the ground, a universe of stars spread out across Graham's vision.

It took him quite some time to locate his legs, and several minutes more to trace those legs up to his feet and the huge gray hand that was dragging him across the frozen ground.

Graham raised his head and saw an equally large figure attached to the large hand. It was a broad form, dressed in strips of poorly tanned leather and wearing a cap on which tufts of mangy fur still hung like the last spectators after the play had ended. Every bit of exposed skin was as gray as November rain.

"Excuse me," called Graham.

The hulking figure did not turn.

"Excuse me," the king said, speaking a bit louder. "I'm awake. I think I can walk on my own."

The creature who was pulling him stopped and slowly turned its head. Its face was like nothing Graham had seen before. Most of the features were pressed together in a space no bigger than Graham's palm: two small red eyes, an even smaller nose, and a pair of ragged ears that were smashed down almost on top of the eyes. The rest of the creature's broad face was occupied by a mouth that looked easily big enough to handle a bushel basket at a bite. From this wide maw, the carious tips of teeth and tusks protruded at all angles. Framing the whole face was a mass of stiff bristles that would have looked at home on the back of a wild boar.

"Uh, excuse me," Graham repeated, feeling considerably less happy about the situation than he had a moment before. "Thank you for rescuing me, but I can get along on my own now."

The creature's red eyes stared back. It blinked.

"Can you speak?" asked the king.

Another blink.

"Do you understand what I'm saying?"

The creature turned and began dragging Graham again, this time face down. Despite numerous protests, it didn't stop a second time or even slow its steady pace. Graham struggled to hold his head off the ground as the creature pulled him between lifeless trees and over fields of loose stones. His chin cut a furrow through the drifts as they went through snow-covered glades. He had to press his lips together and hold in his breath as the creature dragged him across an icy stream.

Graham twisted around to look up at his boot clenched in the creature's hand and cursed silently. Wigglebright had told him that the boots would stick like glue to the mountains of glass and behave as normal boots elsewhere. It seemed the gnome was right. And like normal boots, they had slipped on ice, leaving Graham in this predicament.

The gray creature pulled him out of the stream and into a field of small cobbles. Graham's skull rang as the fist-sized rocks thumped against his head. He felt not unlike a human croquet mallet.

Graham was contemplating whether his head *could* hurt any more, or if he had reached the theoretical maximum for pain generated in one part of the body, when he noticed that the creature was drawing close to one of the hills of dark stone. As they approached, Graham saw black openings yawning in the upper parts of the steep slope. At first he took them for the mouths of caves, but as more details of the place became visible, he realized that the whole hill had been shaped by forces other than nature.

The black stone had been tunneled and carved into a massive fortress. Near the ground, the windows were few. Higher up, they grew more and more numerous, until whole sections of the hillside looked like pieces of rocky lace—though Graham thought that any lace maker would have had to be exceptionally drunk to create such twisted, ugly work. There were parapets and towers, crenelations and cornices, all chiseled from the stone of the hillside. Try as he might, Graham could discern no order to any of it.

The gray creature dragged Graham toward a pair of massive iron doors that were broad enough to admit three wagons side by side and tall enough that those wagons might have wheeled in a house without disturbing the roof tiles. The creature reached up with its free hand and pounded it against the metal of the door.

There was a faint rustling from behind the door, and a small peephole slipped open with a rusty squeak. "Who be there?" called a reedy voice.

Graham looked toward the peephole and tried his best to appear dignified. Considering the circumstances, his best was not much. "I'm King Graham of—"

The gray creature gave Graham's legs a sharp tug and cut off his words. "It's Thragaadash," said the creature. "I'm back."

"You can talk?" Graham said in wonder. "But why didn't you speak to me?"

The creature glanced over its shoulder and favored Graham with a look that would have soured honey.

"Thragaadash be it?" said the voice behind the door. "And I'm supposed to believe that?"

"Open door," growled Thragaadash.

A bloodshot eye appeared at the opening. "Orders I have, don't I? Let someone in who ain't supposed to be in, and it'll be me as is out there in the chill."

Thragaadash tightened one massive hand into a gnarled fist and waved it in front of the peephole. "You don't let in, and your teeth I'll use for cast-a-lot."

"Hmmph." The eye disappeared from sight. "My job am I trying to do."

The peephole squeaked closed. For a few seconds there was silence, then there came the loud clank and grind of a locking bar being lifted from its cradle. With an earsplitting creak, the huge doors cracked open.

Thragaadash put his palm against one of the door panels and shoved it inward. Graham winced as the creature dragged him through the opening and into the tunnel beyond.

The interior of the fortress was not what he had expected. From the forbidding demeanor of his captor and the stern exterior, he had imagined darkness and rough-hewn hovels. But the hallway inside the door was lit by long lines of clean-burning torches. More than that, the floor was actually covered by rich carpet of deep wine red. Compared to the agony of being dragged across the stony ground outside, being dragged over the carpet was merely severe pain.

There was a maze of hallways within the fortress. They went up ramps, around corners, and through a dozen doors. The carpet changed to azure, to green, and back to burgundy. As they took one turn after another, Graham saw other forms moving through the fortress. They were too distant to see clearly, but he got the impression that they were imps. Though he had not arrived by his own feet, it looked as if Graham might have ended in the right place after all.

Finally Thragaadash pushed open a door of dark wood. Graham winced as the carpet ended and his head banged across a floor of gray stone. Thragaadash pulled him around a table, and with no apparent effort, lifted Graham from the ground.

"What are you doing?" asked the king.

The gray creature gave this question no more attention than he had any of the others Graham had asked. Instead Thragaadash produced a strip of brown leather and wound it around Graham's ankles. Hefting the king a bit higher, Thragaadash slipped Graham's bound ankles over a hook projecting from the wall. Without a word, the creature turned and pushed back through the door. Graham heard heavy footsteps move away down the hallway.

"Wonderful." Graham did his best to look around the room. Unlike the halls they had gone through, there was only one torch here and the shadows were thick. At least it was warm. He hadn't been truly warm for longer than he cared to think about.

Gingerly, Graham reached up with one hand and touched the abused top of his head. He was amazed to find that not only was his skull still in place, he even had hair—though he was certain that could he see it there would be a considerable amount of new gray among the blond.

Rapid footsteps approached and the door to the room swung open. In his upside-down view, Graham saw the twisted form of an imp coming toward him.

"Well, well, well," the imp said as it drew near. "Told me he did that his catch was good." This imp was even stouter than others of its kind Graham has seen. Its rough face was round as a melon, and its tummy bulged against its grease-stained clothing.

"Can you tell me where I am?" asked Graham.

"East of the Glass Mountains, west of the sea," replied the imp.

"No, I meant this place."

"Oh." It extended one clawed finger and scratched at its leathery cheek. "Sorrowing Court this be. The pantry at Sorrowing Court."

Sorrowing Court. The name fit well with the gloomy exterior of the place and its home among these dark mountains.

Graham made an attempt to smile at the imp. "Let me introduce myself," he said. "I'm King—"

"Pah," said the imp. "Your fancy introductions save for yourself. Know you well enough, I do."

"You do?"

"Course I do." The imp put a hand to the side of Graham's head and gave a push that started him swinging back and forth like the pendulum of a clock. "The cook here, I be. And you be . . . ," the imp's warty lips turned up in a smile, "lunch."

·19·

The imp hummed a discordant tune as it bustled around the room. It threw open the door to a large cupboard and revealed a selection of blades that ranged from tiny little paring knives, to glistening weapons that could only be called swords. The round-bellied cook reached into the center of the collection and drew out a large meat cleaver.

"This one I'll use," it said, testing the edge of the gleaming blade against the rough skin of its thumb. "Yes," it said eagerly, "this one."

"Look," said Graham. "You can't really mean to cook me."

"Cook you?" The imp walked across the floor and looked into Graham's upside-down face. "No, cook you I'll not."

Graham smiled in relief. "Glad to hear it. Now, perhaps you could let me go?"

The imp frowned. "Can't do that."

"But if you aren't going to cook me then why—"

"Not cook you." The imp leaned down and put

its flat face close to Graham's. "Cook you I won't." A gray tongue slid from its mouth and moved across its lips. "Serve humans raw, we do. With Ilzak sauce and butter. Lots of sauce. Lots of butter. Lots more tasty."

Graham's stomach lurched and he thought for a moment that he might throw up. Or, considering his current position, maybe down.

"Would it make any difference if I told you I was a king?" he asked.

"King?" For a moment the imp looked puzzled, then a smile returned to its rough brown face. It reached out a finger and jabbed it into Graham's stomach. "King full of creamy puffs and honey cakes. King should be very, very tasty." The imp licked its lips again, then turned and scurried back across the room. It flung open the doors to another large cabinet and almost disappeared inside as it searched through the contents.

"Dwarves we cook," it said over its shoulder. "Don't cook dwarf, the meat be tough. Some, they like the tough. Thragaadash!" The imp snorted. "Thragaadash eat dried dwarf on stone plate. Thragaadash even eat the plate. Like that, mountain trolls be. But me, tender be what I like. Human be nice and tender. Tender and juicy." At last it emerged from the cabinet with a shiny brown jug in one clawed hand and a rough cloth sack in the other. "But human be better with sauce. King be most tender of all. King deserves a good sauce and Ilzak sauce best of all."

"Sauce," said Graham. Despite the context, the word caused his stomach to rumble. How long had it been since he had eaten? The blood pounded in his ears. Between his exhaustion and the long period of hanging upside down, he was on the verge of passing out. If he did pass out, Graham suspected that the next plate he saw would be one on which he was the main dish.

"Sauce be important," said the imp. "Any silly troll in the woods can eat human without sauce." It dropped a collection of copper pots and bowls on the counter, then turned his back on Graham. There was a pop as it jerked the cork from the top of the brown jug, then a long gurgling splash as it poured the contents into a pot. Even from across the room, Graham could smell a pungent, musty odor. "Sauce be . . . be . . ." The imp waved the meat cleaver in the air. "Sauce be . . ."

"Civilized?" suggested Graham.

"Civilized!" shouted the imp. "Sauce be civilized." It started to hum again as it stirred into the pot a green powder from the sack. Wisps of ugly purple steam drifted up from the noisome mixture. The imp produced a length of twisted yellow root from a box on the counter and began to hack it into irregular slices with enthusiastic chops of the meat cleaver.

Graham gritted his teeth, held his breath, and pulled himself up until his hands could reach the leather tie around his ankles. If he could only get free . . .

He fumbled at the knots Thragaadash had made, but he could not hold himself still enough to make any progress. After a few moments, the muscles of his abdomen were trembling with effort. Graham let his breath out in a explosive puff and fell back against the wall.

"Say something you did?" asked the imp.

"Just that, I mean." Graham cast around for something to say. "I was just wondering what you put in your sauce."

A look of fury came over the imp's face. It threw back its head and issued a bloodcurdling scream. Then it hurried across the room, grabbed Graham by the hair, jerked his head up, and put the razor-sharp edge of the meat clever against his throat.

"Try to steal Zuzak's sauce, you do!" cried the imp.

"No!" Graham shook his head as best he could with the blade touching his throat. "No, I would never try to steal your secrets."

The glare in the imp's eyes dimmed. "You not?"

"No."

"Oh." The imp turned and slammed the meat cleaver into the nearest counter with a force that left it quivering in the wood. "Be sure you not." He stalked back across the room on its bandy legs and resumed adding ingredients to the pot. "Most famous cook is Zuzak. His sauce all imps want."

"I'm sure they do," said Graham.

He eyed the handle of the cleaver. The imp had left it very close, perhaps even within reach. He stretched out a hand, straining to reach as far as possible. It was not quite enough. The cleaver was only a few inches from his trembling hand. He put his hands on the floor under his head and pushed himself away from the cleaver. As he swung back in the other direction, he stretched out again. This time the tips of his fingers brushed the handle. He swung back and gave another push.

On the third swing, he got a solid grip on the handle of the cleaver. But the hold of the blade in the wood was tight and Graham was left stretched between his feet bound to the wall and his hand gripping the cleaver.

"Hey, what you doing?" called the imp.

Graham twisted his head to look at the stocky cook. "Just trying to get comfortable."

The imp shook his head. "Comfortable you don't need to be. Soon enough is lunch." He walked toward Graham, still holding the heavy metal pot of sauce in his thin arms. "Let go my chopper, you."

With a desperate tug, Graham pulled the cleaver free from the wooden counter. As he flew back toward the wall, he arced his body and swung the sharp blade at the strap between his feet. The edge cut the taut leather easily, along with most of the heel from Graham's right boot. He tumbled to the floor.

"Hold still you!" shouted the imp. "Not even finished my sauce have I."

Graham came to his knees with the sharp blade raised in one hand. "I don't want to hurt you," he said.

"Pah," said the imp. "Soft human. Soft king. Not scared of you am I." He tilted his round head toward the door at the side of the room. "Guards be waiting right outside. One word from Zuzak, and in here they'll be. Better put down my chopper before hurt you are."

Graham surged to his feet and kicked out toward the imp with his right foot. The toe of his boot hit the sauce pot with stinging force, sending the copper container flying from Zuzak's hands. The pot did a flip in midair and came down on the imp's shoulders. Dark liquid and slices of pale root poured down the creature's round body and cascaded from the imp's belly onto the stone floor.

"My sauce you ruined," cried the imp. His voice was made hollow by the covering pot. "Have to start over, I do."

Now that he was on his feet, Graham found that the imp looked much smaller and not nearly so threatening. Graham looked at the blade in his hand. Though the creature had been preparing to serve him up as a human cold plate, Graham was not quite prepared to kill him.

He leaned back, braced himself, and swung the cleaver down with all his might. The blade struck the side of the copper pot as a clapper strikes a church bell. Vibrations rippled through the imp from top to bottom, from bottom to top, and back again.

"My sauce," the imp said forlornly. Then he collapsed to the floor in the middle of the noxious puddle of sauce.

Graham dropped the cleaver on the counter and closed his eyes. "Have all the sauce you want," he said. "I hope it's still good when there's no king to go in it."

The tight leather strap had deprived Graham's feet of blood for so long that they felt like lifeless lumps of stone. He bent and rubbed at his chafed ankles until a sensation of pins and needles replaced the numbness. It was distinctly unpleasant, but at least he knew he would keep his feet.

What he really needed was a good warm meal and a chance to rest. About a year of solid sleep sounded right. Only Graham doubted that he could count on the denizens of this strange fortress to leave him alone even long enough for a catnap. As for a meal . . .

He stood and walked unsteadily across the room to the cabinets where Zuzak had gotten the ingredients for his sauce. There were a number of bags, boxes, and bottles inside. Graham tried them all, but could find nothing that he thought of as edible. He had better luck with the box of roots on the counter. Most of them were the slim yellow root, which Graham did not know and was unwilling to trust. But in the bottom of the box was a single old potato.

The potato was raw and wrinkled, and eyes had sprouted from a half dozen points, but Graham's hunger was not about to be daunted by such minor matters. He pulled the root from the box, brushed off the dirt, and took a hearty bite. He could not remember any meal at Castle Daventry ever tasting so good.

When the meager meal was finished, Graham walked across to the door and eased it open a crack. Despite what Zuzak had said, there was no sign of any guard on duty outside the pantry. He pushed open the door and stepped into the carpeted hallway.

The imp had called this place Sorrowing Court. Somewhere in the maze of hallways and rooms, Graham was sure he would find Queen Ahi'aorina. The sooner he could locate her, the sooner they could both be out of this place and back to their rightful homes. With the snow and ice locked outside, and a little bit of potato on the inside, Graham felt more hopeful of ending this trip than he had in days.

An hour later, much of that hope had evaporated. Sorrowing Court was huge.

Graham wandered down one corridor after another. He passed vast halls with tables that would have seated an army and grand rotundas whose ceilings arched up into an invisible gloom. For all its great size, the riches displayed in Sorrowing Hall were equally impressive. Graham hardly took a step that was not cushioned by fine, intricately woven carpets. Only glimpses of the smooth stone walls were visible behind hundreds of tapestries and paintings. There were more riches in a single hallway at Sorrowing Court than in the whole of Castle Daventry.

The only thing not in abundance in Sorrowing Court was inhabitants. Though Graham twice shied back into the shadows and let individual imps go past, most of the vast fortress appeared to be unoccupied. The sheer number of torches along the walls seemed to demand an army of servitors to keep them burning, but Graham saw none. Not only could he find no sign of Ahi'aorina and her captors, he could not find the door through which he had entered this maze. He passed a large black rat scuttling along one hallway. The rat seemed surprised to see him. Graham leaned against a wall and sighed.

A singular feeling of despair crept over him. He would never find Ahi'aorina. The winter would continue forever. All of Daventry would be lost under a blanket of snow. Deep inside, a voice shouted to get up and move, but it was no more than a whisper. He slumped, pressed down by the weight of his despond.

Graham might have stood there for minutes or hours before the sound of someone approaching

woke him from his lassitude. Two small forms
were coming slowly along the hall. Graham hurried to hide in the folds of a vast tapestry and
watched as a pair of imps went past on their thin
bowed legs. This time, instead of waiting for them
to vanish in the maze of hallways, he crept out of
his hiding place and followed the creatures down
the corridor.

Graham stayed well back and near the wall,
careful to make no sound and ready to hide if the
need arose. The imps gave no sign that they knew
he was there. Within a few minutes, they led him
to a large circular chamber. He stood just outside
the door and peeked around the sill. Other imps
were inside, at least a dozen. The two he had been
following joined a group that were eating from
silver plates spread on ornate tables of black-and-
white marble. Others lolled on scattered cushions
of fine golden cloths. Dominating the room was
a vast couch of red-and-silver velvet. A single imp
lay at one end of the great couch, half-buried
among a stack of pillows, and apparently fast
asleep.

In the shadows behind the couch, a gilded cage
hung from a glistening chain. Over the cage was
draped a flowing silver cloth, hiding the cage's
contents from view. Though Graham could not
see inside, he knew the cage had to contain Ahi-
'aorina.

He leaned back out of the room and tried to
gather his thoughts. An individual imp was no

match for a healthy man. But there were more than a dozen in the chamber. And some of them might be armed. He could try to best the imps and free the faery queen, or he could explore more of Sorrowing Court and perhaps learn something that could help him effect the escape.

Graham had always preferred to solve problems with his wits instead of his fists. After all, it was using his brain that had brought him to the throne of Daventry in the first place. But this time there seemed to be little choice but confrontation.

"If I leave here, I'll probably never find this place again," Graham whispered to himself. He bit his lip and tightened his hands into fists. Looking at the imps, he found it hard to believe that he had let one such creature dissuade him from his previous attempt to rescue the faery queen. He had taken fiercer opponents many times without flinching.

Graham could think of no reason for the terror he had felt earlier. It would not happen again. He might be beaten, but he was not going to run away.

If he could take the first few imps by surprise, perhaps the others would run. If they didn't, perhaps he could defeat them all. Try as he might, Graham could not convince himself that either of these events was particularly likely, but he could think of nothing better. He took a deep breath and stepped into the room.

At least Thragaadash the troll was not around.
If Graham had to battle long odds, it was nice that
all his opponents were smaller than he was. He
strode toward the first imp and prepared to let go
a cry that would send fear into his heart.

A great hand clamped about Graham's torso
and lifted him from the floor. Slowly, he was
turned to face a bearded head the size of an ale
keg. Instead of a shout, what emerged from Graham's lips was nothing but a startled whisper.

"I suppose you'd be Graham," said the giant.
"I am nae surprised to see you."

· 20 ·

Graham would have liked to say something in reply to the giant. Something brave and pithy and worthy of one of Shallan's songs. But the grip of the enormous hand had forced all the air from his lungs. His every attempt to utter a word only brought forth a thin squeak.

The giant's blue eyes, each the size of a man's fist, moved up and down as they examined Graham. Apparently the sight of the human king brought the giant no joy. The broad forehead creased in furrows that were deep enough to plant corn in. Above the jutting shelf of the giant's stiff beard, wide lips were cast down in a heavy frown. They parted for a moment and emitted a sigh so deep it was like the rumble of distant thunder. The huge blue eyes turned away and the giant simply stood there with Graham locked in his tight grip.

"Excuse me," Graham managed in a strained whisper. "I can't breathe."

The strangled remark brought laughter from the imps in the room, but the giant only made another rumbling sigh. He didn't even look at Graham, but at least he did begin to move. With slow, ponderous steps, the giant walked between the tables and approached the large couch. There he paused again and stared off into the shadows.

"Help," Graham tried. But this time there was not enough air left in his lungs even to manage a squeak. He beat against the massive fingers with his fists, trying to attract the giant's attention. The imps found his actions so humorous that they fell laughing from their chairs or pounded the table with their silver plates, but Graham's gargantuan captor seemed to have forgotten he was there.

The imp who had been sleeping on the couch stirred and looked up. When he caught sight of Graham in the giant's grasp, his round face opened in a smile that revealed an improbably large number of curved, needle-sharp teeth. "A visitor it is! My pursuer from Daventry."

At the imp's words, the giant's fingers opened. Graham fell to the floor and lay there gasping for breath.

"He came on his own," the giant said. His voice was slow and flat.

"Told you I did," the imp replied. It jumped from the couch and landed on the floor next to Graham. With its thin arms folded behind its back, it circled around the panting king like a jackal examining a tasty bit of carrion. "Told you he could come to take the faery."

"Take the faery?" For the first time, the giant

showed some emotion. He shook his huge head. "No one takes the faery!"

"Wants her he does," said the imp. "Wants her for his own."

The giant ground his huge teeth together with such force that sparks flew into his beard and sent up puffs of smoke. "The faery is mine."

Graham pulled in a breath, tried to talk, coughed, and tried again. "I'm King Graham of Daventry," he said at last, his voice still raw and hoarse. He stood and made his best stab at a formal bow.

"As I told you it is," said the imp. "He it was that followed me from the Old Wood."

Graham looked down at the grinning imp. "You're the one that kidnapped Ahi'aorina," he said. "You're Kuzgu."

The imp paused in his circling and drew himself up to the limits of his small stature. "Yes, Kuzgu I am called. Kuzgu of Sorrowing Court. Kuzgu who is the chief assistant to the great Lord Dunstan."

Graham looked up at the giant. "Are you Lord Dunstan?"

The anger the giant had shown only a moment before seemed to have evaporated as quickly as it had come. Once again the great face was turned to the shadows and the vast eyes were unfocused.

"Dunstan he is," Kuzgu said, answering for his avowed leader. "Rules here he does. Rules all who come to Sorrowing Court."

With another thunderous sigh, the giant turned and sat on the couch. Under his immense weight, the wooden frame groaned and popped. "Aye, I am Dunstan," he said. Each word was drawn out like a funeral dirge. "I bid you welcome to Sorrowing Court."

Happy to have had a polite reply, Graham bowed again to the giant ruler. "Thank you, Lord Dunstan. I must say that your abode is truly impressive."

The delay before the giant spoke again was so long that Graham feared Dunstan had fallen back into his brooding, but at last he nodded. "Thank you," he said. "What brings you to these halls?"

Before Graham could reply, Kuzgu jumped between him and the couch. "Comes for the faery he does," said the imp. "Come to take her away from you."

Dunstan blinked. "You would take away my one happiness?"

Graham started to say something, then closed his mouth and gave it more thought. Certainly he needed Ahi'aorina. That was the point of this whole long, difficult journey. In his experience, lying about such things could lead to a great amount of trouble. But if he admitted that he actually intended to take the faery back to Daventry, there was no telling how the giant would react.

"I would like to see her," Graham said after a moment. "Is it possible I could speak with her?"

The giant peered at him with a calculating expression. "Do you have nae a spark of what she means to me?" he asked.

"No." Graham looked past the giant to the covered cage. "Though I've followed her across the land, I've never understood why she was taken. Why have you brought her here?"

In reply, the giant stretched up one long arm and grasped the corner of the silver drape. With a sharp tug, he pulled the fabric free and let it flutter to the floor.

Ahi'aorina sat in the middle of the cage with her knees drawn up to her chin. Her pale tresses spilled down over her legs in an uncombed mass and her face was fixed in an expression of despair. Despite her forlorn appearance, Graham felt a lifting of his heart the moment the cover was taken from the cage. In the dimly lit room, Ahi-'aorina's milky skin seemed to glow with a light from within. A faint smell of flowers and growing things wafted through the room, banishing the odor of cold stone. Just seeing her brought back a feeling that he had almost forgotten in the days of ice and snow.

Graham took a step toward the cage. "Spring," he whispered.

"Now you see," said Dunstan. "She is all that warms the spirit. All that cheers the heart."

"Ahi'aorina!" Graham called. "Are you all right? I'm here to help you."

The faery did not stir. If she heard Graham at all, she gave no sign of it.

"Wants no help from you," said Kuzgu. "Fine is she. Well do we treat her."

"She is my dear one," rumbled the giant. "Now you can surely see why she belongs here."

"Here?" Graham shook his head. He pulled his gaze away from Ahi'aorina and looked up at Dunstan. "Why should she belong here and not in the Old Wood?"

Kuzgu jumped up onto the edge of the couch and stood near Dunstan's left hand. "See!" said the imp. He raised a clawed finger and pointed it at Graham. "Told you he wanted her. Come to take her he has."

"She is needed," Graham said quickly. "Without her, Daventry suffers under a curse of endless winter."

The giant shifted on his oversized seat, bringing more creaking and groaning from the wood. "Aye, your land labors under the chill of snow and ice, but here . . ." He paused and spread his huge arms in a gesture that took in all of Sorrowing Court. "Here we are blighted with a winter of the soul. Only the warmth and good cheer that this wee one brings to our home keeps us from sinking into black despair. Before my dear one came, there was only darkness in our hearts. She is needed here more than she is needed in your land."

Considering what he had seen of the giant's behavior, Graham wondered just how depressed Dunstan had been *without* the cheering effects of

Ahi'aorina. "I appreciate that she helps you," he said. "But surely the needs of thousands of people can't be ignored."

Dunstan blinked. "Thousands of people?"

"The citizens of Daventry," said Graham. "The farmers cannot till their frozen lands. Food supplies are running low. Soon there will be starvation."

"Starvation," repeated the giant. "That would be wrong."

"Lies!" screamed Kuzgu. "Speaks lies he does. No one starves. Only want the faery for himself he does."

"You must believe me," said Graham. "All Daventry will die without the faery queen's return."

Dunstan's face grew hard. "Kuzgu is my most trusted friend," he said. "When I was living high in the mountains, it was he that led me to this hall. When I could not discover the secrets of this place, he gave them to me." The giant reached up with a massive hand and touched Kuzgu with surprising gentleness. "Kuzgu told me that bringing the faery here would help dispel my gloom, and he was right. I know I can trust Kuzgu. Time and again his words have shown me the path to take. Why should I trust you instead?"

"Because I'm telling the truth," said Graham. He bit his lip in frustration. "If you don't care about the people of Daventry, then what about Ahi'aorina's own people?"

"What?"

"The faeries of the Old Wood. Without her leadership and power, they are lost. The weaker ones may soon die if she is not returned."

The giant's forehead creased in distress. "Faeries can die? But I thought . . . I thought they knew no suffering."

"More lies," said Kuzgu. "Not like you and me are faeries. Not feeling of pain or sorrow."

"No sorrow?" Graham shook his head. "Just look at Ahi'aorina. Can't you see that she is in pain?"

"Pain." Dunstan turned to look at the cage and its small inhabitant. "Kuzgu said she could nae feel pain," he said, but his words were halting, uncertain.

"She wants to be free," said Graham. "She wants to see her friends, and Qilli'ehennan."

"Qilli'ehennan," said a soft voice. "*Lo'ahima-sa'evannan.*"

It took Graham a moment to realize that it was Ahi'aorina who had spoken. When he looked up at the cage, he saw that the faery queen had raised her head and was looking toward Graham with eyes of glowing green. "Did my Qilli'ehennan send you?" she said in her soft voice.

"Yes," said Graham. "He told me what had happened and helped me to find you."

With a rasping scream, Kuzgu leaped from the side of the couch and struck Graham in the chest. Despite the imp's small size, the force of his jump knocked Graham from his feet and sent him rolling across the floor.

"Enchantments!" cried Kuzgu. "Magic is this one, full of dark spells."

"I'm not . . . ," started Graham, but the imp cut him off before he could say more.

"Seeks to blind us he does. Traps of silver words he weaves with a tongue of deception. Even the faery is charmed by his spells." Before Graham could rise, Kuzgu bounded over and glared down at him with yellow eyes. "The faery he wants, and anything will he say to get her."

Dunstan leaned down from his couch and glared at Graham. If he had been confused before, Kuzgu's words seemed to have banished that confusion. The only expression remaining on the giant's face was rage. "No one may use magic in Sorrowing Court. That is the first rule of this place." He smashed his huge fist into the floor beside Graham. "You must leave this hall right away."

Kuzgu hurried to the giant's side. "Lord Dunstan," he said. "Tricky is this one, tricky indeed. Send him away you can, but back he may come."

Dunstan ran a hand through the stiff bristles of his beard. "You could be right," he growled. "What would you suggest?"

The imp showed his sharp-toothed smile. "Sure must we be, sure that no more trouble can this one cause." He rubbed his rough palms together, producing an unpleasant buzzing sound. "The slizard we need."

"What's a slizard?" asked Graham.

The giant leaned back on his couch. "Do we have to use the beastie? It is nae something I like to do."

"No," called one of the imps seated at the stone tables. "Instead we should eat him. Humans be most tasty. Only a few travelers have come this way, and we are hungry."

"No," said Dunstan. "I thought I ordered that nae more travelers were to be eaten."

"And listen we do," said Kuzgu. He threw a fierce glare at the imp who had spoken. "No travelers do we eat."

Dunstan nodded. "Now, you really think the slizard . . ."

"Yes, yes," said Kuzgu. "Only through the slizard will we be sure."

Dunstan frowned. "Aye." He raised his voice into a commanding roar. "Bring forth yon terrible slizard!"

Graham scrambled to his feet as several of the imps hurried from the room. He had never heard of a slizard, but he had no doubt it was some fearsome beast. Several times in the past, Graham had faced death at the claws of some slavering monster, and he had always managed to elude destruction. Still, he knew that the past was no guarantee of the future. He braced himself to face whatever huge creature stalked these halls.

But when the imps returned, they had no monster with them.

"Are you ready to meet your doom, King Graham?" asked the giant.

Graham peered down the hall behind the imps, thinking the slizard might be found there. He saw nothing. "Where is it?" he asked.

"The dreadful slizard is at hand," proclaimed Dunstan.

One of the imps stepped forward and placed a small container on the ground. It was silver, no bigger than a snuffbox, with ornate carvings along the side and a bright green emerald fixed on the top. The imp hooked a clawed finger under the lid, flung it open, and leaped back. All over the hall, imps hurried to stand well back of the small box.

Nothing happened.

After a minute or more of looking at the open box, curiosity drove Graham to step forward and peer inside. Nestled within the red velvet interior of the box was only a small lizard. Its body was mostly green, with strips of deep orange along its back and red spots along the neck. Its feet were pale yellow, as was the tip of its tail. It looked up at Graham and blinked. Its eyes were a warm amber. Its face was frozen in an expression that looked like a mischievous smile. It was really quite a pretty little thing.

Graham turned away from the box and looked back at Dunstan. "This is it? This is your slizard?"

"Aye," said the giant.

The lizard crawled over the lip of the box and out onto the floor. The nearest imps let out a shriek and backed away. One of the imps picked up a chair and started smacking the ground between himself and the tiny lizard.

"Be careful," said Graham. "You'll hurt it." He went over to the small creature and sat down, his hand in front of its pointed nose. The slizard crawled up onto his palm.

"I don't see what's so fearful about it." He looked down at the little creature and studied its bright colors. Graham shook his head and started to look back at the giant. "It's only a—"

Just then there was a sharp pain on the tip of Graham's nose and a wave of dizziness washed over him. There was a rushing noise, and a tumbling, falling sensation. Suddenly, he was looking up into a face of such scale that it made the giant seem like an ant.

He screamed, and threw up his hands to protect himself. Or at least, he tried to throw up his hands.

Graham stared numbly at the four-toed foot that had replaced his hand, then back up at the cyclopean head looming above him. On second glance, those monstrously large features seemed all too familiar. It was the same face that he had seen in the mirror most every day of his life.

"What's going on," he said, but what came out

of his mouth was a series of reedy peeps and whistles.

The giant that looked like Graham drew back and another figure came into view. It was Kuzgu the imp, only he was now as tall as the great trees of the Old Wood.

"The slizard has done its work," said the towering imp. Its voice was as deep and thundering as the crack of doom. It raised one gigantic foot and held it over Graham. "Now ends King Graham."

The foot whistled down with the unstoppable force of a falling mountain.

· 21 ·

Graham rolled into a ball, threw himself hard to the right, and came up running as fast as his four little yellow legs could carry him.

All over the room huge imps got to their feet and ran toward him, rumbling with thunderous laughter. Graham ran away from one imp, and darted right between the feet of another. A dozen times one of the giant feet came within inches of crushing him. Finally he was able to shoot around a gargantuan chair, slip under the shadow of a table, and temporarily elude his flock of giant pursuers.

He stopped against the base of a towering table leg, and caught his breath for a moment. His mind was still reeling, unable to accept what had happened. One moment the room had been of normal size—and he had been his normal size—and now . . .

A plate big as a house crashed to the floor beside him. Startled, Graham ran halfway up the table leg before he realized what he had done. Though the leg was made from the same polished stone as the rest of the table, Graham stuck to it as neatly as a picture on a frame.

He lifted one of his feet from the smooth stone and looked at it—really looked at it. It was covered in fine yellow scales and had only four blunt digits. Graham tried to flex his toes, but there was only the tiniest of movements. There was no doubt that his foot looked very much like that of the lizard he had seen in the box. He was a lizard.

No, he was a slizard. Apparently the little beast had the ability to trade bodies with other beings. It really was quite an awesome power. No wonder Dunstan and his imps had held the creature in such respect.

But now that the slizard had exchanged bodies with him, what was Graham going to do? He certainly couldn't go home like this, and neither could he free Queen Ahi'aorina. He had to think of something.

His thoughts were interrupted by the appearance of a huge eye. "Here he is!" boomed a deep voice.

Graham managed to dodge a slap from a giant hand, slipped down the table leg, and sped off across the floor. This new body could react with amazing quickness, but its endurance was not good. Already Graham felt very tired. He needed to rest. But if he was going to rest, he first had to evade the imps.

He put his muzzle down and charged right

through the middle of the crowd of imps, running right over one set of wrinkled brown toes. When he reached the far wall, he didn't slow down, but charged straight up the close-fitting bricks and slipped behind the hanging tapestries. The thick cloth muffled the voices of the imps, but Graham could still hear them coming after him. A moment later, there was a series of heavy thuds and the imps began to pound their hands against the tapestry in hopes of squashing the lizard king.

Graham's legs burned, and even with his mouth gaping open he could not seem to get enough air, but he could not rest yet. He pushed himself onward, climbing higher and higher on the wall until he had left the banging of the imps far below. Then, still under the cover of the hanging tapestries, he walked along the wall until he came to a corner. Only then did he slip a little higher on the wall and peek out over the top of the tapestry.

Dunstan's hall and the crowd of imps were nowhere in sight. Graham ducked back behind the tapestries and closed his eyes. What to do?

In the first moments after the slizard had worked its magic, he had seen his own face. That could only mean that his own body was not destroyed, but was still there with the imps. Perhaps it was mindless. Perhaps it was now under the control of whatever intelligence had lived within the slizard. That he didn't know.

As long as his body was still intact, there was the chance that Graham could regain it. He tried to think of what had happened just before the slizard had changed places with him. He had been looking at the slizard. Maybe that was all there was to it. If he could get close enough to his own body to look it in the eye, maybe the slizard's magic would be reversed.

He would certainly have to try. The alternative was not worth thinking about.

After a few minutes, the burning feeling in Graham's legs died down. He felt energetic enough to slide above the tapestry and peek around the corner. He could see shapes moving in the vast room, but little more. His lizard eyes didn't seem to be designed to make out objects at a distance. If one of the blurry forms moving around the room was his own body, he couldn't tell it.

From the way the figures were moving and the distant shouts that reached his lizard ears, Graham knew they were still hunting for him. He wouldn't be able to just charge back into the midst of the imps, at least not until they had calmed down. One good thump and he would be nothing but lizard jelly on the floor of Sorrowing Court. If he was going to get his own body back, he was going to have to have a plan. Graham turned away from Dunstan's hall and walked off down the side of the corridor.

If Sorrowing Court had seemed huge before, now it was a world in itself. Each hallway was endless, each room a yawning cavern.

Graham walked along the walls in some places, and at other times along the floor. He tried running, jumping, and climbing on the tapestries. He soon found that it was easier to depend on the stickiness of his feet and clamber over the stone walls than to risk getting tangled in the folds of cloth. It was a good thing to know. If he were going to stand a chance of getting past Dunstan and the imps, he would have to know the limits of this new body.

Down one of the hallways Graham spied a long silver mirror adorning a wall. He could not resist strolling up onto the glass for a better look. The marvelous yellow feet took him right up the smooth glass as easily as he had walked along the floor.

There was no doubt about it, he was a lizard. He tilted his head from side to side and blinked his slitted orange eyes. He examined his bright green snout and lifted his head to get a good look at his cream-colored underside. He twisted around to get a better look at the stripes along his back and tail.

He was, as he had observed before the switch, quite a handsome little creature, with bright colors and a clean design. Though his body was small, it was quick and agile. The ability to run up walls was quite an advantage. Graham could imagine many other forms that would be much more unpleasant than the one he currently occupied.

However, he was sure he preferred his old two-legged body. He took one last look into the mirror and moved on down the hallway.

At least he still had his own mind. His memories were intact, and he still had the intelligence of a man. At least, he thought he did. Would he know he had got stupid if he was too stupid to notice? Graham comforted himself with the idea that even pondering such a question was surely beyond the reach of a normal lizard.

The tail that jutted out from his spine was certainly a novel piece of anatomy. Most of the time, it seemed to have a mind of its own. It shifted and turned to the side as needed to balance any movement that Graham made. He found that if he tried, he could move and curl the tail in any direction—a sensation not unlike having an extra finger tacked onto his back. However, moving his tail intentionally made him feel clumsy and out of balance.

At the next turn in the hallway, he came across something curious. Behind the covering tapestries, the wall at this place was of a very different construction. Instead of the neat, polished blocks that formed the walls in the rest of Sorrowing Court, this section was made of pieces of broken stone and rough plaster. It was well enough covered by the wall hangings that in his usual form, Graham might never have noticed the hidden repairs. But traveling under the tapestries made them obvious.

In the center of the rough wall, Graham found a fissure that was wide enough to admit his tiny body. The tight press of the cool stones against his body felt comforting. He was tempted to stop and take a nap there in the shelter of the wall. But a strange sound from the other side of the wall caught his attention.

He wriggled through the crack and found himself in another passage. This corridor was very different from any he had seen in the rest of the great fortress. The walls here were simple cut stone. So was the floor. There were no plush carpeting, no rich tapestries. Everything was covered in a blanket of fine dust. Not a single torch was visible, though a dim, pulsating light leaked into the hallway from somewhere in the distance.

The deep humming sound that he had heard in the fissure was much louder here. Graham moved up onto one of the walls and crept toward the noise. The stone here was colder than in the other halls. With each step, Graham could feel the warmth being sucked from his feet and belly. It made him feel tired and sluggish.

He closed his eyes, just to rest them for a moment. Sitting there sideways on the wall, he fell into a dreamless doze. When he awoke, he still felt stiff and sluggish. Warmth was what he needed. He wasn't sure how he knew this, but there was no doubt in his mind that his energy would only return when he found somewhere warm. Warmth and something to eat. His stomach rumbled—a sensation that was apparently the same for both man and lizard.

Moving with all the speed his chilly body could manage, Graham moved on down the wall toward the source of the humming sound.

The sound grew louder and louder, eventually reaching a volume Graham could feel in the soles of his sticky feet. The light increased along with the sound, dancing and flashing from some indefinite point ahead. And if there was light, wouldn't there be warmth? He hoped so.

Finally Graham entered a room where beams of brilliant light sprayed out in all directions and the stones shook with a deep-throated tone. The light ranged in color from beams of deep indigo to shafts of startling crimson to fingers of pale yellow. Like the light, the sound was also more complex than it had seemed at a distance. It was not one tone, it was many tones—maybe all tones—being sounded all at once. The source of all this sound and light was hard to make out in all the glare.

Graham closed his translucent outer eyelids and squinted his slitted eyes, but he still saw little but a shadowy form in the center of the room.

Even though he couldn't see the source, there was no doubt that whatever was causing this was magic—and powerful magic, at that. Whoever had created this thing might be able to help Graham with his problems.

Moving carefully, he crept over to the nearest

beam of light and stuck in a single sticky toe. He half-expected his foot to burst into flame, but the light beam caused no pain. The light was only light. Graham crossed the intertwined beams and approached the brilliant point at the center of the web of light.

There was a chair in the center of the room. He could make out that much. And a figure seated in the chair.

All of the light and sound seemed to be centered on this seated form.

The figure in the chair seemed to be that of a man, but Graham could make out nothing of his features. The magical light flowed over his body, swirling into a shell of white that masked any glimpse of the person underneath.

There was no doubt that this was some sort of powerful magic spell, though its purpose was unclear to Graham. Whoever this person was, he seemed to be frozen here.

Dunstan and Kuzgu might have been responsible for this trap, but somehow Graham didn't think so. He didn't understand enough about magic to discern the complete nature of the light web, but he knew enough to know that this spell was a very strong one. Neither the giant nor his imp struck Graham as a wizard of the caliber to craft such a spell.

If neither of them had done it, then who had? The only way Graham could think of to answer that was to free the figure in the center of the trap and ask him. But he was not even sure how to begin unraveling a spell as complex as this light web. Besides, in his current form, he might free the magical prisoner and still be unable to communicate.

Graham was suddenly convinced that he had missed something important. Kuzgu said he had kidnapped Queen Ahi'aorina in order to make Dunstan happy. That much seemed true, but was it the imp's only motive? Whoever this person was pinned down by magic light, perhaps he had something to do with the other events in Sorrowing Court.

What to do first? Graham wondered. He had to think, but no matter how long he thought, the situation didn't seem to become any clearer.

A flicker of movement caught Graham's eye. He tensed, afraid that one of the imps was coming to stomp him.

It was a moth. Attracted by the cacophony of light, the inset whirled and wheeled around the room.

Quickly, Graham hurried across the floor and scurried up a wall. He stationed himself near a pool of white light and waited. Moments later, the moth fluttered near.

Graham's long, sticky pink tongue shot out and snagged the bug in mid-flight. He reeled it in and crunched it between rows of tiny sharp teeth. The moth was dry, but it satisfied the emptiness in his stomach. He looked around the room carefully, hoping to spot another meal on the wing.

Deep inside the fortress of Sorrowing Court, King Graham of Daventry hunted bugs for his supper.

· 22 ·

Hunger was one sensation that was the same for man and lizard. The sensation of being absolutely, completely stuffed was another.

Graham rolled over belly-up, stretched all four legs into the air, and uttered the bleat of a satisfied lizard. The magic lights had attracted a bumper crop of flying insects, and Graham had gorged until the scales over his tummy were stretched to their limits.

This really wasn't such a bad place after all. Fairly warm. Dark. Plenty of bugs. He should just get Valanice and the hatchling and . . .

Graham shook his head. What was he thinking? He was not a lizard, and neither was anyone in his family. He tried to picture Valanice, but her image would not come. If he stayed like this for much longer, would he forget that he had ever been a man?

One part of his mind insisted that he should be disgusted even at the idea of eating bugs. But the rest of his mind was fully in agreement with his stomach. For the moment at least, he was a lizard, not a human king. Though he had to hold tight to his own memories, it was quite clear that no servant was likely to appear and produce a plate of rare beef with a side of crisp vegetables. If he was going to eat, the menu was going to be full of things with six legs.

Now that his stomach was satisfied, Graham was able to turn his thoughts back to his other problems. The glowing figure in the chair was quite a puzzle, but it was not a puzzle Graham was prepared to solve. Even if he were to have his own body back, he would need someone with more knowledge of magic to explain the web of light.

He could not very well go to Dunstan or Kuzgu for help. That left Ahi'aorina as the only one likely to free the magical prisoner. Which meant that before he could free the man in the lights, he had to rescue Ahi'aorina from her cage.

Dunstan would probably be staying close to the faery as much as he could, leaving Graham few opportunities to get close to her unobserved. If the imps were always hanging around, it would be even tougher. He would need to study the room, and watch how the imps and the giant went in and out. There might be a time when they all were off elsewhere, leaving Graham time to free the faery queen.

When it finally came time to set Ahi'aorina free, he would surely need to get his own body back. The cage would have to be opened, and he couldn't imagine how he might do that when he

weighed less than most keys. But if he was going
to scout the activity in Dunstan's hall, remaining
a small wall-crawling lizard had a distinct advantage.

When he put it all together, Graham had the
beginnings of a plan. He would return to the hall
where Ahi'aorina was held and carefully observe
the situation. Once he had spied out a weakness,
he would find a way to get his own body back.
Then he would set Ahi'aorina free. Then he
would get Ahi'aorina to help him free the figure
in the lights. Then it was back to Daventry and
the arms of Queen Valanice.

Of course, not one piece of Graham's plan
would hold up to careful scrutiny, and he knew
it. There were a thousand things that might go
wrong, and only one way in which they could go
right. Graham would simply have to press on and
hope that luck was on his side.

He scrambled out of the room of lights and
back down the cold, dusty hallway. As he was walking along, he noticed that the dust was not uni-
formly distributed across the hallway. Someone
had been there. In fact, there was evidence that
someone had been passing back and forth this
way with regularity. He didn't know what this
meant, but it was another piece of information to
keep in mind.

The crevice in the wall was much tighter than
it had been on the way in.

One too many moths, thought Graham. I'm going to have to watch it, or I'm going to be one chubby lizard.

Once through the wall, he found it wonderfully warm back in the luxurious carpeted hallways of Sorrowing Court. The combination of the increased warmth and the belly full of food sparked renewed energy in Graham. He trotted down the hallway with confidence. He felt good. Perhaps things really would work out.

It was at that point that he noticed that, though his legs were still moving, he wasn't going anywhere. He turned his muzzle and saw a rat standing close behind him with one heavy paw pressed firmly on Graham's tail.

The rats in Sorrowing Hall had been noticeably large even before Graham's transformation. This one seemed as large as a horse. Its dark gray fur bristled in all directions and its claws were like gleaming black daggers. It looked at Graham with shiny black eyes and wiggled a nose decorated by stiff whiskers as long as Graham's whole body.

"I don't suppose you're a transformed king?" said Graham, producing a series of long lizard squeaks. "You and I could be on the same side."

The rat leaned forward and bared its teeth. It displayed quite an impressive assortment of dental hardware.

"No," Graham said. "I didn't think so." He gave a hard tug and succeeded in freeing his tail from the rat's grip. The rodent hissed and lunged for him. Sharp white incisors clicked together only a fraction of an inch from Graham's head. The king turned and ran for the wall.

The rat was fast. Before Graham had gone more than a few inches, the furry monster was standing in front of him with its mouth ready for a large bite of lizard.

Graham stopped short and dodged left just as the rat leaped. Claws raked down Graham's side. His scales protected him, but the rat's blow sent him tumbling across the carpeted hall. He managed to get his feet under him and tried to run again, only to receive another stunning blow from the rat.

It let out a low growl as it slowly advanced on its prey.

Swift as his four legs were, Graham could not outrun this hunter. He knew that, and obviously so did the rat. It was taking its time now, sure that the meal was almost won. If he were going to escape, Graham would have to count on his human mind instead of his lizard body.

"Have at you!" he shouted. He lowered his snout and charged full speed at the rat.

The furry predator snarled and leaped.

When they were almost nose to nose, Graham bounded into the air. He planted his front feet on the rat's snout, shoved down hard, and flipped completely over the animal's back. Before the rat could turn, Graham opened his mouth and bit down hard on the animal's hairless tail.

The rat gave a whistling bark and surged away. Its movement threw Graham across the hallway. He got up and sped to the nearest wall. Slipping under the tapestry, he climbed the bricks as fast as he could and kept going until his legs were again burning with exhaustion.

That was close, Graham thought.

He reminded himself that there was obviously more for him to worry about in the halls of Sorrowing Court than just imps and giants. Obstacles that he had ignored as a human could be deadly to him now. He inspected his side. A few scales were missing, but there was no visible blood. That was no guarantee that he would get off so lightly the next time.

There was a rustling in the tapestry. Before Graham could react, the rat had climbed up the cloth to a spot right in front of where he was hiding. There was a ripping noise as sharp incisors began to gnaw their way through the cloth.

Graham was not rested, but he had no choice but to move on. He climbed up and up, with the rat following his every step. Finally he reached the top of the tapestry. If he could go farther, the rat would be unable to follow. He hoped. But before he could break free onto the bare wall above, a dark snout appeared, blocking his path.

Whoops! thought Graham. Wrong way.

He spun around and headed back down the wall. All the way down, he expected to feel the rat clawing at the tapestry that shielded him, but this time there was no sign of the hunter. Graham slowed up a bit, fearing a trap. When he reached the bottom, he peeked out cautiously.

Still no rat.

He emerged onto the blue carpet and looked around. Then he looked up. There was the rat, still looking for him at the top of the tapestry.

"Let's see you catch me now!" Graham squeaked. The rat turned its head and glared down at him. For a creature the size of the rat, that wall had to be like hundreds of feet for a man. Graham would have plenty of time to escape. Why, with the distance it had to cover, getting back to the ground would take the rat at least—

The rat leaped from the top of the tapestry and thumped onto the carpet two inches from the end of Graham's snout.

—half a second.

Graham gave a full-throated squeak of terror and ran at top speed down the hallway. A door loomed up on the left. Graham headed for it with the hot breath of the rat streaming down on his tail.

Inside the room was a bare stone floor cluttered by a collection of wooden tables and counters. Graham snagged a table leg with one sticky foot, pivoted neatly, and scrambled up to the lip of the table above. Aching with exhaustion, he dragged himself over the edge and collapsed among a wide assortment of root vegetables.

The table shook as the rat tried to climb up.

Graham stuck his muzzle over the edge and
peered down. If his pursuer were able to climb
up to this perch, Graham knew he would be too
tired to get away again. Already his legs hurt so
badly that letting the rat chomp on him didn't
sound half-bad.

The dark-furred rodent hugged the table leg
and struggled upward. It hugged tighter and
shimmied up an inch. Its claws scraped against
the wood. Another inch. Then it lost its grip and
fell hissing to the floor.

Graham leaned back, a lizardly grin on his hard
lips. He could hear the rat pacing around below,
its claws tapping against the room's stone floor.
The hunter had been stopped, but it had not
given up. If he were going to leave this table without the rat on his heels, he would have to think
of a way to escape this furry danger. Perhaps if he
waited, it would simply tire and go away. Considering how he felt, waiting seemed like a capital
idea. He rolled over on his side and curled into
a tight green ball.

After a few minutes of rest, the ache in Graham's muscles receded. The lizard body tired
quickly, but with food, warmth, and rest, it also
regained its energy more rapidly than a man. Graham stretched out his legs and tail, then he
walked across the table to check on the rat.

It was still there.

The rat rested on its furry haunches right below
the table, staring up at Graham. Though he was
no expert at reading rodent faces, Graham was

sure those shiny black eyes were full of rattish anger.

He looked around the room for possible escape routes. This appeared to be another kitchen or pantry, with pots and pans hanging from hooks overhead and stacks of dishes on high shelves. He saw a rack holding several large knives, but at his current size, there was no way he could wield them against the rat. Even if he cold hold them, the counter where they sat was several feet away— a veritable lizard-scale canyon. All the other tables in the room were at least as far away as the one with the knives. Graham's table had provided a refuge, but it was also a little wooden island.

He looked to the materials at hand. On his table there were only a few round yellow new potatoes and a double bunch of small carrots. If he had still been a man, they would have made a nice meal, but they were not exactly the best weapons in the world.

Graham narrowed his orange eyes. He went back to the edge of the table and took a good look at the position of the rat. Maybe the potatoes were just what he needed.

He eyed the roots around him and went over to one that looked particularly nice and round. With the tip of his muzzle, Graham rolled the potato toward the edge of the table. The vegetable far outweighed Graham's scaly body, but the table was smooth and the potato rolled without much difficulty. When Graham had the potato teetering on the edge of the table, he ran to double-check the position of the rat. Perfect.

He went back for another potato and lined it up beside the first. Then another. Soon one whole side of the table was lined with a row of vegetable ammunition.

He took one more look at the rat. "Prepare yourself, furry," he called down to the animal. With that, he shoved the first potato overboard. There was a thud, and a satisfying squeal of pain.

Graham ran down the line as fast as he could, shoving each potato over the edge as he passed. The sound of potatoes thumping into the floor was like a hailstorm.

A moment later, the rat ran squealing from the room.

"Tell all the others," Graham called after it. "Tell them this is one little lizard that you don't want to tangle with!"

With his enemy routed, Graham slipped over the edge of the table and climbed down the leg. The hall outside was clear. Apparently, being bombarded by vegetables was not something with which the rat was prepared to cope. Feeling like a king again, Graham sauntered down the hallway.

When he approached the room where Ahi'aorina's cage hung, Graham walked over to the wall and slipped under the protective cover of the tapestries. As he turned the corner, he could hear the imps laughing and stomping around. He walked along until he was near the center of the room, then ducked down to have a look.

Dunstan reclined on his couch. His chin was down, and his stiff beard brushed against his chest. So far as Graham could tell, the giant was asleep.

But the room was far from empty. There were a full dozen imps in attendance. Several were snoozing in the chairs, round heads lolling on tables. Another lay sprawled on the floor. From the cups that were spilled beside them, Graham suspected the sleeping imps had partaken of far too much strong drink.

The imps who were still awake were gathered in a loose group around a table at the center of the room. Also near this table was a singular figure. It was taller than the imps, and wore a dirty jerkin over equally dirty wool pants and boots. It was Graham's human body.

Graham was tempted to rush across the floor and stare his body in the eye right then and there, but he held himself back. There was a plan. Before he regained his body, he first had to observe. He had to learn what the imps did and when they did it. Besides, even if he managed to regain his body now, he would be right in the middle of a dozen imps. He had no doubt that next time Kuzgu would find something even worse than the slizard.

Thinking of Kuzgu, Graham looked up toward the corner of the couch. There was no sign of the imp leader. Apparently, Kuzgu had business elsewhere.

The imps at the middle table suddenly gave out a burst of rattling laughter.

"Funny is this!" cried one of them. "A most wonderful joke."

Graham saw that his old body was crawling about the floor on its hands and knees. The look on its face was distinctly unhappy as it moved around clumsily. One hand slipped on a fallen plate and its chin fell to the ground. It got its hands back under it only to get its feet tangled together. It twisted around to free itself and only succeeded in falling again.

But the imps weren't content to leave the body to its own indignities. One of the bark-skinned creatures dug a handful of greasy stew from its plate and flung it into the face of the crawling body. It winced and tried to hide under the table, but the imps kicked at it, driving it out onto the floor again.

"Who be you?" called one of the imps.

The body looked up and blinked through the mask of dripping stew. "I, Graham," it said.

The answer brought another round of laughter from the imps. "Right you are, King Graham," said one of them. It picked up a gnawed bone from its plate and tossed it at Graham. "Eat, Kingy, Kingy. Eat our scraps."

Graham felt a surge of anger. The imps were making sport of him, forcing his poor body to grovel on the floor. He would show them. Why, he would run out there and . . . and . . . Bite them on the toe?

No. Graham had to get his own body back before he could get his revenge on these creatures. Once he was himself again, he would show these creatures just how dangerous it was to anger the king of Daventry.

"Again!" shouted another imp. "Say again!"

"I, Graham," said the crawling body.

The imps laughed so hard that two of them fell from their chairs.

"Again!" cried the imps.

"I, Graham," said the body, its voice confused and frightened. "I, Graham. I, Graham. I, Graham."

The lizard on the wall watched the scene with cold determination. Not for long, it thought. Not for long.

· 23 ·

Queen Ahi'aorina of the Old Wood, Spirit of Spring, was dying.

She was immortal, of course, but she was dying all the same. For most of her nearly infinite years, she had lived among the massive trees and blooming flowers of the Old Wood. The life of the forest had flowed from her, and through her. Each creature of the Wood, from the humming insects to the browsing deer, had been a part of her life.

Now she was alone, separated from all that she had known. Her beloved Quilli'ehennan was not here. Her coterie of faery girls were not here. The great trees, with whom she had had so many slow, wind-whispered conversations, were not here. There was no one to talk to but Dunstan, and all he ever wanted to speak of was his own giant sadness. The imps did not want to talk at all. They only wanted to taunt her and throw scraps of food into her cage.

Even the sky and the earth were denied to her by the dead stone walls of this massive keep. She could feel her energy growing weaker with each day she was away from her home.

She reached out listlessly and ran her fingers down one of the bars of her golden cage. The imps had transferred her to this new cage when they carried her into the dark fortress. It was larger than the cage in which they had carried her from her home, but not by much. Instead of wood, the bars of this cage were smooth gold. And not just gold. If it had been normal metal, she could have bent it to her will and freed herself in moments. But the cage had been formed by magic, and some of that magic still lingered.

Ahi'aorina understood the magic which held her well enough. If she had been outside the cage, she had little doubt that she could have unraveled the threads of the spell and freed any prisoner held inside. But she was the one inside. From the inside, any attempt to pluck out a single piece of the spell only pulled the cords of magic tighter. If she were going to be freed, it would take the help of someone else.

The imps laughed again as they made sport of the human king. Ahi'aorina looked at the blond man and frowned. She had not known who he was when he first tried to rescue her, though she had suspected that he might be the one that Quilli'ehennan would choose to send. The king of Daventry was well known, even in the Old Wood, and well liked by those who had encountered him. He had known the name of her beloved.

And he had argued for her return. Ahi'aorina had hoped that he would best the giant and the imps, and set her free. Instead, they had bested him.

Lost in her own waking drowse, Ahi'aorina had not seen quite what the imps had done to the human, but it was obvious that he was now all but mindless. Her potential rescuer had become nothing but another toy for her captors.

She turned her head to look at the sleeping giant. Barely visible under the skirt of his beard was a thin leather line. Though she couldn't see it at the moment, Ahi'aorina knew that somewhere along that line was the key that Kuzgu had used when he locked her into the golden cage.

If they had been in the midst of the forest, she might have called on her powers. With a whispered word, fast growing vines could have bound the giant's limbs. A wave of her hand could have summoned a sapling to lift the giant's key and carry it to her hand.

But that was all a dream. Ahi'aorina was trapped here, away from friends and forest. Away from all of nature.

She was dying.

A tiny scratching sound came from the wall to her left. With everything that was going on in the room—imps laughing, talking, plates rattling—she might have easily missed the noise. But to her ears, this was by far the loudest noise in the hall, because it was a natural sound. This was not a noise of man or imp. This was the sound of some small wild creature.

She looked carefully at the wall. At first she saw nothing but the gaudy tapestries, but then she spotted a small green face looking at her from under the billowing cloth.

"Hello, little one," she called. "Are you trapped in this place, too?"

The lizard emerged from under the wall hangings, revealing a body striped with orange and spotted with red. There were many lizards in the Old Wood. With few exceptions, Ahi'aorina found them pleasant little creatures. Clean and well mannered, if a little too serious and too caught up in their own affairs. This particular sort of lizard was not a type she had seen before, but it was a pretty little thing. Seeing it in this place of stone and sadness made her feel better.

The lizard looked at her with attentive orange eyes. "If only you could understand me," it piped.

"But I can understand you," said Ahi'aorina.

"What?" The lizard blinked in surprise. "You really know what I'm saying?"

"Of course I do." Ahi'aorina held herself a little straighter and tried to look dignified. "I am Ahi'aorina, Queen of the Old Wood. All the voices of field and forest are within my understanding."

The lizard scampered around the wall with excitement. "That's wonderful," it croaked. "Really wonderful. I have something very important to tell you."

Ahi'aorina smiled. It was so like a lizard to think anything he knew was important, but it was nice to have someone to talk with, even if that someone was a lizard. "Of course you do," she said. "What's your important news? Have you caught any good bugs today?"

"No," said the lizard. "I mean, yes, I have. But that's not my news." The little creature fixed her with an orange stare. "I've come to rescue you."

"Rescue?" Lizards did take themselves seriously, but this seemed a bit extreme.

"I'm King Graham of Daventry," piped the lizard.

"You're King Graham?" Ahi'aorina looked across the room to where the imps were having sport with the simple blond man. "I wasn't aware that the King of Daventry was a lizard."

"I'm not," said the lizard. "I mean, I'm not *usually* a lizard. You see, Dunstan put this lizard in front of me. It did something. I'm not sure what, but something. Now I'm in the lizard's body and I guess the lizard's in mine. After they made the switch, the imps tried to crush me, but I hid behind the tapestry and got away."

Ahi'aorina frowned. She had known some very serious lizards, but she had not known them to lie. While she had never heard of an animal capable of what seemed to have happened here, she knew there were yet many strange things in the world of which she had not yet learned.

"If you are truly Graham," she said, "then who sent you here to rescue me?"

"King Quilli'ehennan." Quickly, the little reptile poured out the story of Daventry's sudden change of weather, the meeting with the king of the Old Wood, and of the long, difficult journey that had brought him across the Glass Mountains to this dark fortress.

The sound of her dear Quilli'ehennan's name alone was enough to send a thrill of hope through Ahi'aorina.

"I was not conscious through most of the trip here, but I do remember some of your valiant efforts to free me from the imp." She extended a pale hand as far as she could toward the lizard. "Come to me."

The tiny creature hesitated only a moment before jumping onto Ahi'aorina's palm. As she drew him back through the bars of the cage, she felt a sudden thrill of magic. This was no normal lizard. It was an enchanted creature.

"It's true," she said. "You really are King Graham."

The lizard rose onto its hind legs, balancing the unnatural posture by using its tail as a prop. Slowly it sketched a formal bow before falling back to all fours. "Lady Ahi'aorina, all Daventry suffers endless winter without you, and the spirits of the Old Wood wail in mourning. I must free you from this unjust imprisonment and return you to your home."

New energy ran through Ahi'aorina. "I believe you, King Graham. What should we do now?"

The lizard spun around on her palm and looked out through the bars. "I came back to this room to watch Dunstan and the imps. I was hoping to find a time when there were was no one in the room so I could set you free."

"I've been here for days," said Ahi'aorina, "and I've not seen such a time. Dunstan sleeps here and takes most of his meals here. Even when he is gone, there are always several of the imps nearby. Kuzgu, the one who took me from the wood, has ordered them to keep an eye on me."

Almost as if Ahi'aorina's words had called him, Kuzgu strolled into the room. The bowlegged imp walked along with an insolent slouch and a smirk on his twisted face. He held a length of gnawed pink bone to which a few scraps of bloody meat still clung. He shoved a chair away from a table and rested his food on a large bone plate.

Ahi'aorina had noticed the plate before. The other imps ate from silver plates, which most would have considered more lofty than bone, but Kuzgu insisted on his bone plate and was always angry when there was not such a plate waiting for him.

"The idiot is here, I see," Kuzgu called to the other imps. "Amuses you, does he?"

One of the imps drove a foot into the backside

of King Graham's human body. "A jester is this one."

"Not speaking of the human was I," said Kuzgu. He lifted his gory meal and pointed the long bone toward Dunstan. "Of this one did I speak. The biggest fool of them all."

While the other imps howled with laughter, Kuzgu bounded onto the couch at Dunstan's side. The imp leaned down and waved the bone in the giant's face. "Sleep, giant. The thing you do best it is."

"I thought Dunstan was the leader," said Graham.

Ahi'aorina raised the lizard close to her face. "Squeak quietly," she said. "You don't want them to know that you are here."

"Dunstan," Graham peeped softly. "Do the imps always act like this toward him?"

"Yes," Ahi'aorina said with a nod. "When the giant is awake, they pretend to follow him. But as soon as he leaves or falls asleep, they say terrible things. Kuzgu seems to be the real leader."

Graham was silent for a moment. "There is something going on here that I can't puzzle out," he said at last. "Dunstan said that it was Kuzgu who led him down here and showed him how to get into Sorrowing Court. Why would Kuzgu do that?"

The faery queen shook her head. "I don't know," she said. "The giant is so sad when he is awake, he never wants to talk of anything but his own sorrow. Most of the time he simply sleeps. The time he spends asleep grows longer with each day."

"Well, we need to get you out of here," said Graham. "Do you have any ideas?"

"There is a key," said Ahi'aorina. "A small key of ivory and gold. Kuzgu gave it to the giant when we arrived, and now Dunstan keeps it around his neck day and night." She pointed to the giant. "Look close and you can spy the cord that holds the key."

The lizard crawled up to the tip of Ahi'aorina's fingers for a better look. "I'll have to get my own body back before I can let you out," he said. "I would never be able to get up here with the key while I'm this small."

"Can you really regain your human form?"

"I don't know. I think I remember how it was done to me; all I can think is to try the same thing."

Ahi'aorina nodded. "Let us hope you are successful, but once you are back in your human body, you will have a hard time taking the key from the giant's neck unnoticed."

"I can't rescue you like this," said Graham.

"I agree," replied Ahi'aorina. "You could not get the key up to this cage. But it may be that you can get it from the giant while still in this form and then use it once you are returned to you own true body."

The lizard nodded. "It's possible," he said.

"I think that's what we should try. If you can loose the key from round his neck and secret it in some place where you can find it later, then we will both be closer to freedom."

"All right. But before I try it, there is something else I need to tell you." The lizard turned to look at Ahi'aorina's face. "I found a room not too far from here. There's a man sitting in a chair and he's surrounded by magic."

"A man? A human man?"

"I'm not sure," said Graham. "There was all this light around him. It was so bright that it was hard to see."

Ahi'aorina tapped a slim finger against her chin. "Magic light. What did this light look like?"

"There were beams of all colors. They seemed to be coming from the man and shining to all corners of the room. There was a noise, too. A loud noise."

"What you're describing sounds much like what I have been told of the *e'llaiomenheae*. A kind of glamour manarvel."

"What's a glamour manarvel?"

"A spell which drains energy from the one it holds," explained Ahi'aorina. "Sometimes one wizard may capture another and set such a spell to add to his own pool of magic energy."

"Do you think Kuzgu's behind it?" asked Graham.

"The imp showed considerable magical skill in taking me from the Old Wood and bringing me here." She looked over at the sleeping giant. "Perhaps he draws power from both this imprisoned figure and from Dunstan." She thought of the weakness and lassitude she had felt since entering Sorrowing Hall. "Perhaps he draws power from me, as well."

"But there are no lights around you and Dunstan," noted the lizard.

"There are other ways, more subtle ways, to drink of someone's power." Ahi'aorina ran her free hand along one of the smooth bars of her cage. "These is magic in this cage that keeps me from feeling anything of the spells that go on outside. Once I am free from here, I will have a better sense of what this imp has done."

She was interrupted by another burst of laughter from the imps. Kuzgu was down on the floor with the rest of them. As Ahi'aorina watched, the imp mocked the plodding movements of Dunstan. His antics brought cheers from the other stout imps. Behind him, the real Dunstan slept on, oblivious to the rude show going on at his feet.

"Now that I have thought of it, I know that this sleep that plagues the giant cannot be natural," said Ahi'aorina. "Kuzgu must be working some spell on him. If he really is draining energy from Dunstan, it could explain the terrible sorrow that consumes him."

"Then Dunstan is another victim of Kuzgu," said Graham.

"Yes."

"We'll need to free him, too."

Ahi'aorina smiled. "I have heard stories of King Graham's kindness. I can see that these stories are true."

"Thank you," said the lizard. "However, our first step is still to get you free of this cage." He turned again and looked at the room. "With all those imps dancing around, I'm going to have a hard time getting over there unseen."

"Oh," said Ahi'aorina. She glanced toward the giant's couch. "That is one problem I believe I can solve from here."

"How?" asked Graham.

Ahi'aorina stood up in her cage, leaned back, and threw the king across the room.

24

Graham had to bite his long, sticky pink tongue to keep from screaming as he flew toward the couch. The distance was no more than a few yards, but when your body was the length of a finger, a few yards was a long way to go with no ground under your feet.

The faery queen's aim was good. Graham struck the couch with a soft thud only a few feet from Dunstan's massive head. He clung to the scarlet cloth and waited for his heart to stop thumping against his belly. On the floor below, the imps laughed and joked, oblivious to Graham's presence.

Above him, the shaggy head of Dunstan rose from the cushions like a hairy mountain. Graham crawled over to the valley between the giant's head and shoulder. He eyed the visible section of cord. It was thin, hardly more than a string. Better yet, the knot that bound the ends of the cord together was easily accessible just above the dark shadows of Dunstan's beard.

Being very careful not to step on the sleeping

giant, Graham advanced on the cord. He was
fairly certain that his footsteps would not awaken
the giant—if Dunstan could sleep through the action of Kuzgu and the other imps, Graham didn't
think anything he did was likely to wake the sleeping giant—but Dunstan didn't have to wake to
smash Graham. All he had to do was scratch some
sudden itch, or swat at a tickle he might think was
a fly.

Graham reached the knot and examined it. It
didn't look too tough. A simple in and out. He
should be able to untwine it in no time. He
grasped the cord with his front paws and pulled.
And tugged. And twisted.

Lizards have no thumbs. It was a trivial fact,
something that Graham had never considered before. Suddenly he found this piece of knowledge
of utmost importance. His yellow feet were just
not suited for delicate work. They were superb at
sticking to walls, but untying cords with them was
worse than trying to thread a needle with mittens
on.

Graham thumped his tail against the couch in
frustration. There was no way he was going to be
able to untie the cord. He would just have to wait
until he was back in his own body.

He was about to sneak away when he took another glance at the cord. Wait. It *was* quite thin.
Maybe thin enough that there was a way for even
a lizard to take care of it. Graham opened his
mouth and bit down hard on the leather string.

His small, cone-shaped teeth were good at crushing insects, but they were not so well designed for slicing. Still, he could feel them sinking into the leather. He whipped his slender head from side to side and bit down harder. With a satisfying snap, the cord broke in two.

Graham let go of the cord and stepped back to watch where the key fell. Only the key didn't fall. The severed ends of the cord dangled loose, but the key—wherever it was—did not move.

He had assumed the key was hidden behind the giant's beard, but he hadn't seen it. It might be pinned between Dunstan and the couch. Or Ahi-'aorina might have been wrong. It might not be on the cord at all. No, it had to be there.

No matter where the key was, it would probably fall free when the giant woke and stood up. The trouble was that if the key went thudding to the floor while Dunstan was awake and the imps quiet, it was bound to be noticed. Graham had to get the key now, while there was still a chance to hide it. If the key were buried under Dunstan, then there was little Graham could do about it, but if it were in the giant's beard, there was still the possibility that Graham might work it free.

He stepped onto the giant's shoulder and pushed the point of his muzzle into the beard. The hairs were stiff as broom straws. They parted only reluctantly as he shoved his way in. Pushing through the beard, Graham felt as if he were forcing himself into the densest of canebrakes. He could scarcely see beyond the green tip of his own nose. He wished heartily that he had a sickle with which to clear a path. While he was at it, he wished he had a hand that could hold a sickle.

It took some time for him to burrow through the outer fringes of the beard and catch his first glimpse of the pale skin at the giant's throat. It was dark here—a bushy, beard-shaded twilight—but his lizard eyes seemed to penetrate the gloom better than human eyes might. He managed to locate the dark strip of the leather cord, and using it as a guide, he went deeper into the forest of hair.

He was beginning to fear that the key might really be under the giant, when he saw the first glint of something gleaming and pearlescent ahead. He pushed through a particularly tight thicket of hairs, and there it was: a small ivory key with a golden handle that was covered over in the crabbed, obscure symbols of some magical script.

Though the key was small, it was still almost as large as Graham. Extracting it would not be a simple chore. Graham sat back and thought. First things first. There was no way he was going to get the key all the way back to the point where he had bitten through the cord. Which meant he had to sever the cord again. He took a good grip on the cord and worked his teeth in. It resisted the bite more than it had the first time. He moved over to another spot and bit again, twisting his head to pull at the cord.

The ground under Graham's feet shook as Dunstan stirred in his sleep. Before Graham could move, huge fingers dug through the beard and scratched against the giant's chin. The small lizard was tossed aside like a rowboat in a storm. Dunstan's head turned to the side, and for a moment Graham feared that the giant might roll completely over, crushing him against the couch as surely as a bug was flattened under a man's foot. But the giant's hand pulled away and Dunstan settled back into his sleep.

The cord snapped in Graham's teeth and he hurried back to the key. He tried to get a grip on it with his mouth, but the shaft was too round and slippery. Besides, it had a sharp, bitter taste that was most unpleasant to his lizard tongue. He would have to think of some other way to move it.

The loop at the top of the key turned out to be the solution. It was just the right size for Graham to slip his head through. With the loop riding against his narrow shoulders like a miniature horse collar, Graham pushed his way down Dunstan's beard.

It was slow going at first, but once the loose end of the broken cord had slipped from the loop, it became easier. Graham's neck ached from the strain of moving the heavy key through the dense hair, but he kept moving. Ahead of him, the light was growing brighter as he approached the end of the beard. It became easier to move as the thicket of hair grew sparser. A few more steps and he was standing on the velvet cushions beside the giant's head.

He carried the heavy key over to the edge of the couch and pulled his head free of the loop. It was a long drop to the floor. Though there was carpet and the noise in the room was considerable, there was still the chance that the imps might hear the key fall. There was little choice. Graham could think of no way he could carry the heavy key down the side. He put his nose under the key and shoved it off. It fell, bounced, and lay glittering on the floor right beside the couch. The imps went on with their party.

Good, thought Graham. Now all he had to do was get down there and shove the key somewhere out of sight. The first part of the plan was going well.

He turned and found himself staring right into a pair of bloodshot yellow eyes.

"What we have here?" said Kuzgu. "Why, King Graham the belly crawler, it is."

Graham yelped and dashed away. A rough brown hand came down around him and plucked him from the couch. Two thin twisted fingers gripped his tail and held him dangling in the air.

Kuzgu brought his smirking face close to Graham. "King Graham, lost weight you have. Feeling well, are you?" The imp answered his own joke with a bout of rattling laughter.

"Let me go, you pencil-armed, potbellied,

squinty eyed, stumpy little mugwort," shouted Graham.

The imp gave an elaborate, mocking sigh. "Your voice, too, is sick. Not a word can I understand. How sad this is." He gave a shark-toothed smile. "A solution I have. Put you out of this misery I will." He tilted back his head, opened his mouth, and held Graham above his gaping maw.

Graham whipped his body back and forth once, then again. On the third swing he planted his front feet against Kuzgu's palm and held on. Then he opened his mouth and bit down hard on the tender flesh between the imp's thump and forefinger.

Kuzgu shrieked and threw his hand back and forth. Graham was flung loose. He tumbled through the air and landed roughly in the center of a plate filled with smelly, oily, half-rotten fish.

"What this!" shouted one of the imps.

Graham scrambled out of the plate onto the surface of the stone table. The tines of a fork clanged down behind him, barely missing his tail. A knife flashed on his left, and Graham squeaked as it nicked green scales from his side.

"Catch him!" cried Kuzgu. "Smash him."

Graham tore across the table just ahead of a deadly array of attacking kitchen utensils. Spoiled vegetables, spilled ale, and soggy bread went flying as the imps tried to catch the intruder among their plates. Gaining the edge of the table, Graham took a deep breath and leaped for the ground.

He hit the carpet running. No time to worry about the key. There were too many imps after him. He had to get away and hide until they had calmed down again. Once they had given up the search, then he would return for his own body and the key.

Feet stomped. Food was thrown. Chairs were overturned. But Graham dodged every obstacle and made it to the base of the wall just ahead of a crowd of angry imps. This time they didn't give up when he slipped under the tapestry. Hands tore at the cloth or tried to pound Graham into lizard jelly. He scrambled up out of the imps' reach and stopped to take a breath while the wall under his feet vibrated with their efforts.

"Get away this time he must not," called Kuzgu. "Kill him we must."

Graham climbed to the top of the tapestry and popped his head out. He looked down and saw that the imps were spread out in a line along the wall. They seemed very serious about finding him. In places, they had already pulled whole lengths of tapestry down and flung it to the ground. He would have to move soon if he didn't want to be left with nowhere to hide.

Then he noticed a lone figure standing in the center of the room. It was his body. His human body. It was the first time Graham had seen his body away from the imps, and it might be the last. He couldn't afford to miss this chance.

He gritted his little teeth and looked down at the imps. They stood between him and the body. Some of them were still tearing or pounding at the tapestry, but others stood back and scanned the base of the wall. There was little chance Graham could evade notice if he tried to go down. That left only one direction.

Graham tilted back his muzzle and looked up. Though he had gotten used to traveling along the walls, he had never thought about the ceiling. The ceiling in this room was plain gray stone. It was smeared by the soot of burning torches and stained by splatters of food from overenthusiastic imps, but at least it was flat and smooth. Graham moved up to it and cautiously transferred his front feet from the vertical to the horizontal surface. He tugged against his sticky pads, testing the strength of the hold. So far, so good.

The transfer of his hind feet to the ceiling was a little more difficult, and far more frightening. When it was done, Graham was upside down. He looked down at the floor far below, and his little lizard stomach did a flip-flop. He remembered standing not so long ago on the tall parapet of Daventry Castle. His altitude now seemed much higher.

With his heart pounding against his ribs, Graham crept slowly across the ceiling. He took a few glances down to make sure that he was headed in the right direction, but for the most part he kept his muzzle close to the ceiling and looked straight ahead. If he was very careful, he was able to convince himself that he was safely on the ground and not dangling high above.

When he next looked down, the top of a blond head was almost directly below. Graham crawled a little to his left, checked again, and took a single step to the right. Trembling, he lifted one foot from the ceiling. Then another.

Dangling upside down from his hind legs, he took a last, deep breath, then pulled both remaining feet free at the same time.

His aim was not quite up to that displayed by Ahi'aorina. He missed the blond head. In fact, he missed his body entirely and thumped on the floor at its feet. The fall was enough to knock the breath out of him. A cloud of flickering moths swarmed around him. He gasped and shook his head. The phantom moths disappeared.

Graham jumped onto the foot of his standing body and scrambled up the leg and over the chest to reach the shoulder. The body turned to look at him, and he watched his lips turn up in a gentle smile.

''I, Graham,'' it said.

''No, you're not,'' said Graham.

He stared into the blue eyes that had been his until the switch. He concentrated on switching back.

Now, he thought. Put me back.

Nothing happened.

Voices rose from across the room. "See him I don't," said one of imps.

"Escaped us again he has," called another.

Kuzgu growled. "Keep looking."

Graham looked into the body's empty eyes. He had to make the switch before the imps came back and saw him. He had been lucky enough to avoid them so far, but luck would only hold out so long.

"Switch," he squeaked softly. "Change. Swap. Trade."

Still nothing happened.

Graham muttered lizard curses. He tried to think of what had happened right before he had traded places with the slizard. He had been kneeling beside the box. The imps had stood well back.

The search party was giving up. "Not here is he," said an imp.

"All right," said Kuzgu. "Catch him next time we will." The imps turned away from the wall and started back toward the table.

Graham had looked down at the box. There had been a pain in his nose, and then . . .

Graham blinked. A pain in his nose.

He leaped from the shoulder and closed his muzzle on the tip of the great pink proboscis. At once there was a shock of dizziness and a sharp pain in Graham's nose.

He reached up his hand and pulled a little green lizard away from his face. He staggered and looked around in amazement.

The world had shrunk. Graham was huge and all his limbs were the wrong length. He had the wrong number of fingers. Colors were wrong. Sounds were wrong. Where was his muzzle? Where was his lovely tail?

He was human again. He glanced at the lizard in his hand, then shoved it into a pocket and buttoned it closed.

A wiry hand landed on his side and shoved him around. Graham looked down into the face of Kuzgu.

"Mushbrain," said the imp. "What is it you do?"

Graham looked at the imp. "I, Graham," he said.

25

Kuzgu looked into Graham's face and snorted. "Worthless you are. Not funny anymore."

"Like him we do," said one of the other imps. "Gives us someone to kick he does."

"Kick us all day you do," said a tall imp.

"Quiet!" shouted Kuzgu. He glared at the imp who had spoken. "What is funny I say. What is not funny I say. Who is kicked I say."

The other imps grumbled. "No fun do we have," said a thin imp. "Nothing to do."

Kuzgu crossed his twig-thin arms. "Without me still in stinking holes you would be. Eat you do from silver plates only because of me." The other imps mumbled something in response and Kuzgu stepped toward them and continued to yell.

While the imps continued their argument, Graham sidled over to the couch where Dunstan still slept. The key was lying on the carpet in plain sight. Graham glanced at the imps, then tapped the key with the toe of his boot, sending it sliding under the edge of the couch.

"Worthless I said and worthless did I mean,"

shouted Kuzgu. He pointed to an imp whose left ear was marked by an ugly tear that caused it to hang down at the end. "Buzgut! To the kitchen take this one. There some use he may be."

"No humans are we to eat," said the taller imp who had spoken before. "The giant will be angry."

"As big a mushbrain as this one is the giant," said Kuzgu. "Soon we will need him no more." He waved to the dog-eared imp. "To the kitchen with the human. His bones we will gnaw while the giant sleeps."

The imp grinned and walked over to Graham. "Come along, lizard brain. Almost time for supper it be."

"I, Graham," said Graham.

The imps snickered as Graham followed Buzgut out of the grand hall and down a corridor. His guide turned left, then right, then right again. Wherever they were going, the walk was quite lengthy.

The slizard wiggled in his pocket. Graham hooked a finger inside and looked down at the little creature. It blinked up at him for a moment, then snuggled down in the bottom of the pocket and closed its orange eyes. It seemed to find the warm, dark pocket a fine place to stay. Considering some of the feelings he had had while a lizard, Graham could well understand.

He hoped the slizard had not been seriously hurt by its adventures. Though the creature's power was truly awesome, Graham did not feel that the little beast was actually malicious. In the end, the exchange with the slizard had allowed him to learn things and do things that would have been impossible for a man. He supposed, in a way, that the slizard had done him a favor. He patted his pocket softly and let the slizard rest.

Finally Buzgut pushed through a door and led Graham into a kitchen full of huge pots and stacked silver plates. Where the other rooms that Graham had entered at Sorrowing Court had looked almost as clean as the halls of Castle Daventry, this room was a mess.

Spilled food had crusted on the stones of the floor and molds grew like weeds. Dirty utensils and dishes dripping with grime were heaped in the corners of the room. A huge black stove sat in the center of the room with greasy smoke leaking at every seam. On top of the stove was a large pot full of some boiling green gruel. The smell in the room was a terrible mixture of old onions and rotting seafood.

"Ay!" called Buzgut. "Where be you?"

There was a clanging from the far end of the room and another imp appeared carrying a pot and a large wooden spoon in his hands. Graham recognized this one as Zuzak, the imp chef who had wanted to baste him when he had first entered Sorrowing Court.

Zuzak's yellow eyes went wide when he saw what was waiting in his kitchen. "Careful be you," he called. "Dangerous be this one."

Buzgut grunted. "No danger now. Introduced him to the slizard did Kuzgu." The imp made a slurping sound. "No brains has he now."

"Slizarded be he?" Zuzak walked closer. "Too bad. Kuzgu I thought he might bash."

"Careful," said Buzgut. "Long are Kuzgu's ears."

Zuzak waved his spoon in the air. "And ugly is his face. Sent you here did he? The new helper be you? A helper I need badly?"

"Came here I did only to deliver this brainless human, not to cook."

Zuzak dropped his pot on the table and frowned. "Promised me a helper three days ago Kuzgu did. Cook, cook, cook I do while the rest of you eat, eat, eat. Not for this did I come all the way from Zakizga to this Sorrowing Court."

"To Kuzgu complain," said Buzgut. He took Graham by the arm and pushed him toward the cook. "Chop this one for supper says Kuzgu."

"Let him chop. Lazy he be."

On the table to his right, Graham spotted a black skillet of heavy cast iron. While the two imps bickered over their leader, Graham edged closer to the table.

"If leave here you would, then make this human tasty," said Buzgut. "In a nasty mood is Kuzgu."

"Pah." Zuzak spat a wad of phlegm onto the floor. "Always in a nasty mood be Kuzgu. Thinks this whole place be his." He stuck his spoon into the pot on top of the stove and stirred the goop inside.

"Kuzgu the magic has," said Buzgut. "Listen to him you don't, and worm food will you be."

"So says Kuzgu," replied the cook. He took the spoon from the pot and made a face as he tasted the contents. "But little magic have I seen since to Sorrowing Court we came. Much yelling have I seen Kuzgu do. Much magic have I not seen."

Buzgut looked alarmed. "Test him I would not."

Zuzak threw the spoon back into the bowl of bubbling liquid. He looked toward Graham and scowled. "Test him I won't. At least not today." He waved toward Graham. "The brainless one bring. Carve him I will."

Graham picked up the skillet and swung it hard into the face of Buzgut. The sound of the impact was like an axe biting into a thick tree, but the imp did not go down. Surprised, Graham pulled back his arm to deliver another blow.

Buzgut gave out a weak laugh. A handful of sharp, curved teeth sprayed from his mouth and rattled across the floor. The dog-eared imp fell backward and lay still. Graham turned his attention to the cook.

Zuzak backed away with his hands held over his face. "Hit me not," he whined. "From the last time be my ears still ringing."

Graham lowered the skillet a few inches. "I

don't want to hurt you," he said, "but if I let you go, you'll tell Kuzgu that I'm free."

"Kuzgu? Pah! Pah, Kuzgu!" Zuzak shook his head. "Lied to me did Kuzgu. Nothing do I owe him."

"If you're not going to Kuzgu, then what will you do?" asked Graham.

Zuzak looked at the door. "Home do I want to be. Home in Zakizga. Leave this place I will and cause you no trouble."

Graham looked at the imp for a long moment. Imps were capable of lying—he had known that before he reached Sorrowing Court—and Kuzgu's deception of Dunstan only reinforced that knowledge. But not all imps were bad, just as not all humans were good. There was something in Zuzak's rough face that made Graham want to trust him.

"All right," he said at last. "Leave Sorrowing Court right now, and I will do nothing to stop you."

Zuzak smiled. "Home am I going. Kuzgu I hope you hit till he be nothing but a smudge on his fancy carpet."

Graham laughed. "Have a good journey, Zuzak." He raised the skillet and pointed it toward the imp. "Be sure you don't eat any humans along the way."

"No, no," said the cook. "No more humans do I eat. Not even with sauce. Humans be too dangerous to prepare."

The imp slipped past Graham and hurried out of the kitchen. Graham followed him out into the hall and watched as Zuzak disappeared down the long corridor. He hoped he had made the right decision. In the meantime, there were more imps to worry about, not to mention a bespelled giant.

Graham went back into the kitchen and rummaged through cabinets until he came up with a length of heavy twine. He bound Buzgut's thin arms and legs together. He then dragged the imp through the kitchen and left him sitting in a storage cabinet with a pile of rutabagas for a seat.

With Buzgut secured, Graham hid the skillet just inside the kitchen door and retraced the path the imp had followed from the grand hall. When he came within sight of Kuzgu and the others, Graham slowed down. He wandered back and forth across the corridor, trying his best to look aimless.

In only a few minutes, one of the imps spotted him. "Look!" he called. "Back again is the human."

"What?" Kuzgu surged to his feet and ran over to Graham. "Where is Buzgut?"

"I, Graham," said Graham.

Kuzgu snarled. "An idiot is Buzgut. More ale than blood has he in his veins." The imp leader signaled to a table at the edge of the room. "Gunzuk, Nuzgo. To the kitchen take this human."

Two of the smaller imps jumped up from the table and hurried to Graham's side. "What of

Buzgut?'' asked one of them.

"His teeth will I pull," said Kuzgu. "Right away must he return or thrash him I will."

The imps nodded and pushed Graham along the hall. This pair turned out to be talkative. All the way to the kitchen, Graham heard a list of complaints about Kuzgu and how things were run inside Sorrowing Court. He had almost decided to give them a chance to flee, when they began to talk about how things would be once Kuzgu was out of the way. Graham's jaw grew tight as he listened to the two imps exchange a growing list of cruelties they would inflict on the remaining imps and the other inhabitants of the court—including particularly nasty plans for Ahi'aorina.

Within a few minutes, both the imps had joined Buzgut in the closet and Graham was on his way back to the grand hall.

If Kuzgu had been surprised to see him the last time, Graham's second return caused the leader of the imps to spray ale across the table. "Bark-headed fools!" He dashed over to Graham and peered past him down the hallway. "When I catch them, funny they will find this not."

"I, Graham," said Graham.

Kuzgu paced around the hall. Six other imps remained in the hall, but only three of them were still conscious. Kuzgu paused by each of them in turn. "Kuzgu is soft, think you. Kuzgu will do nothing, think you." The imp paused to pound his fist against the nearest table. "Not soft is

Kuzgu! Too easy on you have I been." He stalked between the tables looking at one imp after another.

The tall imp who had spoken out before mumbled something under his breath. At once Kuzgu spun around and ran over to the him. "What is it you say?"

The imp jumped up from his chair. "Not your slaves are we. Promises you made. When will they be kept?"

Kuzgu was silent for a long moment. The rough skin of his face went from deep brown to bright red. "Another promise I make to you. To the kitchen you will take this human. Those who have defied me you will bring back." He pointed a clawed finger at the tall imp's face. "Do these things not, and promise to see you dead I do."

For a moment Graham thought the tall imp would refuse, but after a second he got up. "Pobnuz, Rotzok. With him you go," said Kuzgu.

The three imps pushed Graham down the hallway roughly. As soon as they reached the kitchen and went inside, Graham grabbed his skillet and turned to face them.

"I'm giving you a chance," he said. "You can leave Sorrowing Court, or you can face me."

One of the imps growled and jumped forward. Graham felled him with a single blow of the skillet.

A second imp held up his hands. "Hurt me not. Hurt me not." Graham stood aside as the imp turned and fled from the room.

Only the tall imp remained. His yellow eyes studied Graham. "The others you have killed?"

Graham shook his head. "No. At least I don't think any of them are dead. I hit them over the head and tied them up in the storage bin."

The imp grinned. "Silly they will feel when they wake."

"Are you going to leave?" asked Graham. "I'll stand aside if that's what you want."

The imp thought on this for a moment. "No," he said. "Stay I will."

Graham frowned. "I don't want to hurt you."

"Hurt I don't want to be," replied the tall imp. He looked toward the door. "Kuzgu, he I would want to hurt."

"Do you mean you'll help me?"

The tall imp nodded. He held out a wiry hand. "Lugmut I am called."

"I'm Graham." He took the imp's hand and shook it firmly.

"Your name I know," the imp said with a laugh. "Said this enough you have."

Graham laughed. "What now?"

"Now Kuzgu we get." Lugmut left the kitchen and went back down the hallway at a trot. As they approached the hall, he slowed and whispered to Graham. "Surprise him we will. Lizard brain should you play."

"Don't worry," Graham replied. "I'm getting good at it."

Kuzgu looked up as they strolled into the room. He thumped his ale cup against the table and his face blazed with scarlet fury. "What now is it? Where are the rest?"

"A creature there is," said Lugmut. "See it you must."

The leader of the imps frowned. "A creature has them? What kind of creature?"

"Come and see. A dangerous thing it is."

Kuzgu looked as if he might explode into steam, but at last he nodded in agreement. "All right."

All the way back to the kitchen, Kuzgu grumbled. The other imps were lazy. The other imps were ungrateful. The other imps were in for it when he got his hands on them.

When they reached the kitchen, he looked inside. "No creature do I see."

"It is there," said Lugmut. He raised his hand and pointed to Graham.

A puzzled look crossed Kuzgu's face. "This pitiful thing? Not even a human is it." He thumped his hand hard against Graham's chest.

"I, Graham," said Graham.

"See?" said Kuzgu. "Two words only can it say. The brain of a lizard it has."

"Oh, I wouldn't be too sure of that," said Graham.

Kuzgu's eyes widened in surprise.

Graham balled his hand into a fist and punched the imp square in his wrinkled nose.

· 26 ·

Kuzgu staggered back from Graham's blow.

"Get out now," said Graham. "Leave this place, and despite all that you have done to deserve punishment, I will grant you mercy."

"Not I," said Lugmut. He jumped forward and put his hands around Kuzgu's thin arms. "Made us bring the faery here all the way from the Old Wood you did. Promised us treasures. Promised us magic."

"Yours they still can be," said Kuzgu. There was a note of desperation in the imp's voice. "Only capture the human we must. A danger to us all is he."

The taller imp shoved Kuzgu back against the wall. "The only danger is you. Hurt the faery you did when she had done you no ill. Made all of us help you. Made us work too hard and treated us like slaves did you. Bring the faery all the way over the mountains we did. Only to watch her die."

"Work too hard. Slaves." Kuzgu's lips twisted in an ugly snarl. "If your ugly nose it bit off, work you would still not know. Feed you I did. Cared for you."

Lugmut shook Kuzgu so hard that his round head thumped against the wall. "No more of your food do I want. My payment I will take, then home will I go."

Graham stepped up to the tall imp and put a hand on his gnarled shoulder. "Let him go, Lugmut. He doesn't have the other imps to command, and we are far away from Dunstan. There's nothing he can do to us now."

"Owes me he does," said Lugmut bitterly. But he released his grip on Kuzgu and stepped away.

Graham stepped forward and looked down at the imp that had been at the heart of so much trouble. "I could let Lugmut kill you now," he said. "I might even do it myself. Taking Queen Ahi'aorina has devastated Daventry, and other lands besides. By now, people may have already died because of your actions and who knows what has become of the faeries of the Old Wood."

Kuzgu looked at the king defiantly. "To make Dunstan happy was all that I wished."

"No," said Graham. "I don't think so." He stared hard into the imp's yellow eyes. "Dunstan said that you were the one that brought him here, and that it was you who put him in charge of Sorrowing Court. You pretend that he is your leader, but I've seen how you treat him when he is not watching. You have no real love for the giant.

Dunstan isn't really the chief of this place at all, is he?''

The imp returned Graham's stare, but he did not reply.

Graham gestured to the row of torches that burned along the wall. "Sorrowing Court is filled with magic. These torches burn all day and night and they never burn out. The pantries hold far more food than I've seen you gather." He planted his hands on his hips. "Something in this fortress is producing a wealth of magic energy. I've already seen one human who is bound in a trap of magic."

This piece of news seemed to startle the imp. His eyes widened and he looked away down the hall.

Lugmut was also surprised. "Another human is in this place?"

Graham nodded.

Kuzgu looked back at the king. "How could you have found him?"

"How I found him isn't important," said Graham. "But what you're doing to this man, you're also doing to the giant, and to Queen Ahi'aorina. You're draining them of energy to feed the demands of keeping up this fortress."

Kuzgu lowered his head. "Caught me you have. No more secrets do I hold." He let out a deep, shuddering sigh. Suddenly the imp looked very small and very tired.

"The treasure you promised," said Lugmut.

"Lie does it within these halls?"

"Treasure there is," said Kuzgu. He straightened. "Pay you I will." He glanced across the kitchen. "The others. Gone are they? The chance to repay you all would I like."

"Two of them have left Sorrowing Court," said Graham, "but the others are still here."

"Hmmm," said Kuzgu. His eyes brightened. "So there are still nine imps. That's very interesting. It's still possible after all."

Graham frowned. "What's still possible?"

Lugmut tugged at Graham's arm. "His speech. Listen. Wrong it is."

"What do you . . . ," started Graham.

Kuzgu reached into his leather jacket and drew out something of pale pink and blood red. "Here, Lugmut. For all that you've done, I give you this as your payment."

As he pitched the small object toward the taller imp, Graham saw that it was a flower, a small bloom of such perfect beauty that just looking at it made him feel a wave of bliss.

Lugmut's reaction to the sight of the flower was not so rapturous. The imp screamed and threw up his arms. The bloom struck against the imp's hand, and a cloud of golden pollen emerged. Graham caught a whiff of something rotten, something old and spoiled and decaying. At once, Lugmut collapsed to the carpet as if all his bones had been removed. The pink flower settled on his chest.

Graham rushed to his fallen ally and knocked the noxious bloom away with a quick backhanded blow. "Lugmut! Are you all right?"

The imp moaned and opened his eyes, but his gaze was distant and unfocused. "Marsh rose," he said. "Sleep does it make."

"Only sleep?"

Lugmut nodded slowly. "All right will I be."

"I'm glad," said Graham.

"Don't worry about him," said Kuzgu. "Worry about yourself."

Graham looked up and saw that Kuzgu's face was split by a broad toothy smile. "Lugmut is right. You're not speaking the way you usually do."

"Not speaking like an imp, you mean." Kuzgu slouched and scratched at himself with wiry fingers. "Oh, an imp am I. Speak like a little toad I do." His face twisted into an expression of overwhelming disgust. "*Harrraka!* I've had enough of this foolishness."

A tremor ran through the imp's body. He threw his arms wide and his head back. A snarl came from deep down in his throat. Kuzgu's skin began to hump and move. There was a crunching, tearing sound—a horribly wet sound. Kuzgu began to laugh. With every second, his laugh grew deeper and darker.

Thin fingers reached up and took Graham by the collar. Startled, Graham tried to pull **away**. Then he saw it was only Lugmut.

"What is it?" asked Graham. "Do you have some idea of what's happening?"

Lugmut nodded weakly. His mouth opened and he mumbled something, but Graham was unable to make it out.

"What?" Graham put his ear close to the tall imp's face. "What did you say?"

"Run," breathed Lugmut.

Kuzgu's laughter grew into a roar. When Graham looked up, he saw that the imp had nearly doubled in size. The round head had become longer and sprouted a toothy snout. The reedy legs had lengthened, thickened, and acquired a backward canted knee. The chest had widened and rippled with muscles. Everywhere the creature's skin moved as if there were a thousand feverish worms crawling beneath its surface.

"Better listen to your friend, human king," said the thing that had been Kuzgu, in the deep, echoing voice. "The imps are something I must keep intact if I hope to complete my task, but I require no humans." Curving black talons emerged from the ends of its outstretched hands.

Graham turned and pounded away down the hall. Whatever Kuzgu was changing into, he knew he was not prepared to handle the end result on his own. He had to have reinforcements, and the only reinforcement available was Ahi'aorina.

Snarls and howls followed him down the corridor as he took the twists and turns needed to return to the central hall. Graham couldn't tell if the noises were getting closer, but their volume alone was enough to keep him running at top speed.

When he reached the hall where Ahi'aorina's cage hung, it was such a familiar scene that it almost seemed like home. One of the drunken imps had awakened long enough to drag himself to the table and pour another cup of ale. The other two were still sprawled facedown in their drink. Dunstan reclined on his couch, his breathing low and steady as a breeze through the trees.

Graham dashed to the side of the couch and bent to look underneath. For one terrible moment, he didn't see the key. Then he caught a glimpse of its ivory gleam and stretched his arm into the shadows to retrieve it. His fingers closed around its cool length and he pulled it out into the light.

"Queen Ahi'aorina!" he shouted. "I'm coming."

He jumped up and got his hands over the edge of the enormous couch. A bone-chilling howl rang through the room. Startled, Graham felt his feet slip and he slid from the velvet side of the couch. Finally he gained a toehold and pushed himself upward. With two bounds across the cushions, he leaned out and got a hand on Ahi'aorina's cage.

"I'll have you free in a moment, Your Majesty," he said.

The faery queen looked at him with a wan expression. Her skin had turned the deep yellow of old ivory, and her hair was thin as dry moss in the branches of a tree. "I fear it may be too late," she said. "Even now I weaken into death."

"You can't die," said Graham. He tugged the cage closer to the couch and worked the ivory key into the delicate lock. With a twist and a soft rattle of invisible workings, the lock sprang open. The door to the cage swung to smoothly on its golden hinges.

"Come on," said Graham. "We have to get out of this place right now."

Ahi'aorina reached out a limp hand. The pearl tones of her skin had dulled and her fingers trembled with weakness. Graham linked his fingers with hers.

"Step down," he said. "Once we get you away from this place, you'll feel better."

The queen slid toward the door and looked down at Graham. "I do not believe I have the energy to climb down."

"Just jump. I'll catch you."

She nodded. With one hand on the bars, she rose to her feet and stood swaying in the door of the cage.

Graham gave her what he hoped was a reassuring smile. "Hurry," he said. "We don't have much time."

Huge fingers wrapped around Graham's chest and squeezed until his ribs groaned like tree branches in a strong wind. "You are nae going anywhere," said Dunstan.

The giant lifted Graham from the couch and flung him across the room. Graham's heels clipped the forehead of one of the drunken imps in passing, knocking the creature from its chair. From there the king pinwheeled head over heels, bounced from the top of a stone table, and fell to the floor amid a clatter of plates and broken cups.

The wooden frame of the couch creaked as the giant rose to his feet. "Kuzgu warned me you were trying to steal away my happiness," said Dunstan. The floor quaked as he advanced toward Graham. "Now I see that he was right."

Graham shook the cobwebs from his head. "No, Kuzgu was lying to you. He's the one that stole your happiness."

Dunstan reached down, caught Graham, and lifted him until his boots were hanging several feet from the carpet. "Kuzgu is my friend," said the giant. "He brought me into this hall. Everything I have is because of him."

"He brought you here for his own reasons." Graham strained helplessly against the giant's enveloping fingers. "Think back. Before you came to this place, didn't you feel better? Weren't you happier? Stronger?"

The giant's forehead creased in doubt. "I don't know. I cannae remember. It seems there was a time when this sorrow did nae press on me so."

"It's Kuzgu," Graham insisted. "He drains your happiness and your strength to build his own power."

Dunstan's lips formed an immense frown. "You are trying to confuse me. You lie."

"No," said a soft voice. Both Graham and Dunstan turned to see Queen Ahi'aorina standing in the door of her golden cage. "The human king speaks the truth," she said. "Now that the door of my prison is open, I can see the lines of magic which bind you to this place. Kuzgu is drawing your life away, just as he is drawing my own."

"But . . ." The giant seemed to be lost. "Kuzgu is my friend."

A hulking black shape stepped from the hallway. "How touching," said a low, sibilant voice. "A friend until the bitter end."

Dunstan looked into the corner. "Who are you?"

"It's Kuzgu," said Graham. "The real Kuzgu."

The black form moved farther into the room. Its flesh was so dark that it was hard to make out the details of its form. The sparkle of an eye, a glistening fang, a gleaming talon—all the rest was as black and unfathomable as the shadows of the moon.

"Now," Kuzgu rumbled. "If everyone will hold still, we can get this over with quickly . . . and painfully."

Dunstan lowered Graham to the floor. "Are you truly Kuzgu?"

"You have known me by that name," said the dark form. "I have others."

Graham moved away from the giant and searched the room for something that might serve as a weapon. "Be careful," he cautioned Dunstan. "There's no telling what sort of powers he may have."

The giant nodded and clenched his hands into man-sized fists. "Why did you bring me to Sorrowing Court?"

"Why, haven't you enjoyed yourself here?" The darkness advanced on the giant, leaving jagged rents in the carpet where it passed. "Hasn't there been plenty to eat? Plenty to drink?" A shadowy arm extended and a claw pointed at Ahi'aorina's golden cage. "Didn't I fetch this little pretty one for you?"

Dunstan shook his huge head. "You did nae a thing for me," he said. "I can see that now."

Kuzgu laughed. "It's a shame that only now, when it is far too late, you have driven the clouds from your eyes." The black form rippled like a sail in the wind. When it was still again, it had grown to nearly the same size as Dunstan. "Come, friend," said Kuzgu. He held out hands whose claws were longer than swords. "Let us share a friendly embrace."

The giant's face reddened with rage. A rumble began low in his throat and shook the stones of the central hall.

"Hold!" shouted a strong voice. All eyes turned

to see Queen Ahi'aorina jump from her cage and land on the couch where Dunstan had lain. Her pale hair floated around her head in a waving verdant nimbus. Her eyes glowed with all the fires of spring. Her beauty was such that Graham's breath caught in his throat. She was unearthly. A perfection that no mortal woman could ever reach.

Ahi'aorina pointed to the thing that had been Kuzgu. "I know you, *efreeti*. Yours is a dark and miserable race. And yet your power is nothing beside the force of spring."

Kuzgu hissed like a steam kettle about to burst. "I see you as clearly as you see me, little faery. You think you can fool me with this show of tricks? You are weak. Weak!" The dark form moved toward Ahi'aorina. "I have supped on your life for days, and now I will gnaw on the husk left behind."

With a deafening roar, Dunstan charged at the dark shape. Kuzgu met him with slashing talons that sank deep into the giant's arms and back. The two towering figures tumbled across the room and smashed into a wall. Rock dust showered down from above. Dunstan rose snarling from the ground with the squirming Kuzgu in his arms. Veins as large as Graham's forearm sprang up on the giant's neck as he tried to squeeze the life from his infernal opponent.

At first it looked as if Dunstan would succeed. The black shape twisted and squirmed, but the giant only squeezed tighter. Then, with a force that Graham could not imagine, Dunstan's arms were forced back. The darkness surged free. Black claws rose from the melee and stabbed down again and again.

"Do something!" cried Graham.

Queen Ahi'aorina sank to her knees and shook her head. The aura of health and energy that had surrounded her faded. "The *efreeti* is right. I am too weak to oppose him." The fire in her eyes guttered and died.

Dunstan groaned as the talons cut into his flesh. The giant's blood poured onto the carpeted floor.

Graham looked around the room. Two imps still slept through the fight. The one that Graham had accidentally kicked lay on the floor with his eyes staring blankly at the ceiling. All around him were the tools of his meal: knives and forks, plates and cups. Graham considered the knives, but he found it hard to believe that such tiny a weapon would be of any use against such a titanic foe. Still, there was nothing else in the room but tables and plates . . .

Plates.

The bone plate that Kuzgu had eaten from was still sitting on a table. All the other imps had eaten from silver plates, but the leader had insisted on bone.

Graham ran across the room and seized one of the silver plates. With a flip of his wrist, he sent the silver platter flying at the *efreeti.*

The plate sank into the darkness like a stone dropping into a pool. At once the black shape drew back from the giant. Crimson light sprayed from the point where the plate had entered the thing's body. It opened its mouth and uttered a scream that went up and up. Long after the cry had passed the limits of Graham's hearing, he could still feel it ringing in his teeth and vibrating his bones.

The black form began to shrink.

In a moment it was the size of a man. In another it was no bigger than an imp. Then it was nothing but a quivering lump of shadow on the blood-soaked floor.

Dunstan rolled onto his side and looked at Graham. The giant's face was pale, and blood oozed from a dozen or more cuts in his arms and chest. "He was nae my friend," groaned the giant.

"No," said Graham. "No, he wasn't."

The king of Daventry took one of the fallen tapestries from the floor and tore it into shreds. He went to the fallen giant and began to bind his wounds. "He was not your friend, but I would like to be."

Dunstan closed his eyes. And smiled.

·27·

"He will live," said Ahi'aorina. "Though he may wish otherwise." She put her pale hand on Dunstan's forehead and gently wiped his massive brow. "The wounds caused by an *efreeti* do not heal quickly, and there will be much pain."

"I can stand pain," grunted Dunstan.

"I hope so," said Graham. "Because you're about to experience a good deal of it."

All he had been able to find to stitch the giant's wounds was some yards of braided cord taken from one of the tapestries. And all he had to guide it was a nail pried from a cabinet drawer. He pushed his makeshift needle through the skin of Dunstan's arm, braced his feet against the giant's side, and pulled. Dunstan groaned, but the rough cord pulled the wound neatly closed.

"There," said Graham. "I think that's the worst of it for this side. I'll tie up a couple on the left, and a good bandage should do for the rest." He stood and took his gear around the reclining giant.

Dunstan held up his arm and flexed his hand.

"A goodly job," he said. "I've seen much worse on the battlefield."

"Having seen just one of you fight," said Graham, "I don't even want to think of what kind of damage a whole army of giants might cause."

Dunstan gave a burst of laughter, then groaned and put a hand to the wounds on his belly.

"It's good to hear you laugh, Lord Dunstan," said Ahi'aorina.

"Osh," said the giant. "I'm nae lord of anything. I don't want anything more to do with this Sorrowing Court." He looked at the faery queen and a blush came across his wide face. "What I've done to you, lady, that's unforgivable."

Ahi'aorina smiled. "Your thoughts were clouded by the *efreeti*. You were not responsible. Even I had slipped into the despair he fostered."

"I felt the touch of it, too," said Graham, "and it wasn't even aimed at me." He pulled tight the last of Dunstan's stitches, then tied the wound closed with a sheepshank that would have done a sailor proud. "There. I think that should do it. Don't get too active too soon. I don't want to have to do this again."

Dunstan appeared much less concerned with his own wounds than with the pain he had caused Ahi'aorina. "You may say it's nae my fault, but I am shamed nonetheless." The giant shook his head. "I've wronged you both, and a great number of others besides."

"When you learned the true nature of Kuzgu,

you fought valiantly," said Ahi'aorina. "You have nothing to be ashamed of." She smiled.

Freedom from the cage and the end of Kuzgu's spell had obviously done much to strengthen the faery. Her hair had regained something of its luster and her movements showed new energy. But it was just as obvious that she was still weak and far from her best.

There was a thump from across the room, and the clatter of a plate. Graham looked up, ready to face some new foe, but it was only one of the drunken imps. The potbellied creature stirred, blinked its eyes, and settled back into a stupor.

"I believe they could sleep even if the castle were falling down around them," said Graham.

Ahi'aorina suddenly jumped to her feet. "Where is it?"

Graham looked around the room. "Where is what?"

"The *efreeti*." Ahi'aorina hurried around Dunstan and pointed to the ground. "The remains of the creature were over there, but now it is vanished."

Graham dropped the needle and went to her side. The clutter of plates and spilled food still covered the floor, but there was no sign of the small mound of blackness that had been left behind after the silver plate had done in Kuzgu.

"Could it move on its own?" he asked.

Ahi'aorina spread her hands. "I do not know. *Efreeti* are rare creatures, and I have never before seen one brought to this state."

Graham got down on his hands and knees and scanned the floor. Through the debris, he spotted the lump of darkness. It was creeping and twisting along, stretching like some immense vile inchworm as it pushed through spilled food and around fallen chairs.

"I see it." Graham ran over to the moving mass of shadow. Only when he got close to it did he realize something even more frightening than the thing's movement. He skidded to a halt behind the creeping darkness.

"It's growing," he said.

Where the thing had been small enough to fit in Graham's palm, now it was as big as a loaf of bread. And even as he watched, it grew larger still. Ahi'aorina crossed the room to join him. Even Dunstan got onto his hands and knees and crawled over for a look.

"What do we do with it?" asked Graham.

"I can smash it," suggested Dunstan.

Ahi'aorina shook her head. "I fear that would have little effect. The *efreeti* are not creatures of the natural world. Only powerful magic can bring them into being. Though silver can wound it, I am not sure it is even possible for one of them to be destroyed. At least not without magic just as strong."

The shadow slug swelled again, reaching the size of a small dog as it moved past one of the stone tables and headed into the hallway.

"We're going to have to do something," said Graham. "In another few minutes, we'll be fighting it all over again."

Ahi'aorina held her hands over the moving spot of darkness and closed her eyes. "It draws energy from the magic stored in these walls," she said. She pulled back her hands, opened her eyes, and shook her head. "If I were stronger, I could use my own magic to thwart it. But I have not the power to work a magical barrier."

Graham bit his lip and watched the thing bump and slide over the carpet. He could always bat it with another silver plate, but if it kept coming back, that was far from a perfect solution. He needed something that would keep Kuzgu from returning.

A smile came to Graham's lips. "I know what to do," he said.

"What?" asked Ahi'aorina.

Graham walked over to the crawling shadow, took a deep breath, and lifted it from the ground. It felt a little like holiday pudding—less than solid, but more than liquid. But if it was a pudding, it was the heaviest and the coldest pudding Graham had ever felt. Within moments of lifting the thing from the carpet, his fingers had gone numb and his arms were aching with the cold. He turned and staggered across the room with the toilsome, frigid bundle in his arms.

"Help me," he called through gritted teeth.

Dunstan looked at him as if he had gone mad.

"What are you doing with that?" asked the giant.

"The cage." Graham was forced to dodge as a waving psuedopod of darkness emerged from the central mass and swatted at his head. "The cage," he said again. "We'll put it in there."

Ahi'aorina brightened. "Of course," she said. "The cage kept me from drawing any power from outside. It should bar this creature as well."

The amorphous mass wavered, shook, and swelled in size. Its weight increased with its size. Graham's knees trembled as he labored to take another step. "Yes," he grunted. "Now if you could . . ."

"Here," said Dunstan. He reached down and wrapped his huge hand around the quivering blob. "Let me have it."

Graham gratefully released his grip on the freezing bundle. As Dunstan shoved the shapeless mass through the open cage door, Graham struggled onto the massive couch and ran across the cushions to help the giant.

Dunstan was having some difficulty getting the creature free of his hand. "This thing is stickier than a honeycomb and colder than midwinter," he grumbled.

"Let me know when you're ready." Graham got one hand on the door and waited.

The giant suddenly pulled his hand away with a sound like a cork slipping from a bottle. Graham shoved the door home with a solid click. He turned the key in the lock and pulled it free.

For a moment, the darkness boiled furiously. Misshapen limbs appeared, rang against the thin bars, and fell apart as quickly as they had formed. The shadows stilled.

"Looks like we've done it," said Dunstan.

A single eye appeared in the side of the inchoate mass. Below it a jagged slit—like a child's parody of a mouth—grew and opened.

"Free . . . me. . . . ," said the thing that had been Kuzgu.

The voice was hardly more than a whisper, but it was oddly compelling. Without even thinking, Graham raised his hand and started to put the key in the lock.

"No!" shouted a voice at his back.

"Free me," repeated the darkness. "Free me and all your desires will be fulfilled."

An image of Castle Daventry appeared in Graham's mind. Valanice and Rosella were waiting there for him. The fields around the castle blazed with spring flowers. There was warmth, and love, and comfort to be had—all at the turn of a key.

"No!"

A stream of green light washed over Graham and sent him tumbling from the couch to the floor. He lay looking up at the cage, the key still in his hand.

"Dunstan," called Ahi'aorina. "Find the cover. Put it over the cage."

The giant's hand reached down beside Graham

and came up with the length of shimmering cloth that had swathed the cage on Graham's arrival at Sorrowing Court. Carefully, Dunstan wrapped the cover around the cage until all sight of the golden bars and their dark prisoner was obscured.

Ahi'aorina leaned over Graham. "Are you injured?"

Graham shook his head and sat up. "Only my pride is wounded," he said. "Thank you."

The faery extended a slim hand and helped Graham to his feet. "I wish I could have been more subtle," she said. "But I only have so much magic and there was not much time."

"I'm glad you acted as fast as you did. Subtle would be nice, but I'd rather be alive." Graham tugged open his pocket and dropped in the ivory key. The slizard woke for a moment, then curled around its pale new companion and settled back into its nap.

Dunstan leaned over the couch and looked down at the two small figures. "Can we leave this place now?" he asked. "I want to be out of here before that thing finds a way to escape."

"I agree," said Graham. "We'll free the imps, and then we can be on our way."

"Free the imps?" said the giant.

Graham nodded. "I flattened most of them with a cooking skillet and left them tied up in a closet."

Dunstan laughed. "Did you? That should make for quite a tale."

"Yes," said Graham as he rubbed his chin. "And I knew just the man to tell it. Or rather, to sing it." He could only imagine the laughs that Shallan would have gathered with his ballad of a skillet-wielding king. Not to mention the verses the bard could have wrested from the other things that had happened in Sorrowing Court.

"But now that you've caught the imps, are you sure we should let them go?" asked Dunstan. "They did help Kuzgu."

"They did, but I don't think they did it on their own. I think they were under the influence of the *efreeti,* just like you." Graham suddenly thought of Lugmut and how he had left the imp lying in the hallway. "One of them even helped me, and Kuzgu attacked him. I hope he's still all right."

The cage overhead shook and bumped. The giant looked at it and frowned. "So we stop to free the imps you captured. Then we can leave?"

"Yes."

"What about the *efreeti*'s other prisoner?" asked Ahi'aorina. "The one who languishes in a glamour manarvel?"

Graham snapped his fingers. "I forgot all about him."

"What is this?" asked Dunstan.

"There's a man hidden in a secret corridor behind one of the walls," explained Graham. "It looks like Kuzgu has him wound up in some kind of magic trap similar to the one he was using on you and Queen Ahi'aorina. Will you help us free him?"

"Of course," said the giant with an enthusiastic nod. "You've freed me from Kuzgu's spell. It's only right that I should return the good deed."

Graham led the way out of the central hall and down the corridor. He had not traveled this way as a man, and he found it hard to judge the distance. Several times he stopped to pull up sections of tapestry only to find the wall underneath of the same neat construction as the rest of Sorrowing Court.

"I know it's around here somewhere," he said.

"Try just ahead," suggested Ahi'aorina. "I can feel magic there."

Graham pulled up another section of tapestry. Sure enough, the wall it covered was rough and ill made. The crack he had slipped through a few hours before now appeared no wider than the tip of his little finger.

"This is it," he said. "The man I saw is in a room behind this wall."

Ahi'aorina held her hands in front of the wall and nodded. "The magic here is powerful." She ran her fingers around the edge of the affected area. "It appears that this may serve as some sort of door."

"Where?" Graham joined her in feeling along the stone. "You're right. It has to open somehow. I saw footprints inside."

Dunstan leaned down and stared over their

shoulders. "If you don't know how to open the door, then how can you know what's inside?"

"I was a lot smaller then," said Graham.

"What?"

"It's hard to explain." Graham thumped his fist against the stone. "I can't find any kind of release or handle. How does this thing open?"

"I know how to open it," said Dunstan.

"You do?"

Dunstan nodded. He pushed his small companions gently away and took a closer look at the door. "Yes," he said after a moment. "I can open it."

He tightened one hand into a massive fist, drew back his arm, and smashed the secret door from its hinges in a cloud of plaster dust and loose stone.

"It's open," said the giant.

· 28 ·

"It looks like the hinges were on this side," said Graham. He pushed through the shattered door and kicked debris out of the way. "Not that it matters now."

Ahi'aorina stepped over the fallen stones and joined him in the hallway. "The magic is stronger than I thought," she said. "Much stronger." The faery shivered. "You can feel it in the air like the breath of winter."

Rock dust and powdered plaster hung in the air, but Graham could still see the glow of the magical lights down the dim hallway. The thrum of the magic sounded different to human ears— deep, vibrating tones felt through the soles of his boots.

"I'll have to wait for you out here," Dunstan called from just outside the opening he had battered. "I can nae fit in your little toad hole."

Not only was it clear that the giant would never fit into the area behind the secret door, it could barely accommodate Graham. What had seemed a tall, broad passage on his last visit was now revealed a narrow, rude little corridor whose ceiling was so low that it scraped against his head.

Ahi'aorina fit in the restricted space much more readily, though she did not seem to enjoy the walk between the close gray walls. "I will be so glad to return to the Old Wood," she said as Graham led her deeper into the dim passage.

"Many there, and in Daventry besides, await your return," said Graham.

"I will be happy to see my Quilli'ehennan, and the faeries." Ahi'aorina paused and looked wistfully at the stone over her head. "But I think I will be even happier just to see the sky above me and feel the earth under my tread."

Graham stepped through the rough-hewn door at the end of the brief hallway. Like everything else he had first experienced from a lizard's-eye view, the room was smaller than he had remembered—no bigger than a dungeon cell. But the other aspects of the place were just as he had said.

All the shafts of parti-colored light still swarmed about, reflecting from walls and ceiling and floor. The pulsing coruscating glow that surrounded the central figure was undimmed. Even the moths still fluttered about the room, their numbers undiminished by Graham's earlier feasting.

"It is a magic trap," said Ahi'aorina. "I had hoped the *efreeti*'s capture might weaken this spell, but it seems strong." She stepped past Graham and slowly circled the room. The changing beams of light painted her pale figure first blue, then green, then shimmering gold. "It is as I said. These lights are carrying his energy away and spreading it through Sorrowing Court."

"Can you tell how long he's been like this?" asked Graham.

The faery queen shook her head slowly. "Days. Weeks. Perhaps months."

Graham squinted at the brightness coming from the seated man. "He must have an awful lot of magic in him if he can pour out this amount of power for that length of time. Can you tell who he is?"

"No. I can see that he is a wizard of considerable talent, but beyond that I can learn nothing." Ahi'aorina moved to the side of the room. "The only way to know more is to free him from this trap."

"Can you free him?"

"I do not know." The faery queen brushed her hair back from her face and raised her hands to touch a beam of sapphire light. "My powers are based in nature, and there is little of nature here. But I will do what I can."

As Graham watched, the light ray slowly shifted in the faery's grip. She took a step forward, pushing the beam of light down and in as she went. In a few minutes, she had bent the blue ray back on itself. With a flare, it vanished. Ahi'aorina moved next to a pale green ray and began to coax it from its place.

Ahi'aorina's progress was steady, but slow. Graham leaned back against the wall and watched as she snuffed one beam of light, then another. Dozens more remained.

The movement of the moths about the room grew more erratic as the patterns of light shifted. Watching them, Graham felt his stomach rumble. The moths might have filled a lizard's belly, but that satisfaction had gone when he had regained his own form. Somehow, he didn't think the bugs would taste quite so delicious now.

A muffled call from Dunstan brought Graham out into the hallway. "What is it?" he shouted.

"The boggle," boomed the giant. "He strains his bounds."

"What?"

"Kuzgu. He's trying to work himself out of his cage."

Graham hurried down the corridor to the giant's side. "The cage is magic," he said. "Kuzgu can't get free."

Dunstan ran his fingers through his stiff beard. "So you say. But I think you may want to come and tell that to Kuzgu. I heard a knockin' and a bangin', so I went to have a look-see at our dun guest."

"And?"

The giant shook his head. "The coop is bent as an elbow. I don't think we'll grip him much longer."

"Wonderful," said Graham. If Kuzgu escaped from the cage before they escaped from Sorrowing Court . . . "Go and watch him," he said to the giant. "I'll let Queen Ahi'aorina know what's going on."

Dunstan nodded and tramped away down the hall. Graham kicked his way back through the debris of the small corridor and rejoined the faery queen.

Ahi'aorina's work had reduced the scale of the trap significantly. There were now no more than a dozen beams of light remaining in the room, and the glow around the seated man had dimmed enough that Graham could make out the vague shape of the prisoner's features. But those light rays that remained were the largest and brightest of all.

"We have a problem with Kuzgu," Graham reported. "It looks like the cage might not hold him after all."

Ahi'aorina only nodded. She gripped a beam of cyan light and pressed it toward the source.

Graham waited near the door of the room. He bit his lip, expecting Dunstan to come running at every moment with the news that Kuzgu was loose. When the giant didn't return after a few minutes, Graham began to fear that the *efreeti* had already dispatched him.

At last the beams of light had been reduced to one. The magical hum that had filled the room became a crackling, pounding heartbeat. The shroud of light around the seated figure turned into a crawling shell of miniature green lightning.

"Now we will know," said Ahi'aorina.

"Know what?"

"Whether he still lives."

Graham started. "How can he not be alive? So much energy was coming from him."

"Not all magic dies with the user," said Ahi-'aorina. "We know nothing about this man until he is freed."

The sound of huge running feet drew Graham to the doorway. "Dunstan?" he shouted. "I hope that's you."

The giant's broad face appeared down the hall. "It's me, well enough. Kuzgu's not loose yet, but we've only smallish time before he is. Best tell the queen to hurry."

Graham turned back to Ahi'aorina. "Dunstan says—"

The faery queen held up a pale hand. "I heard. I will do this as rapidly as I can."

It was obvious that the last light ray resisted Ahi-'aorina's efforts much more than any of the ones that had gone before. She strained against it like a man pulling against a stubborn mule. Slowly— slowly—the light began to bend.

Sparks dripped from the seated figure. The magical heartbeat stuttered, raced, quieted, then roared. Lightning arched from the glowing man and danced along the walls of the room. Graham stepped back into the corridor, but even there he could feel the hairs on his arms and neck swaying.

A flash of heat surged from the room, blowing

dust and the smaller rocks from the floor. Right on its heels came a wind so chilling that Graham's breath caught in his throat and frost formed along the walls. He leaned into the gelid gale and staggered back into the room just in time to see Ahi'aorina force the light ray home. There was a flash.

When Graham's eyes cleared, he was sitting in the corner of the room. Only a dim glow leaked into the chamber from the hallway outside. There was a smell in the air like that after a summer thunderstorm, but all sign of the magic light and sound had vanished.

"Ahi'aorina?"

"I am here." A pale form moved in the darkness.

Graham put one hand on the wall and got to his feet. "Are you all right?"

"Yes. Tired, but all right."

"What about the man?" Graham stumbled forward with his hands stretched out into the shadows.

"He lives," said Ahi'aorina. "More than that, I cannot say."

Graham's fingers brushed the faery queen's smooth, cool shoulder, then he found the back of a wooden chair. He could feel intricate, obscure carvings in the wood, but he could not make out what the forms were. "What should we do?" he asked.

"Let us get him out into the light," said Ahi-

'aorina. "Though my eyes are not so blind as a human's, I cannot see well enough to help him here."

Graham found the man's arms and got his hands under his shoulders. With Ahi'aorina's help, he lifted the man from the chair where he had sat for so long, and carried him down the narrow corridor to the broad, well-lit hallway outside.

Dunstan was waiting for them. "From the thunder and the lightning, it seems you had yourselves quite a rowdydow back there."

"Queen Ahi'aorina did the work," said Graham. "I only watched." He pulled the unconscious man through the broken door and laid him gently on the carpet.

The giant looked down with interest. "So this is the one what was pinned."

Graham nodded. He turned the man over, and got a good look at him for the first time.

The prisoner appeared to be an elderly man, at least three decades older than Graham. His features were narrow, and though his hair was still black, it only sparsely covered his skull. His eyes were sunken among nests of tight lines. His skin was ashen as death.

"Are you sure he's still kicking?" asked Dunstan.

"Ahi'aorina says he is."

The faery queen emerged from the darkness. "He has languished under the burden of the magic trap for a long time. He should revive anon.''

"I hope that means soon," said Dunstan. ''Kuzgu has that cage about to buckle.''

The man on the floor groaned. Graham held the man's head off the carpet, and in only a few moments his eyes began to flutter. His thin lips parted and he drew a rattling breath.

"Is it finished?" he whispered.

"Rest," said Ahi'aorina. "You are free."

The man's eyelids opened, revealing eyes of pale watery blue, and he squinted against the light. "Who are you? Where is Kuzgu?"

"Don't worry," said Graham. "We've stopped Kuzgu.''

"You have?" said the man.

"At least for the moment." Graham looked down the hallway. "What's your name?"

"Karn Megiddo," said the man.

"I'm Graham, this is Queen Ahi'aorina of the Old Wood, and our large friend is Lord Dunstan.''

"I'm nae a lord," insisted Dunstan. "And if we want to get out of here, we must quit this place before that cursed boggle is after us again.''

The thin man put his hands on the floor and pushed himself to a sitting position. "Can I see him?" he asked.

"Kuzgu?"

"Yes," said Karn Megiddo. He cleared his throat and spoke in a stronger voice. "I want to see how you've captured him.''

Graham nodded. "I can't blame you for wanting to be sure that—'' A rumble sounded down the hall, a noise so deep that Graham felt it in his stomach more than he heard it. "What was that? Is Kuzgu loose?''

"No," said Ahi'aorina. "It is something else.''

The floor jumped underneath them. The distant thunder came again. On the wall, the torches began to flicker and dim.

"What's going on?" asked Graham.

"The magic that was being drained from Karn Megiddo was supporting Sorrowing Court.'' Ahi-'aorina waved her arm at the hallway around them. "Much of what you see here is a product of magic—little better than an illusion. Without the power that was being drawn from him, it cannot be supported.''

As if to underscore her words, the carpet under their feet paled, thinned, then disappeared. In its place was a floor of rough black stone.

"So all the luxuries here are vanishing," said Graham. "We may soon be in darkness.''

The faery queen shook her head. "I fear it goes further than that. Even the structure of this place is supported by magic.'' There was a crash, and the floor jumped under their feet.

"Without magic," she said, "Sorrowing Court will fall.''

·29·

The torches went out before they had gone more than a hundred yards.

At once, the hallways were filled with a darkness so thick that it made the darkest night seem like noon. For the second time on his journey, Graham dearly wished that he still had his tinderbox.

"Well, what do we now?" asked Dunstan. "I'm a giant, not a dwarf. I've got no eyes for darkness."

Streamers of green light flowed down the hallway. Quickly they twisted and gathered into a sparkling ball that bounced in the air above Ahi-'aorina's hand. "There is not enough life here for me to light our way long," said the faery queen. "We must find something else, or face making our exit in darkness."

"Karn Megiddo," said Graham hesitantly. "There was a tremendous amount of light coming from your magic when we found you, perhaps you—"

"No," the older man said quickly. "I've been

drained too low. I don't have enough magic left for making light.''

"All right. We had better move fast then," said Graham. "If we can get back to the central hall, we may find something there that can help." He offered an arm to Karn Megiddo. "Here, let me help you."

"No," said the wizard. "That is, I can make it fine on my own. You go on. Lead the way."

Graham walked side by side with Ahi'aorina, with Karn Megiddo close behind and Dunstan at the rear. All of them were bound within the circle of green light that came from the faery queen's magic.

How many of the twisting corridors of Sorrowing Court were still real, and how many had vanished into the realm of pure illusion, Graham couldn't say. But he would have bet that without light none of them would make it out to see the sky again. Even Ahi'aorina, whose eyes were far better than his own, admitted to being blind in the velvet darkness of this stone labyrinth.

The instability of Sorrowing Court continued to make itself known as they walked. Small stones and loose sand dribbled down through cracks in the roof. Larger falls sounded from the distance. Dunstan had to crawl more than a hundred yards through one stretch where the ceiling had lowered, and twice the whole party was forced to stop and pick their way through piles of fallen stone.

After passing the second of these falls, they

came upon a few sticks of broken furniture, an empty pot, and a threadbare rug.

Graham picked up the leg of a shattered chair. "Looks like this much was real, though it's not good for much now."

Ahi'aorina, who had begun to wilt under the effort of maintaining her magical light, stared around the room dully. "Have we returned to the central chamber?"

"No," said Dunstan. "We've nae come far enough. Not by half."

"Is the central hall where you've bound Kuzgu?" asked Karn Megiddo.

"Yes," said Graham. "At least that's where we left him. I certainly hope the cage we put him in was real."

"It is real enough," said Ahi'aorina. She suddenly folded her legs and sat down on the stone floor. "I was its prisoner long enough to know how real it is." Her voiced was strained and her breath labored.

"Are you all right?" asked Graham.

The faery queen shook her head. "I must rest," she said. "My powers are exhausted."

"Don't fret yourself," said Dunstan. He lifted the worn rug in his hand and wound it round a loose table leg. "I can take care of lighting the path from here."

Graham looked at the giant's contrivance. "That's a fine beginning for a torch, but where will you get the spark?"

Dunstan laughed. "I'm a giant of the Hibestian Range," he said. "I need no help making a spark."

The giant bared his teeth in a wide grimace. Then, with a sideways motion of his jaw, he generated a shower of sparks that tumbled through his beard and onto the floor. Quickly, Dunstan plucked a smoldering whisker from his beard, put it against the cloth torch, and blew the glowing ember into a flame.

"That seems like a very handy talent," said Graham.

Dunstan grinned. "The Hibestian Range is a fierce cold spot. Even a giant can find himself turned into an icehogle when the wind comes down from the peaks. If you're to live there, it pays to have a way to make fire in a pinch."

Ahi'aorina let the magic flame dissipate from her hand as Dunstan's torch grew brighter, but the prolonged effort had left the faery shaken and exhausted. "Can we stay here?" she asked. "Just for a moment."

"Of course," said Graham. The ground shook slightly as some part of the unstable fortress collapsed. "But maybe we shouldn't wait too long."

"Why don't I scout ahead?" said Dunstan. "I will nae go far, but I need to get the best use from this fire while we've got it." Ahi'aorina nodded, and the giant moved away down the tunnel, taking their only light with him.

Graham shuffled through the darkness carefully and took a seat near the faery queen. "Is there anything I can do for you?" he asked.

"You have already done more than anyone could expect," Ahi'aorina's soft voice said from the darkness. "Now we have only to rest and to find our way free from this place."

Graham leaned back on a pile of rubble and tried to get a little rest of his own. The darkness was again so complete that he could not say with absolute certainty whether his eyes were open or shut. The only sounds were the gentle hiss of falling sand and the distant drip of water.

"What about you, Karn Megiddo?" he called, mostly just to break the silence. "How do you feel?"

"I am well enough," said the wizard.

"How long have you been trapped here?"

Karn Megiddo was silent for a few seconds before answering. "I don't know. What day is it?"

"Spring has just begun. Or would have, had Ahi'aorina not been taken from the Old Wood." Graham scratched his chin in thought. "I've lost track of the time myself in this place without sunrise or day. We held the Sun Festival in Daventry a few days before I left."

"It was summer when I came to this place," said the wizard.

"The better part of a year," said Ahi'aorina. "If it is only one year. That is a long time to spend in a manarvel. The wonder is that you were not more badly injured.''

''I am . . . resilient,'' said Karn Megiddo.

A shout came from up the hall. Graham stood, peering ahead for a glimpse of Dunstan's torch. His eyes lied to him several times, finding light where there was none to find, but after a moment the real torch came into view. Soon Dunstan had rejoined the rest of the group.

''There's a big room ahead,'' he said. ''I think it's where the central hall used to be, though there's nae so much flashery as there was before.''

''What about the tunnels leading away?'' asked Graham. ''Are they still there?''

''Some of them,'' said the giant. ''Nae all, though. And there's much rock down ahead.''

''Let's hope that one of the tunnels that remains is the route out of this place.'' Graham turned to look at the others. ''Are you rested enough to continue, Queen Ahi'aorina?''

The faery stood. ''I will get but little rest within these halls, but I am prepared to go on.''

Under the light of Dunstan's torch, the party got under way again. They soon reached a vast round chamber. Translucent draperies of flowstone and dangling stalactites showed that this had been part of a natural cavern, but even here the effects of the magical collapse had caused huge cracks in both floor and ceiling. If this had once been the hall where Dunstan's couch had rested, there was now no sign of it or any of the tables and chairs that had once been scattered around the room.

"Are you sure this is the central hall? Where are the imps who were sleeping in here?" asked Graham.

"We've come the right distance," said Dunstan. "More than that I don't know. As for the imps, either they were part of yon glamour, or I was wrong about them sleeping while the castle fell down about their ears."

Ahi'aorina walked slowly around the room. "The cage," she said. "If this is the hall, then where is the cage?"

Graham spun around. A chill ran down his back. "Over there."

A single piece of twisted gold jutted from a pile of fallen rock. Beside it was a muddy piece of cloth that might have been the cage cover.

"Let's go," said Dunstan, "while we still can."

There was a sliding, scratching sound. From across the room, a fragment of shadow detached itself from the rest of the darkness and stepped into the open.

"It's too late for that," said Kuzgu. "Far too late."

Karn Megiddo stepped forward. "Kuzgu," he said. "You're free."

The *efreeti* hissed. "And so are you, wizard. But don't worry. All the ingredients are still in place. Soon enough you will return to your chamber."

Dunstan stepped forward and waved his torch

at the dark creature. "You'll nae be weaving your cantrip about me again."

Kuzgu laughed. "I have bested you by wit and by strength. I don't fear you, giant."

"Good. You can have me," said Dunstan, "but let the rest of them pass."

"No!" shouted Graham. "We all stay together."

The dark form moved across the floor. "Don't worry, little king, you are all going to be together for a long, long time."

Graham backed away from the advancing creature. His gaze went to the floor and he searched desperately for a glint of silver among the gray stones.

"The plates and knives are gone, human." Red eyes glowed within Kuzgu's invisible face. "There is no weapon left here that can stop me." Kuzgu spread his midnight arms wide as he neared Graham. "And this time I know who to kill first."

With a rippling crack, the ceiling in the room let go.

Dunstan snagged the back of Graham's tunic and pulled him away as a block of stone bigger than a cabin fell on the snarling *efreeti*. With stones of all sizes raining down, they fled from the central chamber just ahead of an avalanche of rock.

Dunstan ran down the largest of the corridors leading away from the room. The rest of the party hurried behind him, trying to keep the giant's leaping torch in view. When Dunstan slowed and the others caught up, the central chamber was far away and out of sight behind the turns of the corridor.

"Do you think that will hold him?" Dunstan asked as Graham came staggering up.

Graham bent double and rested his hands on his knees. "Hold who?" he asked between deep breaths.

"Kuzgu," said Dunstan.

"I think he's smashed flat," replied Graham. "You saw what happened."

"Aye," said Dunstan. "But that don't mean he will nae be trying for us again."

Ahi'aorina stepped past Dunstan and lifted her chin in the air. "We are closer to the surface," she said. "I can smell sunlight not far away."

"I wouldn't mind some of that," said Graham. He looked up and down the hall. "See anything that might be where the kitchens were? I don't want to leave the imps trapped in here while it falls in around them."

"Nothing so far," said Ahi'aorina. "Perhaps we will yet see them along our way."

The rumble of more collapse nearby sent the group on its way again. A few minutes of walking brought them to an intersection where a trio of corridors crossed. By now, Ahi'aorina was able to direct their way, selecting the route that would lead most directly to the outside. Dunstan's torch was burning low, but they didn't devote much worry to it. Sunlight was near.

Even Graham could smell a difference in the air. "We must be getting close," he said. "It looks like we really will live through this."

At that moment, a dark figure appeared at the edge of the failing circle of light.

"Cursed boogle!" shouted Dunstan. "You'll stay dead this time!" He seized a barrel-sized boulder in his free hand and raised it over his head.

"Wait!" cried the shadowy figure. "Only me it is!"

Graham blinked. "Lugmut?"

"Yes, yes. Lugmut it is." The imp stepped into the circle of torchlight.

"I'm glad to see you're all right," said Graham.

"All right I am not!" cried the imp. "Lost I am. Hungry I am. Not all right."

"Osh," said Dunstan. "I take it this wee fiend is on our side?"

"Yes." Graham walked over to Lugmut and put a hand on the imp's shoulder. "I'm glad to see you. Do you know where the other imps are?"

Lugmut nodded. "Not far are they."

"Good. Let's get them and get out."

They trailed behind the tall imp as he took them to a dark opening in the wall. "The kitchens this was," he said. "Heard the others here."

Dunstan went to the mouth of the tunnel and held up his torch. Then he lowered his light and turned to Graham. "I think you'd better come see this," said the giant.

"What?" Graham took the flickering nub of the torch from Dunstan's hand and stepped up to the dark tunnel. Inside were only a few piles of dirty brown roots, some broken bits of wood, and one gray mountain troll. The troll lay on his back on the stone floor. There was an expression of great contentment on his scrunched face, and his belly was distended like a man who had devoured three melons at a sitting.

"Thragaadash!" called Graham.

The troll raised its head from the ground and blinked its small eyes. "Wha'?"

"Where are the imps, Thragaadash?"

"Not here." Thragaadash suddenly sat up and his wide mouth dropped open a bit. "I know you," he said. "You're lunch!"

Dunstan leaned down at Graham's side. "He's nae meal today, ye ugly wart."

Thragaadash looked at the giant for a moment, groaned, and lay back down. "Giants no good. Meat all stringy."

"Where are the imps?" Graham repeated.

"Gone." The troll waved a hand at the ceiling. "All gone."

"You're sure you didn't eat them?"

Thragaadash frowned. "Imps even worse than giants." He patted his protruding stomach. "Ate rutabagas," he said. "Imps got scared when dark come. Run away."

Graham was quite certain he was going to regret his next question, but he felt compelled to ask it anyway. "What about you, Thragaadash? We're leaving this place. Would you like to come with us?"

The troll raised its head again and surveyed the group. "You let Thragaadash eat faery lady?"

"No."

"Umph. Thragaadash never gets to eat faery lady."

"Well, you're not going to eat one now," said Graham. "Do you want to go with us or not?"

The troll rolled over on its side and closed its eyes. "Not," it said. "Thragaadash like dark."

Graham looked at Dunstan. "Do you think he'll be all right here?"

"Who knows?" said the giant. "But he doesn't want to leave, and I'm nae carrying him."

Lugmut came bouncing over. "Leave him you should," said the imp. "When hungry they are, mountain trolls forget their friends."

Graham sighed. "I guess that's it then. Everyone we can get out is out." He turned to Ahi-'aorina. "Is this still the way out?"

The faery queen nodded. "No more than a hundred strides."

"Then let's go."

Within a few steps, the darkness of the corridor was relieved by a faint blue glow. In another dozen strides that glow became bright enough to cast shadows behind the five travelers. The air became cleaner. And colder.

Blinking against the light of a bright morning,

they emerged from Sorrowing Court. The entrance that had been blocked by tall iron doors was now nothing but the rough mouth of a cave. High up on the mountain they could see fissures and rents in the stone. Clouds of dust and smoke trailed away in the wind.

"I feared I'd nae see the light again," said Dunstan. He walked a few steps out onto the frozen glade at the base of the mountain, jumped into the air, and landed with a thud that shook the earth.

"Be careful," said Graham. "There's one mountain falling already."

Lugmut wrapped his thin arms about himself. "Cold it is," he said.

"Not for long," said Ahi'aorina. The change in the faery queen was almost immediate. She raised her face to the sun and drank in its light like a thirsty man quaffing from a bucket. Her skin grew bright and gained a shimmer of colors that no human could name. She went from pretty, to beautiful, and beyond that to something almost too glorious to bear. At her feet the snow began to melt. Grass sprang up. Tiny flowers of white and palest blue crept over the dark stones. Quickly the circle of green spread until all of the group were caught in a bubble of warmth.

Graham closed his eyes and drew in a deep breath. "Spring," he whispered.

He sat down among the fresh grass, feeling as if his legs weighed forty stone. Each. Soon they would have to get up and begin the trip back to Daventry, but for the moment all he wanted to do was rest. He opened his eyes and watched as Ahi-'aorina danced around the glade at the foot of the mountain, banishing winter as she passed.

Karn Megiddo stepped away from the cave mouth and brushed rock dust from his dark doublet. "I really must thank you all for saving me," he said. "I am in your debt."

Graham smiled. "You don't owe us anything," he said. "Where will you go now? Is your home close by?"

"I'm afraid my home does not exist anymore," said Karn Megiddo. "Now, you're sure you don't feel that I'm in your debt?"

"Not at all."

"Good." The wizard rubbed his hands together. Sparks of dazzling silver light moved among his fingertips. "That will make it so much neater when I kill you."

The smile froze on Graham's lips. "You don't really mean to kill us."

"Oh, I do," said Karn Megiddo. "I really do." In the sunlight, the wizard's face looked paler than ever, and his eyes were flecks of pure black. He held up one long, bony hand and a bolt of jagged lightning arced from his fingers to strike at Graham's feet.

Ahi'aorina stopped her dancing. Both Lugmut and Dunstan turned toward the wizard.

"What's this then?" asked the giant.

Graham was afraid to take his eyes away from Karn Megiddo. "He says he's going to kill us."

Dunstan snorted. "What? We didn't rescue him fast enough?"

Karn Megiddo turned and looked at the giant with an expression of terrible scorn. "You great shrub-faced idiot," he said coldly. "If you hadn't removed me from the spell chamber, then I would have required no rescuing."

Dunstan growled and raised a knotted fist, but Ahi'aorina laid a small calming hand against the giant's side. "The glamour manarvel held you in its grip," she said to Karn Megiddo. "If we had not removed you, then you might never have been freed."

"Oh, I would have been freed," said the wizard. He turned away from the others and paced around the circle of grass with his hands clamped at his back. "It was designed that way. Once the spell was completed, the manarvel would have unraveled of its own accord."

"What spell?" asked Graham.

"The spell!" cried Karn Megiddo. "The spell that I have worked on for over two decades and which you," he leveled a finger at Graham, "you have destroyed in only a few days."

Graham shook his head. "I don't know anything about this spell. We thought you had been imprisoned by Kuzgu."

The wizard spat on the ground. "You would. No, I bound myself in the manarvel."

"But why?" asked Ahi'aorina. "What could you hope to gain by imprisoning yourself?"

"Only my full power could sustain Sorrowing Court and prepare the way for the great spell." Karn Megiddo raised one arm, and rippling sheets of lightning rolled up to gather in a whirling, spitting mass at his hand. "For everything to work out, I had to leave it to my assistant to gather the ingredients in my spell while I held open the door that prepared the way. In only a few more days, I would have been ready."

Graham stared at the miniature storm which spun around the wizard's hand. "What was this spell supposed to do?"

Karn Megiddo sneered. "Make perfect cream horns with just a touch of butter," he said. A lightning bolt seared the earth in front of Graham. "What do you think it was supposed to do, fool? It would make me the most powerful magician east of the great sea! Sorrowing Court would have been the center of the world, and I would have been capable of feats never imagined!" For several seconds, the magician simply stood there, panting through his clenched teeth.

Graham exchanged a glance with Dunstan. The giant nodded and began to move slowly around behind the wizard. Ahi'aorina held her hands low, but Graham could see the sparks of green fire that moved along her fingers. The grass around Karn Megiddo's feet became thick and tangled, binding the wizard to the earth. Lugmut simply turned and began to sneak away.

"We're sorry we caused you such a problem," Graham said. "We really didn't mean to." He kept one eye on Dunstan as he spoke. The giant selected a boulder from the ground that was nearly as big as a horse, and slowly lifted it over Karn Megiddo.

"You're not sorry at all," said Karn Megiddo with a sneer. "I don't know you, but I know your kind. Out to set the world to rights. To keep anyone from gaining the whip hand."

Graham shrugged. "It seemed the right thing to do."

"Well, stop it!" shouted the wizard. "This doing the right thing causes no end of bother for people like me."

He flicked one hand casually over his shoulder and a thick bolt of lightning smashed into Dunstan. The giant was knocked a wagon length away. The heavy stone slipped from his hands, bounced once against his shaggy head, and thudded into the grass. Like an oak tree split by an axe, Dunstan slowly toppled to the ground. Karn Megiddo raised his other hand, and a second bolt sent Lugmut tumbling out beyond the circle of spring to land in a drift of snow. Steam rose from the imp's sprawled form.

"Stop!" Graham started forward, but Karn Megiddo raised a hand in warning.

"Enough wasted time," said the wizard. He tapped a finger against his chin. "I'll need a new assistant. You'll have to do for that."

Graham shook his head. "I won't help you."

"Quiet." Karn Megiddo looked at Ahi'aorina. "There are other giants, and more than enough imps in this world, but you are the one irreplaceable part of my spell. You will have to stay here until I am once again prepared."

"You can't hold onto Queen Ahi'aorina," said Graham. "Without her, winter will cover the land."

"Should I care?" asked Karn Megiddo.

Graham clenched his teeth. "No crops will grow. People and faeries both will starve."

"Magic is my only crop," said the wizard, "and power is my harvest." His narrow features drew together in a look of disgust. "Believe me, once I have my powers, these sniveling peasants will wish they could only starve."

"No!" Graham leaped for the wizard, and managed to get one hand on the man's blue doublet before he was slapped to the ground by a shock which left his ears ringing and his vision doubled. He could barely see Ahi'aorina running toward Karn Megiddo, but he saw the flash as the wizard struck out at the faery.

"Hold still," Karn Megiddo hissed at her. "I can't afford to kill you, but I'll make you wish I had."

The blurry figure of the wizard stepped closer to Graham. "As for you, King Graham, I believe I can find a better assistant than you." Karn Megiddo raised his hand and the lightning around his fist grew brighter.

Something wiggled in the pocket of Graham's tunic.

He looked down to see the tip of a green snout and a pair of orange eyes looking up at him. Quickly, Graham snatched the wriggling creature from his pocket and flung it upward.

Karn Megiddo extended his arm. There was a blinding flash of light.

When Graham could see again, Ahi'aorina was

bending over him. Her cool fingers touched his cheek. "You were nearly lost to this world," she said.

Graham groaned and sat up. "What about Dunstan and Lugmut?"

"Both are injured," said Ahi'aorina, "but they will recover."

A shadow passed over Graham. He looked up to see the narrow face of Karn Megiddo staring down at him.

"Get back," said Graham. "I'll never help you."

The wizard blinked. "I, Karn," he said.

·31·

It took two weeks skirting the south edge of the Glass Mountains for the small group to reach the point of turning north toward Daventry.

It was a lengthy detour, but they had little choice. Neither Ahi'aorina nor Lugmut was equipped to scale the treacherous peaks. Graham, though he still had Wigglebright's glass-conquering boots, had lost his gloves somewhere in the maze of Sorrowing Court. The stitches that Glitterthunk had used in his lacerated palm had finally dropped away, and he had no inclination to slice his hands again. So they went around.

Their passage was much less odious than had been Graham's long pursuit of the imps. Where the trip to Sorrowing Court had taken place in the face of renewed winter, the journey home was taken in spring.

Ahi'aorina grew stronger each day. At first there was only her trail of green footsteps among the snow to mark her passage. But as the day went on, the circle of her power grew wider. When they camped under a tree, Graham would awaken to

find it full in bloom. When they passed through
a field, butterflies and flowers followed in their
wake.

The faery queen's path widened into a green
road, then to a broad swath. On the day they
came down out of the foothills and reached the
bubbling creek that ran from the base of the Glass
Mountains, Ahi'aorina's power was so great that
there was no trace of winter left anywhere in view.
All trace of snow was gone, and summer birds circled in the high blue sky.

They camped that evening on the far bank of
the stream, by the tangled roots of an oak so huge
and ancient that it might have looked at home in
the Old Wood. In the red light of dusk, Graham
went down to the sandbars along the stream and
gathered dry driftwood for a fire. When he returned to the campsite, he found Lugmut laying
out a circle of stones.

"Where is Queen Ahi'aorina?" Graham asked.

Lugmut waved a hand at the nearby woods.
"Gone off she is. To talk with trees, I think."

Graham dropped his load of firewood into the
site the imp had prepared and fished in his
pocket for his tinderbox. "Do you still mean to
leave us tomorrow?" he asked.

Lugmut nodded. "Time it is. Zakizga and Daventry in different directions they are."

"And you're sure about taking your friend here
along?" Graham gestured to a tall figure who
stood quietly by the base of the oak.

The imp looked over at the figure and shrugged. "Needs me he does."

"I agree that he needs someone," said Graham. "But are you sure that Zakizga is the best place for him?"

Lugmut's lips parted in a smile. "Think I eat him, do you?"

"No, but . . ." Graham paused to nurse the fire to life. "It's only that, well, can you trust the other imps there to have the same self-control?"

"Judge us not by Kuzgu," said Lugmut. "No real imp was he."

The figure stepped away from the tree. The blue doublet, so clean when they had pulled Karn Megiddo from the glamour manarvel, was stained and torn. The black hair was wild and uncombed. The figure stumbled as it approached the fire, then looked up sheepishly. "I, Karn," he mumbled.

"Sit down before hurt yourself you do," grumbled Lugmut.

The figure in blue sat down and stretched his hands out cautiously over the flickering flames. "Fire," he said. He looked from Lugmut to Graham and smiled, obviously proud of this extension to his vocabulary.

Over the weeks of the journey, the slizard—they had no other name to call him—had begun to learn a few new words. He still had trouble controlling Karn Megiddo's body, and frequently he fell or had great difficulty with some simple activity. If it had not been for Lugmut, who fed him, and helped him up each time he fell, the slizard would have never made it so far.

Graham looked at the mismatched pair sitting beside the fire and smiled. He had to admit that the imp had taken very good care of the fledgling human. Perhaps going to Zakizga together was exactly what both of them needed.

The sky overhead turned to purple, then to black, and a great snowstorm of stars appeared. A curve of moon shone down, silvering the nearby woods and brightening the landscape. Graham cooked dinner for them all over the fire. Then the three of them lay back and listened to the sounds of a spring evening.

Graham worried a bit about the absence of Ahi-'aorina. Never before had she left them after dark. With her growing power, the faery had also been growing more distant, more alien. Each day she had wandered farther and farther from the path followed by the rest of the party, sometimes being gone for hours at a time. Graham would have liked to have known what Ahi'aorina was doing at these times, but when he questioned her the faery's answers were far from clear.

The soft footsteps around the campsite woke Graham from a drowse. He opened his eyes and saw the silhouette of the faery queen moving about in the darkness. That she had woken him was strange—usually she moved with absolute silence.

"My lady?" he called. "Is everything all right?"

Ahi'aorina moved closer to the flame. As she did, Graham saw that there were several cuts in her pale arms and more on her bare legs. Blood spilled down from her wounds and dripped slowly into the grass.

Graham surged to his feet. "What happened? Who did this to you?"

Ahi'aorina raised her hand. "Hold, King Graham. No one is to blame for my injuries."

Lugmut appeared from the darkness, leading the slizard by the hand. "To the faery what has happened?"

The faery queen looked up at the dark sky. In the moonlight her eyes were silver as scales of a fish. "These wounds are my own fault. I went to the Glass Mountains."

"You did what?" asked Graham.

Ahi'aorina walked away from them and bent to wash her limbs in the stream. "Tomorrow we would be far from these peaks, and I could not bear to leave them without speaking first with their heart," she said. "I went only to the nearest of them, to the one closest to the life and growth. There I spoke to the mountains of how pleasant it would be to have some life on them and about them. I asked them to let some trees grow on their slopes, and to throw off their lifeless silence."

"It looks like they were not very interested in your ideas," said Graham.

"Not at first," agreed Ahi'aorina. "But I believe I have touched something in these cold mountains. They are not dead, only sleeping. Perhaps they will have trees on their slopes one day, and birds nesting in their branches." She stopped and pushed her long, verdant hair away from her face. "Perhaps one day they will even welcome faeries into their new forests."

Graham understood little about faeries. Their lives were too long and many of their motives too mysterious for humans to be comfortable around. But this, this desire to spread life and add room for her people, this was something Graham thought he understood. "I hope it is so," he said. "Is there anything I can do to help you with your injuries?"

"Water will suffice," said Ahi'aorina. "The spring water of this stream is the best remedy I could hope for." She waded into the stream until her long hair lay on the surface of the water.

Graham sat in starlight and watched the queen of the faeries until sleep came over him again.

In the morning, Lugmut and the slizard said their good-byes and marched off to the south. Graham watched them go with more than a trace of sadness. Dunstan had marched for his own home right from the start, but the rest of them had been a company. Graham would miss the imp, and even the slizard.

Ahi'aorina's wounds seemed to have healed overnight, leaving not so much as a scar on her smooth limbs. Graham and Ahi'aorina headed west until they struck the trace of an old trade road.

Then they turned north for Daventry. With the clear, level path before them and the gentle weather that accompanied Ahi'aorina, their progress was swift. Graham hoped that in only another day or two, he would spy the parapets of Daventry jutting above the trees.

On the morning of the second day, they stopped in a small orchard of wild cherry trees so Graham could gather his breakfast. If Ahi'aorina ever ate anything, Graham had never seen it. While he scrambled in the branches, she sat cross-legged on the ground, raising her face to the sun. Graham paused for a moment and looked down at her.

Even in the weakened state in which Graham had found her, the faery queen had been beautiful. Now, as she neared her full health, she had become stunning. Like Quilli'ehennan, her perfection was sometimes almost painful. Graham's principles and restraint were strong, but still he was glad he would not be many more days alone with Ahi'aorina before he was returned to Daventry and Valanice.

Graham's thoughts were interrupted by a disturbance at the far side of the grove. He slipped farther along the branch and spotted four figures picking up fallen cherries and stuffing them greedily into their mouths.

"Tart, wouldn't you say?" said one of the intruders.

"I'd say very tart," said another.

"Not so tart as a gooseberry," said a third.

"But tart all the same," said the last.

Graham felt a spark of anger. He rolled around the branch, dangled for a second by his hands, and dropped to the soft grass. Then he stomped straight over to where the four stood.

"I want my cloak back," he said.

Hogshead looked at Graham with surprise so great it almost seemed his eyes would fall from their sockets. "It's him!" said the beefy blond farmer who was wearing Graham's black cape.

"Aye," said Ramsquarter, who had Graham's knife though his belt.

"The very one," said Lambsfoot.

"Cause of all our troubles," said Brindlenose.

Graham scowled at the four men. "Where's your sister?" he asked. "Did people to throw in the pit get so sparse that you came here to hunt for them?"

"Tilly is gone," said Lambsfoot. "Right, Ramsquarter?"

"Yep," said Ramsquarter. "Isn't it so, Hogshead?"

"Truly it—"

"Oh, shut up!" cried Graham. He looked from one of them to the other and tried to hold back his anger. "Now, I'm going to ask a question, and

I want one of you—that's *one* of you—to answer. Understood?"

All four men nodded.

"Where is Tilly?" he asked.

The men looked back and forth between themselves. Finally scarred Brindlenose stepped forward. "The Laburnum took her," he said.

"Why did they do that?"

Ramsquarter stepped up to answer this one. "They were angry because you and the minstrel got away."

Graham brightened at this news. "So Shallan got away, too?"

"We don't know," said Lambsfoot.

"We didn't see him," added Hogshead.

"But the Laburnum got angry," said Brindlenose. "Didn't they, Ramsquarter?"

"That's right," said Ramsquarter. "Isn't it, Lambsfoot?"

"Stop!" said Graham. "One at a time. The Laburnum came for Tilly?"

"Made a lot of noise," said Hogshead.

"So much that they scared us," said Lambsfoot.

"And there was no one around," added Ramsquarter.

"No one to throw down," said Brindlenose.

Graham's face reddened. "So you threw your own sister down there?"

The four men looked down at the ground. Not one of them was able to meet Graham's eye.

Hogshead sniffed and wiped a thick hand under his nose.

"And when the Laburnum were still angry, you ran away," said Graham, finishing the story for them.

"We were scared," mumbled Lambsfoot in his high, squeaky voice.

Ramsquarter looked up. "But why should we be scared of this one?"

"He's not half our size," said Brindlenose.

"And he's all alone," said Hogshead.

The four men started forward.

"Hold," said Ahi'aorina. The faery queen emerged from the trees and glided swiftly to Graham's side. "He is not alone."

"It's only a girl," said Lambsfoot.

"A pretty girl," said Ramsquarter.

Ahi'aorina made a gesture with her right hand. At once, a cloud of dark hornets came flowing through the cherry grove. The black-striped insects ignored Graham and circled around the four men.

"Return my friend's cloak," said the faery. "And his knife as well."

The men were only too anxious to drop Graham's things on the ground.

"Take away these bees," yelled Brindlenose. He flailed his hands at the circling insects.

Ahi'aorina gestured again, and at once the hornets flew away.

"You'd better run while you can," said Graham. "If I ever see you in Daventry, I'll be only too happy to toss you into my own little hole, the one we call the dungeon."

The four farmers left the grove at a lumbering run and disappeared in the distance. Graham bent to pick up his cloak and knife. "I wish I could do something more to punish them," he said, "but we can hardly march them from here to Castle Daventry."

Ahi'aorina sighed. "A human life is so brief that punishment hardly seems necessary. In a moment, they will be gone."

"It doesn't seem that brief to me," said Graham. He looked into the distance and smiled softly, and not a little sadly. "Though sometimes it seems children grow up overnight."

"Your life need not be so hurried," said the faery.

Graham looked at her with puzzlement. "What do you mean?"

"Come with me into the Old Wood," said Ahi'aorina. "You have earned a place among us. There you will go on while the world goes past. You can have aeons of life instead of mere decades."

"No," said Graham. "It's a tempting offer, but I have a family, and friends, and a kingdom to look after. I think I had better go home and live my life, no matter how brief."

Sadness passed over the faery's face, but she nodded.

Graham and Ahi'aorina walked on through that day. They talked of Dunstan, and whether he had yet made his way back to the Hibestian Range. They spoke of their children, and Graham discovered this was one area where faery feelings and human had much overlap.

Late in the afternoon, they passed a small farm with walls of white stone. Graham recognized it as that of a farmer along the southern edge of Daventry. They were almost home.

A few hours later, when the red sun was just touching the horizon, Ahi'aorina suddenly stopped.

"What is it?" asked Graham.

The faery queen pointed to the trees on the right of the road. "These forests are the beginning of the Old Wood," she said. "I must leave you here and return to my own people."

Though he had been looking forward to getting home from the moment he first left it, Graham felt an unexpected twinge at the thought of leaving Ahi'aorina. "You could walk with me closer to Castle Daventry," he suggested. "The Old Wood goes on for miles."

Ahi'aorina gave him a mischievous smile. "It goes on for more miles than you know. But I can go no farther. The Wood and I must speak, and I will enter it here."

Graham nodded. "All right." He pointed to the tiny bundle in Ahi'aorina's hand. "Would you like me to take that?"

The faery queen raised the small object. She had fashioned the cage from pliable vines and woven grasses found in the vale outside Sorrowing Court. Inside the tiny cage, a green lizard stared out at the world with orange eyes. "I will take it with me," she said. "It will be safer in the Old Wood, removed from those that might free it through accident."

"Do you think he still remembers being Karn Megiddo?" Graham asked.

"Memories can last a long time," said Ahi'aorina.

Suddenly, Graham found the faery queen's arms around his neck. Her lips pressed against his cheek, leaving behind a kiss that tingled on his skin. "My memories of you will be there when Castle Daventry is nothing but a heap of mossy stone," she said. "If you should change your mind, come to me." She drew away from him and began to walk toward the Wood.

Graham felt a bit dizzy. "Perhaps we'll meet again soon," he called. "Come and visit us at Castle Daventry."

The faery queen paused at the edge of the Wood and smiled. "I may," she said. "And should you ever come to visit me, you may call me by my new name."

"New name?"

"From this day," said Ahi'aorina, "I am Culatha alimehenii, She-Who-Was-Rescued-By-A-Human."

"I'm honored," said Graham. "Culatha is a lot easier for a human tongue to wrap around than Ahi'aorina."

The faery laughed. She raised a pale hand and pointed to her left. "There are farms just ahead. If you hurry you may find one with supper still on the hearth."

Graham looked up the road. "No, I'll walk on. I should be at the castle well before midnight."

"I am sorry that you will have to walk these last miles alone," said Ahi'aorina.

"Oh, I'll be fine," said Graham. He turned to look at the faery queen and found her gone. There was only the wood, and the dark shadows between the trees.

"Good-bye, Culatha," Graham whispered.

As he turned and started up the road, he was surprised by a sudden sound. At first he took it for the noise of a woodpecker, but it was not quite that. He turned around and saw a lanky form seated on the stone fence at his back. The man was clapping his hands.

"That looked like the end of quite a tale," called Shallan.

Graham laughed. "I should have known you'd be here to see it."

A tall form stood and moved to join him. "Well," said the minstrel. "It seems I remember the promise of a meal and a place to sleep."

"Of course," said Graham. "Such things always work out for a minstrel."

Together the two men walked up the road to Daventry Castle.

The Epic Fantasy Series Based on the #1 Bestselling Computer Game

KING'S QUEST®

__KINGDOM OF SORROW 1-57297-033-2/$5.99
   by Kenyon Morr

A dark, frigid winter has descended on Daventry, a blizzard that will not stop. Yet beyond the boundaries of the kingdom, it is spring. Dark forces are at work, and the mighty King Graham must find out who—or what— is behind the treachery.

♦♦♦

__THE FLOATING CASTLE 1-57297-009-X/$5.99
   by Craig Mills

On the clouds of a vicious storm, an ominous black castle appears in Daventry, ushering in a reign of terror which claims both the kingdom and its ruler. To save his father's life and the kingdom, Prince Alexander must penetrate the dark forces surrounding the castle...and face the very heart of evil itself.